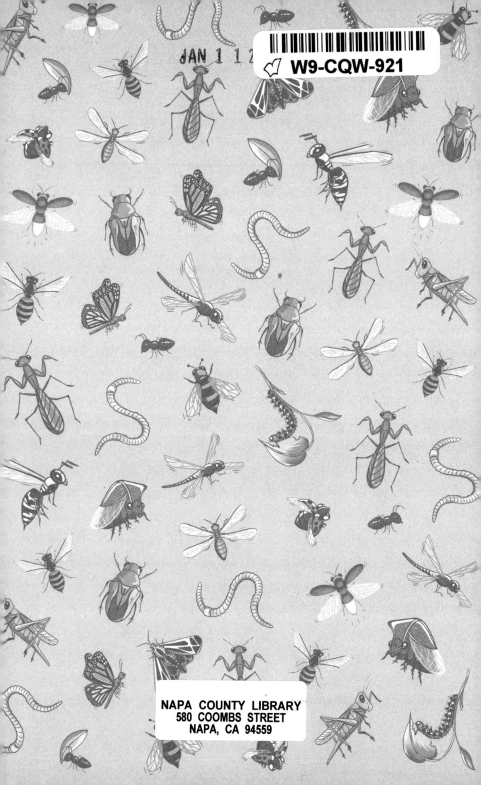

The Big
DREAMS
OF SMall
CREATURES

The Big DREAMS OF small CREATURES

GAIL LERNER

NANCY PAULSEN BOOKS

NANCY PAULSEN BOOKS

An imprint of Penguin Random House LLC, New York

First published in the United States of America by Nancy Paulsen Books,
an imprint of Penguin Random House LLC, 2022

Visit us online at penguinrandomhouse.com.

Library of Congress Cataloging-in-Publication Data
Names: Lerner, Gail, 1970– author.
Title: The big dreams of small creatures / Gail Lerner.
Description: New York: Nancy Paulsen Books, 2022. | Summary: At a secret laboratory devoted
to the peaceful coexistence of human and insects, the fate of the insect world hangs in the
balance of ten-year-old Eden, who can speak to insects, and nine-year-old August,
a bullied fourth grader who wants to squash everything.
Identifiers: LCCN 2022019479 (print) | LCCN 2022019480 (ebook) | ISBN 9780593407851 (hardcover) |
ISBN 9780593407868 (ebook) | Subjects: CYAC: Insects—Fiction. | Ability—Fiction. |
Bullies and bullying—Fiction. | African Americans—Fiction. | LCGFT: Novels.
Classification: LCC PZ7.1.L4683 Bi 2022 (print) | LCC PZ7.1.L4683 (ebook) | DDC [Fic]—dc23
LC record available at https://lccn.loc.gov/2022019479
LC ebook record available at https://lccn.loc.gov/2022019480

Printed in the United States of America

ISBN 9780593407851
1st Printing

LSCH

Edited by Stacey Barney
Design by Jessica Jenkins
Text set in Utopia Std

FOR MY BEAUTIFUL CHILDREN,
RUBY & HART

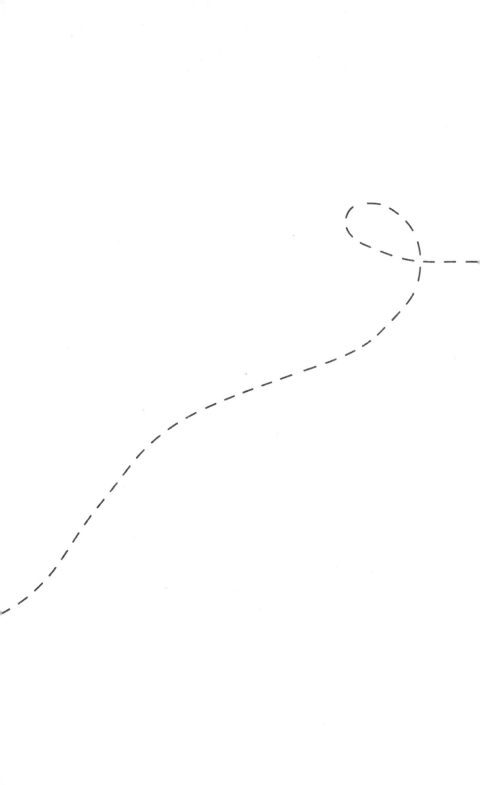

In the Wings

August stood backstage in the darkness, whispering tongue twisters to himself.

"Rubber baby buggy bumpers. Rubber baby buggy bumpers. Rubber baby buggy bumpers. The sixth sheik's sixth sheep's sick. The sixth sheik's sixth sheep's sick."

The area he was standing in was called the wings. When Ms. Batra, the school's drama teacher, first told his class that a stage had wings, August imagined the broad wooden floor taking off, like a giant bird or airplane, and flying in circles above the folding chairs below. He was surprised and a bit disappointed to learn that the wings were actually the dusty space on either side of the stage, where the curtains hung in bunched-up clusters while the performance was taking place.

August peered out at the bright stage, admiring the three cardboard walls that were decorated to look like the inside of a house. Unlike a real house, which had a fourth wall to keep the house warm and private and keep strangers from looking in, a stage set had only three walls on purpose, so the audience could see everything inside: the three chairs, the three beds, and the three bowls of porridge.

August rocked on the balls of his feet, impatient for his first entrance as Papa Bear. He wasn't nervous, just excited. He'd been so eager for this moment that he'd been tearing the pages off his word-a-day calendar without even glancing at the daily word. He'd thought that Thursday, April 29th, would never come, but it was finally here: the day of their first performance for the entire school. The big show for their parents would be that Saturday, but the idea of performing for their classmates was even more exciting. The annual play was the only time August got to be a star at school. For at least a week after each show, kids and teachers from all grades would stop him in the hall and say how good he was.

Today, the lunchroom-slash-assembly-room-slash-theater was packed with kindergartners through fifth graders, thrilled all to be missing class to see a show. August was only in fourth grade, but he'd been in many plays. He'd discovered that he loved acting when his kindergarten class had performed a dance in the school's Spring Festival. August had played a sunflower. The whole dance had only lasted about a minute, but as he moved from lying curled on the floor in green felt overalls, to rising to his feet, to finally standing on his tiptoes as he reached his yellow-gloved hands toward the papier-mâché sun, August realized that he wanted to spend every minute of his life onstage. When he was acting, he was no longer the anxious, chubby-cheeked little nine-year-old who got picked last for Red Rover. He could be anyone or anything: even the tallest, most graceful flower in the field. He dreamed of the day when he would become a real actor on a real stage, instead of in a multipurpose room that smelled like meatballs.

He was thrilled when Ms. Batra announced that this year the fourth-grade play would be *Goldilocks and the Three Bears*, and that it would be longer than any play they'd done before: twenty whole minutes. When August asked if it could be half an hour, Ms. Batra explained that a fourth-grade play couldn't be any longer than twenty minutes; otherwise they would "lose the audience." When she'd first said this, August imagined the entire audience of parents lost in the woods like Hansel and Gretel, but then Ms. Batra explained that "losing the audience" meant that the audience would stop paying attention, and that as actors it was their job to make those twenty minutes as interesting and delightful for them as possible. August thought about his parents, who often came home tired and frustrated by their jobs, and he loved knowing that if he did his job well, he could make their lives more interesting and delightful, even if it was only for twenty minutes at a time.

August adjusted his ears and looked down at the furry brown mittens and slippers that protruded from the arms and legs of his blue church suit. Ms. Batra had glued claws onto them, and August had been so happy with how they looked, she'd had to remind him five times that he couldn't dance around in them until they'd dried. Ms. Batra was so wise and talented. And kind and pretty. She was for sure the best teacher at Madison Prep. Maybe in all of Rhode Island. Maybe in the whole country. August adored the costume she'd made. It was the perfect combination of bear and human, which made it easy and fun to play a wild animal who also had the best qualities of a human father. As Papa Bear, August got to be the kind of dad he wished he had.

August's father had to travel for work all the time. Right now, he was on a two-week trip to Los Angeles, and wouldn't be able to see the play in person. August knew his dad was genuinely sorry to be missing it, and that his mom would video the whole show and send it to him. August's dad would always watch it right away and then call him to talk about it. He loved telling his dad about all the best moments of rehearsal and the crazy mix-ups that happened backstage, but it wasn't nearly as good as having his dad at the show. Not even close. Papa Bear never traveled for work. He stayed home and worked with his family. He, Mama Bear, and Baby Bear foraged for berries in the forest all day, then came home and ate porridge together every night.

Papa Bear also wasn't annoyingly reasonable all the time. On their nightly phone calls, when August would complain that Sheila was bullying him again, his dad would say something like, *Boy, that's sad that she's got to make other kids feel bad to feel good about herself. You've got to wonder what's going on with her,* which wasn't helpful at all. Papa Bear, however, took Baby Bear's side no matter what. When he discovered that an awful girl had broken into their house and smashed his baby's bed, he had no problem scaring her off with a terrifying roar and a flash of his claws. Papa Bear didn't waste time asking, *Why did you break into our house, little girl? Are you hungry? Do you need a safe place to stay?* Instead, Papa Bear just took care of business and made sure she never came back.

But the absolute best part of playing Papa Bear was that Sheila, his real-life bully, was playing Goldilocks. No one had been surprised when she got the part. Sheila, like Goldilocks, was a greedy, bratty girl who wanted everything for herself and would do anything to get it. The only difference between Sheila and Goldilocks was that Sheila didn't have golden locks. She had straight brown hair that she wore in a floppy braid. In fact, August was the only kid who had Goldilocks-style golden curls. His mother let him keep the sides short like all the other boys, but she insisted that he keep the front long, and every morning she'd tug at his curls until they swirled around his bright blue eyes like foam around a tide pool. Secretly, August liked his hair, but he hated the way grown-ups felt like they could reach over and tousle it without even asking permission.

"Maybe," Ms. Batra had said when they were discussing who would play each part, "August should play Goldilocks. After all, it doesn't say anywhere that Goldilocks has to be a girl."

Everyone had snickered at the thought of August playing Goldilocks except Sheila, who was enraged.

"Don't even think about it, Nigh," she'd whispered into his ear, leaning so far forward over her desk that he could smell the Fruit Roll-Up she'd had at lunch. Sheila Morton had been calling him Nigh for over a year, ever since she'd peeked at his report card and seen the long column of *NI*s, which stood for "needs improvement." Sheila had had it in for him since kindergarten, when he'd pushed ahead of her in line for Show-and-Tell. It wasn't the nicest thing in the world, he had to admit, but he'd just gotten a wooden sword for his birthday, and he was dying to show it off. He'd gone on a little too long, though, and Sheila, who wanted to show everyone her tiny new guinea pig, Snowy, had gotten bumped to the next week. By then, however, Snowy had almost doubled in size, and a regular-sized guinea pig wasn't nearly as adorable as a tiny one.

Sheila had never forgiven him for it, and by getting the whole class to call him Nigh, she'd gotten her revenge. August resented his nickname. He only got all those *needs improvement's* because he didn't waste his life memorizing spelling words, or finishing every last worksheet, like all the other fools in his class. They were the real fools, busting their butts for stickers of smiling apples. August knew better. He wasn't going to waste his energy working hard now. He'd wait till he was grown up and a professional actor who got paid in real money and applause, not stickers. But in this meaningless world of fourth grade, where stickers mattered, Sheila's nickname had stuck.

"Don't worry. I don't even want to be Goldilocks. I want to be Papa Bear," he'd told her, and he meant it. If Sheila was Goldilocks and he was Papa Bear, everything would be different. *She* would be scared of *him*. Papa Bear would never duck behind a water fountain and hide like August did when he saw Sheila coming; in the play, Papa Bear would stand up on his hind legs, point his giant paw, and demand that she get out of their house and leave them alone. And Sheila would have to jump up and run screaming out of the cardboard house as fast as she could and never come back.

Unfortunately, in real life, his giant paw was just a little hand, the school was made of bricks, and Sheila wasn't going anywhere. Still, he was going to relish every moment of the play while it lasted.

"Break a leg, Augie," Vincent Vicks said, placing a wicker basket filled with plastic berries on a small table beside him. Vincent was on the stage crew—one of the kids whose job it was to paint the sets, move furniture between scenes, and make sure the actors had the props they needed before they went onstage. The stage crew had to wear dark clothing, so they didn't attract attention to themselves. With his long dark hair, black jeans, black T-shirt, and the dark purple cape he wore to school most days, Vincent was almost totally invisible, which was pretty much how he was every day anyway.

"Thanks," August said quickly, hoping no one had noticed them talking.

Being associated with Vincent could put August at risk of being bullied even worse than he already was, so August did his best to avoid him. In addition to wearing a cape, Vincent had a weird condition where he burped when he got nervous, which was most of the time. Sheila'd started calling him Nurps, which was a combination of *nerd* and *burps*, and got all the other kids to do the same. August felt bad for Vincent. Once Sheila's mean nickname had spread, Vincent's burping problem got even worse, especially when he ate, so he stopped eating lunch in the cafeteria. At recess he'd dangle, friendless, from the monkey bars. August imagined him eating alone in the bathroom, his sandwich perched on his lap, his juice box wedged between his knees, and his cape hanging from the little hook on the inside of the stall door.

But now August's cue to enter was coming up, and he realized that he needed to relax and focus. He'd gotten so tense thinking about Sheila, Vincent, and the whole unfair, inexplicable system that dictated who was popular and who wasn't that his shoulders had risen so high they almost touched his ears. He lowered them, threw them back, and took a deep breath. This was his time to shine.

August turned to pick up the berry basket, and as he leaned down to grab it, he was horrified to see a fat brown cockroach scrambling in the fur of his mitten. He'd heard rumors that cockroaches invaded the lunchroom every night, searching for gobs of mayo and chunks of hot-dog buns, but he'd never actually seen one. He shook his hand violently, desperate to get it off, but instead of falling onto the ground, the cockroach trundled forward, its spiny legs disappearing under the cuff of his suit jacket. August shrieked and staggered backward onto the stage as he felt the cockroach's whisker-thin feelers travel up his arm.

"Aaaaaghhhhh!" he screamed, landing amidst the bright lights, his body jerking and twisting as he struggled to get the cockroach out of his shirt. Totally unaware that all the actors and the entire audience were staring at him with shock and confusion, he tore off his mittens, flung off his suit jacket, and clawed at the buttons of his white dress shirt, ripping it off as he knocked over the cardboard house and smashed the balsa-wood beds in the process. Struggling to stay on his feet, he reached for something solid to grab on to, but his hand landed on something soft and scratchy. It gave way, tumbling to the ground and taking August with it. It was only when he landed, shirtless and gasping on the stage floor, that he realized the thing he'd grabbed was Sheila's curly blond wig. She glared down at him, furious. Her nylon wig cap, bulging with brown hair, made her look like an angry mushroom.

A blast of laughter hit him with such force that if he hadn't already been on the ground, it would've knocked him over. Unlike the delighted laughter of the crowd when he'd frolicked around the stage as Jiminy Cricket in second grade, this laughter was harsh and brutish. The audience and the cast were in hysterics, and Sheila was laughing the loudest of all. The only people who weren't laughing were Ms. Batra, whose mouth hung open, astonished, and Vincent Vicks, who covered his face with his cape, too pained to look. Everyone else from K through 5 was laughing *at* him, not *with* him, at the very moment that they should've been grinning and shaking their heads in admiration of his magnificent performance. Although August was bare-chested in the cold lunchroom, his body burned with shame. Even as his brain throbbed, clouded by humiliation, one thing was clear: it was all the cockroach's fault.

Independence

*E**den perched high in* the branches of her favorite elm tree, looking down at the picnic tables below. It was four o'clock on Thursday, April 29th. In one hour and fifteen minutes, she'd officially be ten years old. In three hours she'd be eating her favorite dinner (spaghetti and meatballs) and her favorite cake (yellow with chocolate frosting) with her parents, but this time alone in the park after school was even more precious.

Eden loved independence. She'd been making her own lunch ever since she was five, which was also the same year she'd learned to wield a deadly weapon. Not many parents would let their five-year-old use a Swiss Army knife, but after seeing her father peel an apple in one ribbon, Eden begged him to teach her. She needed to know how to make one of those lovely apple skin spirals herself. She had been remarkably patient for a kindergartner, and perfected it after only fifteen tries, at which point she and her dad made four apple pies and he told her she could peel all the family's apples from then on, provided that she used the knife only at home, and only if he or her mom supervised.

By the time she'd turned nine, Eden had been peeling apples unsupervised for two years, as well as doing her own laundry, depositing her own birthday checks, and baking chocolate chip banana bread whenever the bananas on the counter got too brown.

"You know, you don't have to do everything yourself," her parents would tell her. "We like doing things for you."

But that wasn't the point. She didn't have to. She wanted to.

Eden didn't just like doing things for herself. She also liked being *by* herself. She couldn't remember the exact day she'd traded the jungle gym for the elm tree, or started reading instead of riding her bike with the neighborhood kids. She knew it was around the time she realized she wasn't into the things most other kids were into, like video games or TV shows. Eden was more interested in nature's organic entertainments: the chorus of crickets outside her bedroom window on a spring night, or a hundred newborn spiderlings tumbling out of one tiny egg sac, like clowns out of a car. And over time she became known as the girl who was always reading by herself: up in the tree, down in the library, sunk into the beanbag chair, always near the group but never part of it.

Kids in her class would shake their heads when they came upon her reading in a tucked-away nook: *What's she doing? Why is she always reading? Have you ever hung out with her? Have you ever been to her house?* They'd say these things aloud as they walked past her, not bothering to hide their curiosity, as if she were a bird they'd noticed on a branch, or a squirrel that had startled them.

One time in kindergarten Eden's teacher had handed out sheets of storybook paper—the kind that had a big blank space for drawing at the top and alternating blue, dotted, and red lines for writing at the bottom. Each kid had to pick an animal and draw a picture of it on the top half and write a sentence about it on the bottom. While most of the kids had chosen big-ticket animals like tigers or pandas, Eden had chosen the woolly bear caterpillar, because she loved how fuzzy and chubby it was, and the way it had a rusty orange band with black ends on either side. It was as if nature had two ideas about what the woolly bear caterpillar should look like, couldn't make up its mind, and went with both. Underneath her picture Eden had written, "The fuzzy wuzzy catirpiler looks lik a stufft animul." Her teacher, Ms. Firth, had peered over her shoulder. *Looks like I have a budding entomologist,* she'd said with a smile. When Eden tilted her head, confused, Ms. Firth explained that *entomologist* was a fancy word for someone who studies insects. Eden, who liked insects *and* big words, was thrilled. And from then on, whenever anyone asked her what she wanted to be when she grew up, she had her answer.

She also knew that if she ever leapt into a group of kids talking about how great the new superhero movie was and said, *Hey! Did you guys know that there's only one kind of human, but thousands of different kinds of wasps and bees?* everyone would think she was even more of a weirdo than they already did.

But now, nestled in the crook of the elm, which was easily the best tree in Edgerton Park, which was easily the best park in New Haven, and maybe even all of Connecticut, she was content. Eden could watch the corrugated leaves turn from chartreuse to emerald without worrying about what anyone else thought of her. Only two weeks earlier, anyone glancing up at the tree would've spotted her easily, but now the leaf canopy covered her, enabling her to watch the families beneath her almost entirely unseen.

Eden, seeing that the elm leaves were finally at their fullest, wrote "Maturation of Elm Leaves Complete" along with the date and year in her notebook. She smiled, pleased that it had happened on her birthday. For the past five years, Eden had been making a chart every spring noting the date that the first buds appeared on various trees, the date they'd begun to open, and the date they'd completed their journey from bud to leaf. It took a lot of scampering up various trees and she had the scratches to prove it, but Eden loved having an ongoing annual project.

Having made her notes, she wedged herself between the same two branches she always did and opened her backpack, pulling out the half a peanut butter and jelly sandwich she had left over from lunch, a freshly peeled apple, and the paperback copy of *The Baron in the Trees* that her mother had given her as an early birthday present. Mom had said that the main character might remind Eden of herself, and she was excited to hear there was a book about someone like her. Eden often thought she was the only person in the world who felt closest to people when she was observing them from far away.

It turned out a lot of kids had the same birthday as Eden. The park was dotted with picnic tables; many of them were draped in festive plastic cloths and piled high with presents. Eden was impressed by how many families were hosting late-afternoon parties on a school day. Those parents were clearly going out of their way to throw their child's birthday party on the actual day they were born, which was much more exciting than just having it on the nearest weekend.

Eden loved spying on the families below, watching big men struggle to blow up little balloons and checking out the kinds of food all the different families set out. When Eden's extended family got together, there was always a ton of food and a huge variety. Eden's mom was Jewish, and her dad was Black. Her mom's side brought big boxes of take-out pizza (all eaten within minutes) and plastic trays of cut-up vegetables (all left untouched), and her dad's side made burgers and chicken, which they cooked on the grills at the park. Both sides of the family brought chips and cupcakes.

Even though anyone could see that Grandma Betty was Black and Grandma Roz was white, both women loved to say what they were all the time. *And I say that as a strong Black woman,* Grandma Betty would say, as if it weren't totally obvious. And Grandma Roz would say, *Of course I'm anxious. I'm Jewish!* as if only Jewish people could be anxious. But it got a little more complicated when Eden's grandmas tried to tell Eden what *she* was. *You're Black and Jewish, honey. You're Blewish!* Grandma Roz would say. And then Grandma Betty would shake her head and say, *Baby, you're Black.*

Eden's parents would tell her not to listen to her grandmothers. *You're mixed,* they'd say. *You're both,* they'd say. *And it's up to you to decide how you self-identify. There's no wrong choice.* But Eden had already decided what she was. She was a strong, Black, anxious Jewish girl on her way to becoming a strong, Black, anxious Jewish young woman. Eden felt comfortable being mixed, because everything about her was mixed in some way: she wanted to be a scientist, and she wanted to write novels; she wanted to seem more normal to other kids, but she wasn't going to stop doing the things she loved that made her weird; she wanted to be a vegan, but she couldn't give up burgers and ice cream. The one thing she did not feel mixed about was telling her Jewish grandma that she had to stop saying *Blewish*. It was embarrassing for everyone.

Above several of the picnic tables piñatas dangled, and Eden watched as lines of squirmy, giggling children waited for their turn to hit the unfortunate donkey, ducky, or SpongeBob their parents had chosen. Eden watched for a few minutes as a pink-, blue-, and yellow-fringed doggy broke open. The children swarmed the candy, stuffing it into little paper bags. Eden nodded; she liked seeing a job well done. She was about to go back to her book when she saw a boy in the middle of the group point to a sturdy oak tree nearby.

"Hey!" he shouted. "There's another piñata over there!"

The boy, followed by all the children, raced toward it.

"Weird! It's buzzing!" he called as he got closer.

As he raised the broomstick, poised to smash it, Eden had a sickening realization: it wasn't a piñata. It was a wasps' nest.

The Pea

August realized that the problem with having a lunchroom-slash-assembly-room-slash-theater was that even if you'd run away from the theater and vowed to never return, you still had to go back there at lunchtime.

He stalled in the doorway, hoping that the usual excitement about it being Thursday and French Bread Pizza Day would take everyone's mind off his failure, but Sheila, Brittany, and Paul all looked up and stared at him, then bowed their heads together and started whispering, loud enough for him to hear.

"He ruined the school show," said Brittany. "You know he's going to ruin the parents' show, too."

"He ruined my wig," said Sheila. "And he's going to pay."

"For the wig?"

"For existing," Sheila said, stabbing her fork into her brownie.

"What are we gonna do to him?" Paul asked.

"I don't know yet," Sheila said. "But it's gonna be bad."

August shuddered. Sheila was capable of terrible things. One time in art class, when they were lying on sheets of butcher paper, tracing around each other's bodies with chalk, Sheila had stepped on his mouth, pressing her dirty sneaker against his lips. She'd told the teacher that she'd stepped on him by accident, but August knew she was lying. That had been last fall. He could only imagine what new nasty tricks she'd learned over spring break.

August noticed that Ivan Linsky, who, as usual, was sitting alone at a table, was staring at him, his brow wrinkled with concern. August looked away. Being seen making eye contact with Ivan was just as bad as being seen talking with Vincent. Ivan, like August and Vincent Vicks, was an outcast. He had bright orange hair and did ballet, which he didn't even have the good sense to be embarrassed about. Ivan was actually proud of being a dancer. He didn't even try to keep it secret from Sheila and the other kids and would occasionally do little leaps in the hallway on his way to class. His mother had been a famous ballerina in Russia, where she grew up, and now she ran a ballet studio in town. She packed Ivan fancy, extra-nutritious lunches every day: a slice of pumpernickel bread, two hard-boiled eggs, and bright red soup in a Mason jar, and Sheila had started a rumor that the soup was made of blood.

It's not blood. It's borscht, Ivan insisted, but from that day on, Sheila, her best friend Brittany, and Paul started calling Ivan Dracula. They didn't stop at name-calling, either. They really leaned into the whole vampire thing. Once when the lunch monitor stepped out of the room, Brittany had grabbed Ivan's Mason jar of borscht and screamed, *Blood!* as she hurled the glass jar to the floor right in front of him. The jar had shattered, and the dark red soup splashed up all over Ivan, staining the white, long-sleeved rash guard his mother made him wear to protect his nearly translucent skin from the sun.

It's Dracula! He's come to suck our blood! Brittany had shouted in a terrible Transylvanian accent as Ivan stood there, his shirt so spattered with red it looked like he'd been stabbed in the stomach. From then on, Ivan almost never ate in the cafeteria. August imagined him gulping beet soup alone at his mother's studio after school. But today, Ivan was in the lunchroom, enjoying French bread pizza along with all the other kids.

"Augie?"

August looked over to see Ms. Batra standing beside him, holding a tray with two plates of pizza. August was worried she'd scold him for ruining the show, but instead she invited him to sit with her and talk. Her dark hair smelled like flowers, and he wanted to press his face into her soft white sweater and cry. He loved Ms. Batra. Unlike his other teachers, who always told him that they knew he could do better, Ms. Batra told him he was wonderful. She'd laugh, delighted, when he made up new lines during the play, and she'd add them to the script so they'd officially become part of the show.

August didn't mean to add lines and didn't like the way Sheila would scowl at him when he unexpectedly got an extra laugh. He didn't want to call attention to himself, but when he was onstage playing a character, his brain just naturally thought up funny things he knew the character would say, and they would pop out of his mouth almost against his will.

Watch out, everyone. Augie's going to steal the show, Ms. Batra would say, shaking her head admiringly, and August imagined himself scooping the entire audience into a bag and sneaking away with them so he could keep all the laughter and applause for himself. But that was all over now.

"I can imagine how upsetting that was," she said.

"Then let me go home. Call my mom. I'm sick. I have a fever. I'm contagious, I know it," he said. "Though I'll for sure definitely be better by Saturday's show."

"Trust me, Augie, I know how you feel."

August felt his throat start to tighten, the way it did when he accidentally ate something with sesame in it.

"No, you don't," he muttered.

"I do. I bet you won't believe me, but when I was in first

grade, almost the exact same thing happened to me."

August couldn't believe it. How could he and smart, beautiful Ms. Batra have anything in common? Still, he was curious. It was hard to imagine Ms. Batra ever being younger than he was. It must have been a very long time ago. She was old now. Probably thirty.

"Come sit down with me, and I'll tell you," she said, waving at a fly that had been making its way around the lunchroom.

August guessed that no one would mess with him if he was with Ms. Batra, so he sat with her at a nearby table.

"I was playing the princess in *The Princess and the Pea*," she began. "I loved my costume. It was a long white dress with a golden fringe that matched my crown. And in the middle of the stage was a stack of mattresses that I got to climb up onto and pretend to go to sleep. It was probably only two or three mattresses, but I remember feeling like it went to the sky, and my favorite part of the whole show was when I got to throw back the covers and say, 'I can't sleep. There's a rock in my bed, and it hurts!' And then the whole class would make a circle around me and sing, 'It's the pea! It's the pea! It's the pea!'"

August laughed. He loved hearing Ms. Batra sing in the lunchroom, as if she didn't care if anyone was listening. She didn't seem to notice that Sheila, Paul, and Brittany were watching them and laughing.

"Eww, look," they whispered, loud enough for him to hear. "His only friend is a teacher."

They cracked up laughing, and August was astonished to realize that he actually didn't care. He had ruined the play, and Ms. Batra still cared about him. She could've been sitting with Sheila, Brittany, and Paul, chuckling with them about how awful August was. Instead, she'd chosen to be with him, even though he'd failed. That's what real friendship was. He leaned in closer to her, eager to hear the rest of her story.

"Then what happened?"

"Well, at the very first show, I threw back the blankets, and just as I was about to say my line, a swarm of moths flew up from under the covers. I was so scared, I peed myself."

August laughed a little. He couldn't help himself. It was so surprising to hear a teacher say "pee," plus he could totally imagine the scene. He looked away so she couldn't tell he was laughing, pretending to swat at the fly that had settled on the rim of his lunch tray.

"It's okay. You can laugh. It's funny now. But it wasn't then. I peed all down my white dress, and everyone could see. And then, when everyone sang, 'It's the pea! It's the pea! It's the pea!' the whole audience laughed. I was so embarrassed, I thought I would die right there on the spot."

August nodded. That was exactly how he felt.

"I swore I'd never be in a play again," she said. "But you

can probably tell that didn't last very long. Augie, one day you will be a wonderful actor, or drama teacher, or whatever you want to be, and what happened today will just be a funny story you share with someone else who needs to hear it."

He thought about what she'd said for a moment. "Can I go home early anyway?"

"I don't think that's a good idea," Ms. Batra said. "If you go home now, it'll only be harder to come back tomorrow. Why don't you stay and have some pizza with me? It looks pretty good."

He had to agree. Only a few minutes ago he thought he'd never eat again, but between her gentle voice, funny story, and the delectable smell of the pizza, he was feeling hungry.

"Thank you, Ms. Batra," he said, chomping down on the pizza. But instead of tasting the irresistible combination of melted cheese and tangy sauce, he felt something zip from the roof of his mouth to the tip of his tongue.

"Aaaaaghhhhh!" he screamed as he realized that a fly was ricocheting in his mouth. It bounced off the inside of his cheek then buzzed all along his gumline, like the world's nastiest electric toothbrush before it zipped out of his mouth. If that wasn't bad enough, August suddenly remembered that flies threw up as soon as they landed on something. He'd read it in one of his Gross but True books. The thought of it made his stomach churn, and he felt a sour taste rise up in his throat.

"Augie? Are you okay? What happened?" Ms. Batra asked.

He tried to stay calm, but when he tried to tell her he was fine, that it was no big deal, the sour taste leapt from his throat to his tongue, and he felt his breakfast shoot out of his mouth and onto Ms. Batra's sweater. The messy streaks of sauce, cheese, egg, and orange pulp turned her clean white sweater into a finger painting. Ms. Batra jumped up, disgusted, and ran from the lunchroom as all the kids erupted in shocked laughter.

"Ms. Batra!" he called after her, but she was already gone.

"Hey, everybody!" Sheila shouted to the whole lunchroom, her crackling laugh harsh in his ears. "Look! Nigh messed up the play *and* puked on a teacher!"

A roar of laughter went up. August looked down at the fly, who, happy to be in daylight again, was lazily circling August's brownie. As he angrily dumped his tray into the trash, he cursed the fly. Ms. Batra hated him now, and Sheila had even more reasons to make fun of him. It was all the fly's fault.

The Piñata

"*N*o!" *Eden shouted, slamming* her book shut so loudly that she startled a blue jay off its perch. She scrambled down the trunk of the elm tree nearly as fast as the jay flew away. She instinctively grabbed her backpack, knocking her book and half a sandwich out of the tree. The waxed paper her PB&J had been wrapped in fluttered down like a leaf. Eden ran toward the nest, which dangled from the oak like a giant gray mango. If she didn't get there fast enough, hundreds of innocent wasps could die.

"Stop!"

Everyone turned to look at the running, hollering girl, but she was a moment too late. Just as she arrived, the boy bashed the nest with the broomstick, smashing a hole in its side. The intricately crafted layers of pulp and paper that the wasps had assembled so carefully shattered into bits and exploded like confetti from a New Year's popper. A cloud of angry wasps streamed out as the entire nest crashed to the ground.

"Bees!" screamed the children as they found themselves in a cloud of angry, stinging creatures that descended on them with stunning accuracy.

"Don't run!" Eden called to both the children and wasps. She knew better than to think the wasps could understand her, but she had the same message for them both. "If you stay still, no one will get hurt!"

But everyone was so busy panicking, no one listened. As parents came running, swatting at the wasps with their hands, Eden scooped the nest up from where it had landed. It was split open at the spot where the stick had hit it, and the gash had widened when it hit the ground. She could see all the larvae inside curling up into themselves as they were exposed to the heat of the sun for the first time. Scared for their safety, she slipped the whole nest into the cool darkness of her backpack, zipping it quickly to protect the larvae.

Eden cared about the children who'd been stung, of course, but she was sure they were going to be fine. They had parents to help them, and all they really needed was some soap and water, and an ice pack. Their parents were already rushing them back to their cars. But the poor larvae no longer had a home or any shelter to keep them safe from the world.

Eden's thoughts were interrupted, however, by the sound of angry buzzing behind her. Eden turned to see a swarm of wasps advancing on her like a tornado: swirling in a circle while somehow also moving forward with relentless force. She recoiled in fear. The wasps, like a battalion of trained soldiers, had already surrounded her and were poised to attack from every angle, making sure she had no way to escape. *Of course,* she thought. How were they supposed to know she was trying to help? In their eyes, she probably looked like another violent intruder, intent on murdering their babies and destroying their home. Still, she didn't want to get stung, so she threw the bottom edge of her jacket up over her head, trying to protect herself from the coming attack.

But no attack came. Instead, she heard a metallic buzzing sound, like tin foil being torn from its roll. It crackled in her ear, and when Eden peeked up from under her jacket, she could see that in addition to the army of wasps encircling her, a single wasp was hovering directly in front of her, inches from her face. The wasp's body was striped with black and yellow and bright as caution tape, and the wasp's message seemed as clear as caution tape, too: *Stay away!* Taking in its narrow waist, pointed abdomen, and regal air, Eden quickly realized that she wasn't being confronted by any ordinary wasp. She was face-to-face with the queen.

The wasp queen emitted a series of high-pitched buzzes,

then watched Eden expectantly, as if waiting for her to respond. Eden stared at her, perplexed. The queen repeated the buzzes again, higher and louder. When Eden still didn't respond, the queen buzzed again, so much louder and higher that Eden thought her eardrum might break. She also thought her brain might break along with it. What was happening? Was the wasp queen actually talking to her? Was she hallucinating? Dreaming? Or was she awake and this was a dream come true? Talking with animals had always been Eden's greatest fantasy. Ever since she was little and had read *The Story of Doctor Doolittle* and *James and the Giant Peach*, she'd spent every birthday wish hoping it would happen to her.

The queen fluttered impatiently, then uttered the sequence again. Eden did her best to decipher their meaning, but the buzzes still made no sense to her. By the fifth time she'd heard them, Eden was ready to give up. She couldn't listen any harder. And then it occurred to her: maybe instead of listening harder, she should try listening softer. Eden closed her eyes and took deep breaths, focusing on listening with her heart instead of her brain. She stopped guessing what the queen was saying in exchange for letting herself empathize with what the queen might be feeling. After a few moments, Eden felt a rippling sensation throughout her body, as if she were a lake that someone had tossed a stone into. Suddenly, Eden felt the love the queen had for her babies, the pride she took in her magnificent nest, and the terror the queen must've felt when she'd realized it was under attack, as strongly as if Eden had experienced all those things herself.

And as soon as Eden allowed herself to feel the queen's emotions, she found that she could actually understand the queen's words, too. The buzzes didn't sound random anymore. They were very specific, and their message was clear:

"Unhand my nest, human. Or face my wrath."

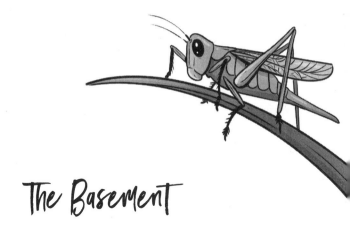

The Basement

August got home from school, ready to put the whole awful day behind him. By the time he'd finished scraping his tongue with a paper towel in the boys' bathroom, lunch was over. He'd been too nauseated to eat anyway, but as soon as he'd gotten off the bus and could see his house at the end of the block, he was suddenly starving, his stomach growling at the thought of his favorite snack: a glass of milk and his mother's homemade strawberry jelly spread thick on a graham cracker. August's mom worked part-time, selling real estate, so some days when he came home from school, she would be there instead of Sabrina, the boring high school girl who stayed on her phone the entire time. Most days when his mom was home, she'd make him do his homework before they did anything fun, but every now and then she'd make an exception and watch TV or play tetherball with him right after snack. He hoped today would be one of those days. But when he opened the front door, he was disappointed to see his mom and her friend Nancy talking in the kitchen.

They were seated at either end of the kitchen table, both wearing workout clothes and drinking from gigantic re-usable water bottles with short, built-in straws, which made them look like toddlers who'd just come from a yoga class. In all the years August's mom and Nancy had been friends, he'd never seen Nancy in anything other than black span-dex that made her pale arms and face look even whiter than they already were. Between her black-and-white body, her short, spiky red hair, and her loud rat-a-tat-tat of a laugh, she seemed more like a woodpecker than a person. Nancy bugged him. She was like a very simple machine that could only do two things: smile and ask what he was up to in school these days.

"Hi, Augie," she said, smiling. "What are you up to in school these days?"

Oh, you know, humiliating myself, puking on my favorite teacher, he wanted to say. But instead he just looked at the floor and said, "Nothing much."

"Tough day?" his mom asked. "How about a little jelly on a graham cracker and a glass of milk?"

"Really?" Nancy said, wrinkling her nose. "That's a lot of sugar. You know, he's much better off having a glass of water and a piece of fruit."

Mind your own business! Don't talk about my snacks!
August wanted to scream. He prayed that his mother
wouldn't listen to busybody Nancy, who obviously didn't
know what she was talking about. Who in the world would
choose fruit over jelly? August hated fruit. It was full of seeds
and pits, covered with bitter skins, and it required so much
chewing. His mother's jelly, on the other hand, was perfec-
tion: sweet and smooth, and it slid right down.

"I think it's okay this time," his mom said, winking at him.

August smiled, grateful that she knew exactly what he
wanted without him having to say anything. He and his mom
were different in lots of ways: his hair was light and wild as a
wave; hers was dark and smooth as a seal. She loved thunder-
storms; he was terrified of them. She liked eating barbecued
chicken with bones in it; he could only handle nuggets. But
she could read his moods like no one else could. He hoped
she also knew that he really, really wanted Nancy to leave.

"How about I see Nancy out, and you run down to the cellar and get a new jar of jelly?"

"Okay!" he said, so excited that Nancy was leaving that he
momentarily forgot to be afraid of the cellar. "Bye, Nancy!"

As August heard the front door close behind Nancy, he
realized he was already at the bottom of the cellar steps, his
fingers on the doorknob. Going down to the cellar alone
always felt risky. The damp, musty air made August feel like

he was heading somewhere ancient and possibly haunted.

Still, he wanted jelly *and* he wanted his mom to think he was brave. He turned the knob and pushed the door, holding his breath as it swung open into the pitch-dark world of the cellar. He groped along the wall until he found the light switch, which always seemed to be in a different place than the last time he'd reached for it. Flicking it on, August sprinted as fast as he could toward the jelly shelves and grabbed the cardboard box of Mason jars. He'd bring them all upstairs and pick the flavor he wanted in the bright kitchen, where it was safe. He turned to run for the door, but stopped short when he felt a fine, silky net press into his face.

"Aaaaaghhhh!" he screamed as he realized he'd run straight into a spiderweb. August threw the box of jellies to the ground, where they landed with a sound that was a sickening combination of a crash and an ooze. He struggled to wipe the web off his face, but it was already tangled in his eyelashes, and a little piece had gotten into his mouth.

"August! What happened?" His mother came clattering down the steps.

"Spider!" he blurted, wishing he had ten more hands to wipe his face with. It felt like two would never be enough to do the job.

But his mother's eyes were elsewhere, staring down at

the cardboard box full of smashed jelly jars. "My jelly," she sighed.

"Can we save it?" he asked, near tears.

"No, Augie, we can't," she said, looking down at the box that had once contained perfectly sealed jars with brightly colored labels. Now it was full of loose goo, which was mixed with chunks of glass. "But chin up. It's a major bummer, but we can always make more. Now, you go get yourself a piece of fruit and get started on your homework."

August plodded up the stairs, too dejected to pet Orso, their shaggy black dog, who was stretched out across the top step, legs in the air and belly exposed, waiting for some love. It had been the worst Thursday of his life. The play, pizza, Ms. Batra's sweater, and his mom's jelly had all been ruined, and bugs were to blame for all of it. Who knew which of life's pleasures they would come for next? August had to find a way to protect himself, his mom, the teacher he loved, and all that was fun, pretty, and delicious in the world. He thought about his options. He could go upstairs, eat an inferior snack, and feel bad about himself, or he could take action and be a hero. The choice was clear.

The Queen

Eden was so astonished that she could understand the buzzing of the wasp queen that she forgot to obey her command. The army of workers began buzzing amongst themselves, swarming into an attack formation. Eden had learned from her studies that all worker wasps were female, and she'd always imagined them as a teeny, tiny version of the Amazons, the mythological army of female warriors. Seeing them assemble for battle in real life was as impressive as it was terrifying. But before they could unleash their power, the queen raised her wing and they all hovered in midair, awaiting further command.

"Unhand my nest, human. Or face my wrath," the queen buzzed, brandishing her stinger like a sword.

Eden's brain and body finally reacted at the same time. She put her backpack on the ground and stepped back to show that she meant no harm. "Your Majesty! I come in peace. You, your nest, and your colony are safe with me."

The chorus of buzzes quickly stopped. Eden watched as a hundred tiny wasp heads turned toward her, then all simultaneously tilted to one side. There was no mistaking it. It was the universal gesture for *Huh?*

Of course, Eden thought. She could understand the queen's language once she'd opened herself up to feeling the queen's feelings, but that didn't mean the queen or her workers could comprehend her human speech, or that they even wanted to try. Eden wondered if they would understand her better if she could make her human language sound more like theirs. But how? The answer came to her immediately: a kazoo!

Eden had three kazoos: a metal one and two plastic, and she loved them, because they were the only instrument she could actually play. Eden's family was full of good musicians. Her mom played flute for the New Haven Symphony Orchestra, and every member of her family played several instruments.

"Everybody should play at least one," they would tell her. It was one of the only things they could all agree on.

Eden loved the idea of playing an instrument and had tried flute for a whole year, but she'd hated every minute of it: lessons, practicing, being bad at it, more lessons, more practicing, more being bad. Everyone told her to stick with it; keep at it; don't give up; you'll get there. Finally, after the millionth brutal hour of trying to get through a G-major scale, she'd thrown her flute across the room and screamed. *Eden!* her mother had said, shocked. It was so unlike her to throw a tantrum, let alone a musical instrument.

I don't want to play anymore! she'd sobbed. *I don't like it! I've never liked it! I hate it!* Eden glared at her mother, ready for her usual speech about not using the word *hate*. Instead, her mother told her it was fine. She did so many other things; she didn't have to play an instrument, too. Eden sighed through her sobs, relieved. But even though she'd gotten what she wanted, she was still unhappy. Eden couldn't handle not being amazing at everything. She refused to try anything new in public until she'd perfected it. Eden knew that making mistakes was how you learned, but it was also what made you look foolish. At school, all Eden had going for her was being smart. If people saw her making mistakes, she'd lose that, too. Her parents didn't understand this strategy. *The perfect is the enemy of the good,* her dad liked to say. *There's no such thing as perfect,* Grandma Roz would explain. *Where are the other two points?* Grandma Betty would ask whenever Eden got a ninety-eight on a lab report. Eden agreed with Grandma Betty. Anything less than perfect was just plain bad.

The next day when Eden had gotten home from school,

her mother presented her with a small box with a red ribbon. Inside was a silver kazoo. *Now you have an instrument!* Eden loved playing the kazoo. The sound was outrageous: a raucous, exuberant mix of goose and lawn mower. No one in the family but Eden and her mom were happy about this. Everyone else thought of kazoos as silly, noisy, goofy-looking plastic things that made an incredibly annoying sound. A few of their neighbors complained. Grandma Betty threatened to stop coming over.

But now, potentially for the first time in all of human history, a kazoo would be helpful. A kazoo would have an actual, valuable purpose. If only she had one with her. Eden could picture all three of her kazoos lined up on her dresser. Why hadn't she put one in her backpack with all her other emergency supplies? Eden decided to try humming. It wouldn't sound nearly as much like buzzing as a kazoo, but it was her next best option. She hummed at the queen and worker wasps, trying to convey her thoughts in bursts of sound. The workers stared at her, confused, then went back to buzzing amongst themselves. Eden knew her humming wasn't working, but the queen swooped closer and buzzed at her quizzically, as if she truly wanted to understand. Eden felt sure that if they were going to have any chance of communicating, she'd need an actual kazoo.

Luckily, she remembered a video she'd seen online that

showed how to make a homemade one with a cardboard tube, waxed paper, and a rubber band. She looked around, frantic. How could she possibly find those things in a park? Wait! She held her hands up to show the queen that she wasn't planning any kind of attack, then darted back to her elm tree. She tore the cardboard cover off her book, which she hated doing but decided was okay in an emergency, and rolled it into a tube, which she held in place with the ponytail holder that was looped around her braids. Next, she covered one end of the tube with the waxed paper from her sandwich, tucking the edges of the paper under the ponytail holder so it stretched tight across the top of the tube. The last step was poking a small hole in the side of the tube, which was easily done with a stick she found on the ground.

Eden hesitated. What if her homemade kazoo didn't work? What if the queen lost faith in her and flew away, convinced that Eden wasn't any help at all? Still, she had to try. She walked back toward the wasps, humming into the kazoo as she went, her heart full of empathy for the queen. It seemed unlikely that humming words through a kazoo would work any better than just regular humming, but it was all she had to go on. Still, she kept moving forward, refining her technique until she'd developed a sound that was a cross between a kazoo and a wasp's buzz. The only way she could think to describe it was a kuzz-buzz.

"Your Majesty, I promise that I'm here to assist you, your nest, and your community in any way I can," she kuzz-buzzed.

There was a long silence as the wheeze of the kuzz-buzz hovered in the air, filling the space between them.

"Thank you, human," the queen buzzed back.

Eden thought she would faint with excitement. It had worked! She and the queen were actually talking! The queen must've also intuited that empathy plus buzzing was the key to human-wasp communication. Eden watched as the queen, seemingly convinced that Eden was a safe human, came closer and circled the backpack, searching for a way in. She was obviously much too tiny to work the zipper.

"Please allow me, Your Majesty."

The queen nodded, giving Eden permission to unzip the backpack and remove the precious nest. She placed it on the ground, careful to put it in the shade. Before she could step away, the queen was already hovering over it, examining the damage. Huge chunks of the nest were in desperate need of repair, and Eden could see that the wasps needed fresh building materials to fix it.

Eden ran to her favorite elm tree and tore a handful of pages from her book, shredding them into tiny strips and putting them down in front of the worker wasps. The workers seized the scraps and immediately began patching up the jagged holes. Making so much repair pulp for the nest all at once took a lot of chewing, and the wasps rotated in and out with incredible efficiency, so some could rest their jaws while others took their place.

Eden didn't need to see the workers' wings and mandibles trembling to know how much of a toll this emergency repair effort was taking on these hardworking creatures. Paper wasps normally took several weeks to build a nest, and now they were racing to do nearly as much work in minutes. Eden knew about the various habits of many insects because she'd been reading about them for years. It had all started on her first birthday, when Grandma Betty had given her the board book *The Very Hungry Caterpillar*. It was the first book Eden had ever gotten as a real, proper present. She took it with her everywhere, and she loved it so much that her passion for it became the stuff of family legend. For years afterward and even to this day, whenever Eden visited Grandma Betty's apartment complex, her grandma would take her down to the card room and tell all the ladies she played spades with the story of how Eden had wedged the sturdy brick of a book into her mouth and chomped on it as soon as she tore off the wrapping.

She always loved books. She thought they were delicious! her grandma would say with a delighted laugh, and the ladies in the card room would chuckle and say, *Aw, silly little baby girl,* then pull out their phones and show pictures of their own grandchildren.

As Eden got older and heard the story repeated year after year, she found both the story and the grown-ups' reactions confusing. What was so silly about it? She'd done what any decent scientist would've done when confronted with something they didn't understand: conduct an experiment with the tools available. Which, in her case, had been five sharp little teeth.

And sure enough, all these years later, it turned out that her history of gnawing at books had come in handy. Eden put down her kazoo, tugged another page out of her book, tore it into tiny strips, and popped a piece into her mouth, wetting it with saliva and doing her best to re-create the wasps' methods.

"What is she *doing*?"

Eden turned to see a boy and a girl watching her from a nearby water fountain. She realized how bizarre she must've looked to them: hunching in the grass, yanking pages from a book and gobbling them up.

"Mom! That girl's eating a book! Mom! Mom! Mom! Mom!" the children called as they ran off, shrieking.

Turning back to her task, Eden applied the damp scraps of paper to the nest, sealing up the gaps. She could feel hundreds of eyes on her, watching to see if this human could be trusted, but they soon got back to work alongside her, as if her presence were the most natural thing in the world.

Being accepted and appreciated right away made Eden feel so light and giddy, she thought she might actually take off and fly herself. She knew it was weird to feel more at home with a species other than her own, but in that moment, helping the wasps, she felt so happy and useful that she decided to stop questioning it and just enjoy being part of a bustling colony.

Eden had done a lot of papier-mâché when she was in second grade. It was one of the things she was sure she was perfect at. By the time she and the wasps had finished, several scout wasps had found a new, more secluded tree for their nest. It was a wide and gracious dogwood, whose branches were decked with white and pink blossoms that would offer privacy and protection. It would also be, the queen pointed out, a glorious playground for her newly hatched babies. Eden, realizing she was the only one strong enough to carry the nest, gathered it carefully in her arms. Once she'd reached the base of the dogwood, she carefully made her way up the slender branches, until the queen pointed out the perfect place for the nest, about halfway out an upper branch.

"Leave it in the crook of the tree, human," the queen buzzed. "That spot is too dangerous for a creature as enormous as yourself. If you venture out there, you will surely topple."

Eden fished her kazoo out of her back pocket. "Please allow me to continue helping you. I'm good at climbing trees. I know I can do it," she kuzz-buzzed.

"Very well," buzzed the queen. "But do take care. A fall from this height would be treacherous. Do not forget that you cannot fly."

"Thank you, Your Majesty," Eden replied, astonished at how easily she'd adapted to talking to an insect. "It'll make it much easier for you to attach the stem."

"I don't mean to be rude and correct you," buzzed the queen. "But we call it a 'petiole.'"

"That's not rude at all," kuzz-buzzed Eden, who actually loved learning new words. She held the nest up to the spot the queen had chosen. "Is this where you had in mind, Your Majesty?"

The queen laughed a tinkling laugh. "It is a tad absurd to hear you say 'Your Majesty' so often. I normally demand it of all my subjects, but I realize now that often all they have to say to me is 'Yes, Your Majesty' or 'No, Your Majesty.' I imagine it must be tedious for you to have to repeat it again and again."

"It is, a little," Eden admitted. "But I want to be respectful, Your Majesty."

"You are impressively respectful, my dear, and you've done me a great service. From this time hence, you may omit my honorific."

"Thank you, Your Majesty. I mean, thank you."

Pleased at their new arrangement, Eden and the queen turned back to their task.

"If you could just reach your tarsal claw a little higher," said the queen. "That would be perfect."

"If I may correct you," Eden kuzz-buzzed. "We call that a 'hand.'"

"You may," the queen replied. "I admire your ability to speak your mind while also remaining courteous."

Eden blushed with pleasure as she thanked the queen. She'd never been this close to a queen before, and she was amazed by how beautiful she was. Her black antennae were tipped with gold, her wings were honey colored, and her black and yellow stripes weren't just solid, repeating bands. The black dripped into the yellow here and there, as if she'd been hand-painted. The shadows were lengthening on the grass as the queen joined Eden on the branch.

"Is there anything else I can do for you?" Eden asked.

"Thank you, but you have already done more for me than I could have dreamed. If only other humans were as kind and helpful as you," the queen buzzed wistfully.

"Oh, there are a lot of humans who do much more than I do," Eden explained. "Doctors, nurses, teachers—"

"Yes, yes," buzzed the queen impatiently. "These 'humans who do,' as you call them, may be 'kind' and 'helpful,' but only when it comes to other humans. And yes, I'm aware that many humans also dote upon dogs, cats, hamsters, and any of the many animals they consider 'pets,' as well as lions, lemurs, and leopards, whom they enjoy seeing in zoos. But when it comes to creatures as tiny as us insects, humans have no trace of compassion."

"I wouldn't say we have *no* compassion—"

"Really? Do you have any idea how many times I've been slapped at by enormous human—what's that word again?"

"Hands?"

"That's it! Hands! I once got swatted the entire length of a picnic table just for landing on an ice cream cake. And look at this," buzzed the queen, soaring over to a nearby garbage can.

Eden jumped down and followed, then peeked inside. There, under a burnt hot-dog bun, was a bright orange can of bug spray. On the front was a drawing of a group of bees and wasps inside a red circle with a red line through it. The drawing was cartoonish, not at all realistic. In it, the bees and wasps were clustered together, standing on two legs, their shoulders hunched, and they all had angry expressions: wild eyes and fierce scowls.

"It would be offensive if it weren't so absurd," said the queen. "Look at my face. I don't even *have* those pointy-downy lines."

"Those are eyebrows," Eden explained. Looking at the can of bug spray made her feel ashamed. As much as she loved insects, she *did* use it on camping trips.

"If anything, we should be using human spray to keep *you* from killing *us*. After all, nothing else has worked. You refuse to listen."

"What do you mean? Have you been trying to talk to us?"

"For ages," said the queen. "Generations ago all the monarchs of the insect kingdom gathered and realized that we needed humans to understand that we are their friends and not their enemies. Each monarch made every effort to communicate with the humans of our land. But when we reconvened to share our discoveries, we each reported that no matter how loud we clicked, buzzed, or whirred, we couldn't get the humans' attention. Perhaps, we thought, they can't hear us, so we began sending bigger groups: entire delegations of fleas, bees, mantids, and mites, telling them to swarm closer and talk louder, but that didn't work either. Whenever the humans saw us coming, they would run away. Finally, desperate to get our message across, we sent our biggest convoy of insects ever: an entire battalion of bees to swarm the humans from all sides, so there was no way they could miss our message of peace."

Oh no, Eden thought. She could imagine the disaster that must have ensued even before the queen described it.

"It was a massacre," the queen continued. "The humans attacked with bug sprays and fly swatters. Thousands of innocent bees were sprayed and smashed to death."

"That's terrible," Eden replied, suddenly aware that her eyes were filling with tears.

"A tragedy," buzzed the queen. "It is incomprehensible to me how humans can adore honey but hate the bees that make it."

"I know. It doesn't make any sense. And there's no excuse for what they . . . I mean, *we*, did," Eden kuzz-buzzed, feeling not so great about being a human after hearing the queen's story. "But I'm pretty sure the humans who were swatting at you today didn't hate you. They were scared of you. After all, you *did* command your army to sting their babies."

"Without regret or hesitation," buzzed the queen. "Make no mistake: threaten my sisters and babies, and I will destroy you."

"Understood," kuzz-buzzed Eden, aware that her cardboard kazoo was getting so soggy from her saliva that it was turning to mush. If she and the queen were going to continue talking for much longer, she'd have to get one of her proper ones from home. "But I bet those people didn't understand what you were trying to tell them."

"How is that possible?" demanded the queen. "We've made strenuous efforts time after time. We are desperate to make you understand that you must become our allies, for your sakes as much as ours. Do you humans understand that our planet cannot survive without us to pollinate it, or do you not?"

"Um, it's not that simple."

"How is it difficult?" asked the queen.

Eden didn't want to tell the queen the truth, which was that many humans already knew that the planet wouldn't survive without insects, but most of those humans were scientists, journalists, and kids. Unfortunately, a lot of other humans felt the same way about scientists and journalists that they did about kids: that most of what they said was made-up nonsense that wasn't worth listening to. But Eden didn't want to tell the queen the truth, because Eden believed humans could be better than the queen gave them credit for.

"Is the future of the world so unimportant to your species that only one human will take the time to learn our languages?"

"Wait," Eden buzzed. "Insects have more than one language?"

"Certainly. We have well over five thousand."

"And you all understand each other's languages?"

"Obviously not. We must learn them if we care to communicate with each other. Is it not the same with humans?"

"It is! I speak English, but I'm learning Spanish in school. How many insect languages do you speak?"

"Oh, at least a few hundred," the queen explained, smiling at Eden's look of astonishment. "It's not as hard as it sounds. All the Stinging and Biting languages such as Bee, Flea, Tick, and Louse are fairly similar, as are the Flying and Fluttering languages like Midge, Moth, Gnat, and Butterfly. The Earth languages like Termite, Beetle, Cicada, and Collembola are the most challenging. It's difficult to get the pronunciation right unless you're actually eating dirt while you're talking."

"But if you can learn so many insect languages, why haven't you learned to speak any human ones?"

"I've tried," buzzed the queen. "Many of us have. The problem is that we lack the vocal organs to create your language. You are proof that humans, if they have sufficient curiosity, have the anatomical capacity to learn our languages. Therefore, it is humans who must learn to speak and listen to us. And yet, despite all of my efforts, you are the only human who has ever tried to speak with me, let alone succeeded."

"Then let's find more humans who can or are willing to learn!" Eden exclaimed. She felt pretty sure that if she and the queen could find enough people willing to learn and teach each other insect languages, the skill would spread across the country and eventually the world, the way seeds are spread by wind and rain. The truth would be impossible to ignore because it would be everywhere. "Maybe we could even start a school!"

The queen sighed. "I've heard rumors that a place like that exists, but I fear it's the stuff of myths and legends. Honestly, it is impossible to believe that humans would be sensitive enough to create such a place."

"It also seems impossible that we found a way to talk to each other," Eden buzzed. "But we did!"

"True indeed," mused the queen.

"And we'll find others, too!" Eden exclaimed.

"But who are they? Where are they? And how will you locate them?"

"I'm not sure," Eden admitted. "But I won't find anyone by staying here. Let's go. The only way to find something is to look."

"Now?" the queen buzzed. "But my babies. It's their bedtime."

Eden smiled. She knew how much her mother and father hated missing her bedtime. There had been so many nights when they'd rushed into her room, their foreheads glistening with sweat, and she knew they'd run from work to their cars and up the stairs to her bedroom to make it home in time to kiss her good night.

"You take care of them, and I'll get started."

"Thank you, human," buzzed the queen.

"Please, call me Eden."

"Ah. Eden. I was wondering what your role in human society was. Is an Eden a queen, a worker, or a drone?"

"Eden is my name, not my role. And humans don't have just one role. We have many. With my parents I'm a daughter; at school I'm a student; with my mother's sisters' children, I'm a cousin."

"That sounds complicated indeed," buzzed the queen. "And what do you suppose is your role with me?"

"With you . . ." Eden considered the question a moment. "With you, I'm a friend."

And with that, she slung her backpack over her shoulder and headed out, leaving the queen to ponder what a friend was, and what one might do.

The Gumball

The bell above the door jingled as August entered the hardware store. It was small and cramped, with boxes of nails and bolts stacked to the ceiling, and rows of snow shovels hanging on hooks. The floor appeared to be covered with an intricate floral carpet, but closer inspection revealed it was actually just concrete that had been spattered over the years with drops of spilled paint. August could've easily written his name in the coating of dust that had settled on the countertop.

By now it was nearly four o'clock. He'd had to walk slowly, pulling up his waistband as he went, since his pockets were so full of change that they'd nearly pulled his pants down with every step. He'd plucked every silver coin out of his money jar and added them up, plus the five-dollar bill he'd swiped out of his dad's jeans. August had decided it wasn't technically stealing, since the pants had been in a pile on the laundry room floor when he'd gone through the pockets. His parents were always telling him how important it was to save money, and this time he'd literally saved the money from getting ruined in the dryer. If anything, they should be proud of him for taking it. In total, he had twenty-seven dollars and eighty-five cents, and he'd brought it all.

August had visited the hardware store many times, but he'd never been there on his own, or spoken to the clerk before. Just the thought of it made him nervous. The clerk was tall and wiry, with arms so skinny that August could see all the individual muscles moving under his chalk-white skin, the blue veins twisting alongside them like snakes among stones. The word *CANDY*, written in all capital letters, was tattooed on his neck. August couldn't be sure, but he assumed that CANDY was someone's name, instead of the food. August loved candy, but not enough to have it permanently written on his body.

"Can I help you?" the clerk asked.

"Um, yeah, I'm looking for bug killer."

"Bug killer? You mean, like, pesticide?"

"Yes! Pesticide." August liked the sound of the word. It sounded official and powerful: like it could really get the job done. "I need a kind that kills cockroaches, moths, flies, and spiders."

"Wow, sounds like you've got quite the infestation," said the clerk, scratching at the *A* in *CANDY*.

"I do," August said. He didn't know what an infestation

was, but he also didn't want to tell the clerk that he really needed the pesticides to save his acting career, make Ms. Batra love him again, stop giving Sheila reasons to bully him, and keep his cellar safe for jelly. August wanted to keep it simple: get the poison, then get out of there before his mom realized he wasn't home.

"Unfortunately for you, you need at least three different kinds to take out all of those guys." The clerk's fingers had drifted to the *ND*. He scratched at it so hard, August expected the letters to come right off.

August reached into his pockets and dumped his coins on the counter, where they settled into a wide, sloping pyramid. "Is this enough?"

"Not nearly," said the clerk. "What are you doing here by yourself, anyway? You shouldn't be spending your allowance on this stuff. Go home and get your parents to take care of it."

August sighed. He knew his parents wouldn't "take care of it" or spend a penny on poisons. They'd say that it was just one cockroach, one fly, one spider, and a moth situation that hadn't even happened to him. They'd say he should just let it go.

"Can't. They don't think it's a problem," August explained. "Can I at least afford one kind?"

By now, the clerk's fingers had migrated to the top of his head, where he dug into his dark hair with his nails. He'd started to seem more like a professional scratcher than a clerk. "Prolly. Which bug's giving you the biggest problem?"

August thought about it for a minute but couldn't decide. For his life to get better, he had to take out all four kinds. "I don't know. They're all the same amount of bad. Don't you have one kind that works on all of them?"

"We almost did," said the scratcher. "Till Ol' Man Wannaberger got fired."

August bit his lip to keep from laughing. *Wannaberger*?! What kind of a wacky name was that?

"He designed all different kinds of bug poisons. Giant tanks of 'em. The best in the world, and all developed and manufactured right here in the store. And rumor has it that the very last poison he invented was his masterpiece. Folks said it could kill every type of insect and was so deadly you'd just need one drop to kill any bug within fifty miles."

"Whoa. That sounds exactly like what I need," August said. Watching the scratcher scratch himself so vigorously made August think of all the times he'd scratched himself bloody, all thanks to mosquitoes, lice, and ticks. They'd ruined s'mores, and summer camp, and were the reason Ms. Batra had had to take all the hats and wigs out of her costume trunk. Maybe he should get rid of those bugs, too, while he was at it. After all, no one liked mosquitoes, lice, and ticks. He'd be doing the whole world a favor. "Is it real? Does it work?"

"Who knows?" the scratcher said. "No one ever got to try it 'cause Ol' Milt got fired before he ever got to sell a drop."

"Why?"

"Welp, he started . . . imagining things."

"What kind of things?"

A bald man with a belly as round as his head stepped out of the cleaning supplies aisle, holding an upside-down mop. He and the mop looked like a couple: a narrow woman with long gray hair standing next to a wide guy in dark green coveralls with no hair at all.

"You talking about the day Milt came in with the ant?" he asked the scratcher.

"Yeah," the scratcher said, turning to August. "We were both there."

"Yup. It was five years ago. April sixth. I remember 'cause it was my first day, and—" The bald man paused, wrinkled his nose, pulled a kerchief out of his pocket, and sneezed into it with surprising daintiness.

"Bless you," August said.

"Thanks. Anyway," continued the sneezer, "Milt comes strolling in here and tells us there's someone we have to meet. Then he opens his hand, and there's an ant in it."

"An ant?" August asked.

"Yup. He says it's got a message for us, and we need to listen real good."

"But ants can't talk," August said.

"You know that and we know that," the scratcher said. "And I start thinking, *Maybe the poor guy's losing it. I mean, he is in his nineties.* But we don't wanna be rude, so we stand real close and watch as Milt puts the ant on the counter, unbuttons his jacket, and we see he's got a washboard strapped to his chest."

"What's a washboard?" August asked.

"You never heard of a washboard?" the sneezer said. "I think we've still got one in the back." He disappeared into the aisle and returned with a long, rectangular wooden frame and, inside the frame, a wide metal sheet covered in horizontal ridges.

"Back in the day, before washing machines, people used to take those down to the river and scrub their clothes clean on it, but now people mainly use them to play music," said the scratcher, and the sneezer pulled a bottle opener off the shelf and demonstrated. August had never heard any other sound like it. It was wheezy but lively, and somehow made the dark, cramped store seem brighter.

"But it wasn't like Milt was playing music for us," the scratcher explained. "He was playing it for the ant, and as soon as he stopped, I'll be darned if the ant didn't puff up its little chest and start rubbing its leg up and down its belly the exact same way."

August's neck was starting to hurt from looking from one man to the other. He could tell they'd been friends for a long time by the way they were telling the story together. Their rhythm was so natural and easygoing, he felt jealous. He wanted to have a friend like that, but he couldn't imagine it happening.

"We all thought it was a cute little party trick," the sneezer said. "But then Milt gets this deadly serious look on his face and says, 'Did you hear that? Unless more people start caring about bugs, the planet's gonna be destroyed.'"

August stared at them open-mouthed. "Destroyed? Like, explode? Like in a movie?"

"I dunno," said the scratcher. "Your guess is as good as ours 'cause we weren't about to ask any follow-up questions to a guy who's playing a busted cookie sheet and telling us that an ant can predict the end of the world."

"Pretty weird stuff, if you ask me," the sneezer said.

"Uh, yeah," August agreed.

"Anyway," added the sneezer. "That's when Ol' Milt tells us he's gonna spend the rest of his life trying to undo all the damage he's done with all the bug poisoning and whatnot. And the ant's gonna teach him how."

"But that doesn't make any sense," August said.

"You know that, and we know that," said the scratcher. "But from then on it all changed. Milt stopped making pesticides and started telling customers not to buy 'em, either. Finally Mr. Martinez, who owns the place, told him to stop coming back. He was bad for business. We never saw him again, until one morning—"

The bell on the door jingled, and a freckly woman in jeans and a wide-brimmed hat entered the store.

"One morning what?" August asked.

"Hold up," the scratcher said, turning to the woman. "Can I help you?"

August had gotten so immersed in the story, he'd forgotten the scratcher was also a clerk.

"I hope so," she said. "I'm painting my sunporch, and I'm hoping you can help me find the perfect shade of white."

"Oh, we've got loads of whites," the scratcher said.

"I'll get the color fans from the back," the sneezer offered.

August waited, fuming, staring at the display of clocks mounted on the wall as the woman monopolized both clerks for a full four minutes and eighteen seconds, yammering away at them as she riffled through dozens of paint samples, asking pointless questions about different shades of white. August was outraged. White was white, wasn't it? How many whites could there be?

"Which is better?" she asked the clerk. "Eggshell White or Cottage White? White Birch or White Whisper? Do I go with a bright white like Snow, or a soft white like Cloud?"

They're all the same! August wanted to shout, but he kept quiet.

At five minutes and nine seconds, August broke down and put a quarter in the gumball machine. He'd been planning to resist getting a gumball so he could spend all his money on poisons, but he could already hear the satisfying crack of the gumball's hard sugar shell as it gave way to the soft, dense center and taste the sweetness that would soon flood his tongue. He gave the handle a crank and listened for the metallic thump that meant it had landed at the bottom of the chute. He lifted the tiny metal door, hoping for a red. Instead, he got white. He stifled a scream.

"I'll think about it," the woman said as she stepped outside.

August, relieved that the interloper was finally gone, raced back to the counter, his mouth full of gum. "Theh wha happa?"

"Oh, yeah, right," said the scratcher. "One morning I come in to unlock the place. Everything's normal, no sign of a break-in, but all the poisons are gone. Every last one."

"He took them with him?"

"He must've," said the sneezer. "We never saw Milt again. Some folks say he moved back to Newport to live in the Windward, the fancy-pants mansion he grew up in."

"That's one story," the scratcher said, shrugging. "Other folks say the mansion got torn down. Some people think he moved back in with his mother, but that can't be right. That would put the old lady at about a hundred years old."

"More like a hundred and twenty," said the sneezer.

"If you think that's weird," said the scratcher, "some people say he planned to build some kinda lab or something and teach other people to talk to bugs."

"Rich folks are funny like that. Spending a lotta money on big ideas that don't make any sense," the sneezer added. "Never could figure out why Milt even worked here in the first place. The guy was born as rich as they come."

The bell on the door jingled, and the woman in the wide-brimmed hat strode in again. "You know what? Now I'm thinking beige. But which beige is best? Tan, Taupe, Stone, Bone, Sand, Beach, or Bark?"

The scratcher turned to August. "Sorry, but she's a paying customer."

"No problem. You guys have told me everything I need to know. Thank you," August said, turning to include the sneezer, but he was already gone.

August scooped his coins off the counter and stepped out into the bright sunlight, triumphant. He hadn't gotten any poison, but at least his next move was clear. He was going to find Ol' Man Wannaberger and figure out where he'd put those poisons.

The Calling Card

*E*den hadn't been to the library in a long time. She and her parents used to go twice a week when she was little, and she would come home weighed down with tote bags full of picture books, still aglow from the splendors of Story Time. Eden adored Story Time. At four o'clock on Tuesdays and Fridays, she would race up the main stairs to the children's section, flop down on the nubby orange carpet that demarcated the Story Time circle, and rest her cheek on the ratty embroidered pillow with the multicolored fringe that was so well worn, she'd come home with strands of pink and green silk entwined in her hair. Eden loved being read aloud to, and even more than that, she loved feeling lost in the smush of bodies as all the kids wriggled together, listening to *Ruby's Wish* and the *George and Martha* series. During that lovely, lazy hour, it was hard to tell where one child ended and another began, as if they were all part of one big litter of puppies. Eden knew that soon they would all go back to their separate homes and families, but in the warm jumble of Story Time, it felt like they were all one big family.

The library website clearly said that Story Time was for kids five to seven, so Eden woke up on the morning of her eighth birthday full of dread. Her mother couldn't understand why she was moping in bed instead of bounding downstairs, and her cheerful father, who usually was very patient with his often moody daughter, got downright irritated when she didn't seem excited about the chocolate chip pancakes he'd made. He banged his coffee cup down with a frustrated "What is it now?"

"Story Time!" she blurted in a rush of hot tears. "I'm too old for Story Time!"

Her parents burst out laughing.

"Story Time?" her mother chortled. "You don't need Story Time, sweetie. You read harder books than I do."

"Thank goodness. I thought it was something *serious*," her father said, missing the point entirely. "You can still go. Under seven is a guideline, not a law."

But Eden knew Story Time was over for her. She was a big kid now and had to make room for the new waves of little ones who would be hurling themselves onto the center of the bright rug and leaving their drool trails on the fraying pillows. As much as she'd miss Story Time, she certainly didn't want to turn into one of those brutish older kids at the playground who would monopolize the bucket swings even when there was a line of preschoolers eagerly waiting to get on. Instead, she stopped going to the library almost entirely and started spending her odd-jobs money buying books from used bookstores, partly so she could mark them up and make notes in the margins, and partly so she wouldn't have to walk by Story Time and endure the lonely sound of people laughing at words she couldn't hear. Any other information she needed she got from her phone. The only reason she was at the library today was that the internet had failed her.

After leaving the wasp queen, Eden had spent an hour trying every possible combination of search words she could think of, hoping to find some kind of information about insect-human communication. If there were other people who could speak an insect language, or would be willing to learn one, she needed to find them, and fast. On her way out of the park, Eden had searched for a bee, hoping to find out if kuzz-buzzing worked with insects that spoke the other Buzzing languages, but she couldn't find one. She did come across a cricket and an acorn weevil and tried empathizing and kuzz-buzzing with them, but they'd just looked at her blankly and scurried away.

Eden's discovery that she could speak to the wasp queen via kazoo was momentous, but it was just a start. She had no idea if she could talk to any other buzzing insects, or any way of knowing if the cricket and weevil couldn't understand her or just weren't interested. But Eden also knew that no one would believe a little girl who said she could talk to insects. They would think it was cute when she said that humans and insects needing to be friends was a matter of life and death. It was all just too preposterous. And the only way to get someone to believe something preposterous was to help them experience it themselves. If the mythical place that the queen had heard about was real and Eden could find it, she could give people the chance to talk personally with bees and beetles and hear their stories. She and the queen really would be able to save the world, person by person and bug by bug.

Eden took a deep breath. She could feel that she was getting ahead of herself. She did that sometimes, getting so worked up about a big idea or new experiment that she'd make too big a deal out of something that wasn't actually all that major. Her sincerity and enthusiasm were two more things adults tended to laugh at, as if it were bad to get really excited about something. *Slow your roll, baby. Act like you've been here before,* Grandma Betty would say. And Eden would try her best, but it just wasn't her nature.

Besides, Eden knew that she and the wasp queen didn't actually have the power to fix the entire world. There would still be famines, wars, and melting icecaps. Over the years, humans had damaged their planet very badly. It was more fragile now than it had ever been, and it couldn't be fixed all at once. But if she could assemble a team that could actually help humans and insects understand why they needed to be partners instead of enemies? That really *would* be major.

But for all her online searching, she'd found nothing: no mention of the fantastical school or any evidence of previous insect-human communication. Was it possible nobody but Eden had ever talked to a bug before? Or maybe someone had, but it was before the internet existed. Eden realized she was going to have to do this the way people used to back in the day, and look in real, old-fashioned books in an actual, old-fashioned library.

She zipped through the empty aisles until she found herself in the entomology section. Eden scanned every book, flipping through thousands of pages. Many of them contained exquisite illustrations of insect anatomy. Any other day she would've stopped to look more closely at the delicate veins that patterned a fly's wing, or the perfect point of a hornet's stinger, but she had no time for that today. Her optimism dwindled as she made her way through the shelves. She'd skimmed almost every book but still had found nothing. When she picked up the very last book in the section, she felt certain it wouldn't contain any useful information, so she was quite surprised when a pale yellow rectangle fluttered out. Eden stooped to pick it up off the carpet and discovered it was a little card, embossed with delicate black script. It read "Tillie Wannaberger" and below that "The Institute for Lower Learning, Where Humans and Insects Intersect."

Eden sank to her knees, astonished at her find. Could this be the place the queen had told her about? Was it possible that it actually existed? Eden examined the card more closely. The card was about the same size as the business cards her grandpa Abe used to keep in his wallet before he retired. Below the text was printed "1048-R." Eden squinted at it, wondering what it could mean. On her grandfather's cards, the number beneath his name was his office phone number. This number was much too short for that, plus it had a letter and no area code. But Eden couldn't think of anything else it could be, so she dug her phone out of her backpack and dialed the peculiar number.

Don't get your hopes up, she thought. *It's probably not even a real—*

"Good evening. You've reached the Institute for Lower Learning. How may I help you?"

Eden was so surprised, she forgot to speak. She listened, frozen, to the crackle that punctuated the silence. It sounded like she was calling someplace very far away, or very ancient.

"Hello? Hello, is someone there?" the woman asked.

"Hello!" Eden finally managed to say. "My name is Eden Evans. I found your card, and I'm very eager to talk to you."

"And why is that?" the woman asked.

"I was, well . . ." Eden began. She realized that in her hurry to dial the number, she hadn't taken a minute to figure out exactly what she wanted to say, let alone practiced saying it. She had to just go for it. "I was wondering if the phrase 'where humans and insects intersect' had anything to do with . . . humans talking to insects."

There was silence on the other end of the line that lasted so long, she wondered if they'd been disconnected.

"May I inquire," the woman said, "why you'd care to know?"

Eden took a deep breath.

"Because I can talk to paper wasps. Actually, so far just one paper wasp. The queen. But I think all paper wasps. I mean, I understood what the worker wasps were saying, but we never actually spoke. Ugh, I really should've tested that. I guess I don't actually know everything for sure, so maybe just forget I called, and—"

Eden forced herself to stop talking. She could tell she was rambling.

"Forget it?" said the woman. "To the contrary, I must know more. We've been looking for someone with skills of that nature. Are you available to come in for a meeting with our Director tomorrow morning? Say, nine fifteen?"

Eden hesitated. Tomorrow? Tomorrow was Friday. And not just any Friday: it was the last Friday of the month, which was the day the class celebrated all of the month's birthdays. Eden had been waiting for the final Friday of April all year. There were going to be decorations and games, and her parents were going to bring cupcakes. Eden groaned. Her parents! How was she going to explain all of this to them?

"I do hope tomorrow morning isn't a problem. It's the best time for our Director," the woman said.

"Oh, yes! Absolutely," Eden said. The opportunity to meet the Director of this mysterious place was more important than cupcakes and worth any amount of explaining, no matter how complicated. "That will be no trouble at all."

"Very good," the woman said.

"Wait," said Eden. "Where are you? What's your address?"

"Excellent question. We're in the Windward estate, just east of The Breakers. Go to the information desk and ask for Tillie Wannaberger. I shall meet you there."

"I'll be there. And thank you! Thank you so much."

Eden, who'd been holding her breath the whole conversation, gulped for air. Excitement bristled through her, as though her body were one of the books whose pages she'd just skimmed. But where, she wondered, was the Windward estate? She searched on her phone but found nothing. Next, she typed in "The Breakers." This time, something came up right away. The Breakers was a mansion in Newport, Rhode Island. It had once been a private home, but now it was a museum.

Next she clicked on Maps. Newport, Rhode Island, was 101 miles away from her home in New Haven, Connecticut. It wasn't *that* far. No matter what it might take, she would find a way to get there.

The Windward

Upstairs in his room, August couldn't stop thinking about the collection of poisons and strange Ol' Man Wannaberger, who'd made them. The sneezer and scratcher hadn't given him any clear answers about where Milton might be now, but they'd both talked about some combination of him moving back to Newport, living in the Windward, and going to stay with his mother. The detail about Milton's mother was the most confusing. The sneezer had said she would be about a hundred and twenty now. August didn't know anyone who was that old.

Luckily, he did know a little something about Newport. It was also in Rhode Island, and only two towns away from his. August's home state had the totally boring distinction of being the smallest one in the country. It was shaped like a graham cracker whose bottom right edge had crumbled off. Each crumble was a small island or peninsula, and the inlets between them led to the cold and choppy ocean. Newport was at the very bottom right corner of the state, and it was so special and fancy that August's class went on field trips there every year.

Newport was filled with the kinds of mansions the clerk had told him about. They were museums now, but they were originally built in the late 1800s as private homes for some of the richest families in the country. These people had so much money, they didn't even live in their specially made mansions year-round. They were just summer homes: places to have giant parties and dances, and to change out of their suits and gowns into "swimming costumes" (which is what they called bathing suits back then) before they clambered down the rocky stairs to swim in the brisk Atlantic. The houses were so impressive, they even had names: The Breakers, Marble House, Rough Point, and Kingscote.

The tour guides, who were basically professional goody-goodies who never grew out of wanting to show off for the teacher, loved to share every single detail about these mansions. Although August had toured several of these imposing homes many times, staring up at their frescoed ceilings, silk-curtained ballrooms, columned entryways, and steep sloping roofs, he'd only heard about the Windward once.

He and his class had been touring The Breakers, perhaps the grandest of all the grand houses, and he'd been staring out the window while the tour guide droned on about all the impressive guests who'd stayed there, when he spotted a little shack tucked behind a dense spread of pines. It looked like a miniature version of the elegant homes, no bigger than a two-car garage and so tangled in vines that no one would've even noticed it unless they'd been told to look.

"What's that?" August had asked, pointing.

"That's the carriage house of the old Windward estate," the tour guide said. "It's sad, really. The Windward was the love-liest of all these homes, but it was torn down about five years ago. That's all that's left of it."

The abandoned shack looked way more interesting than the big, stuffy Breakers, where all the cool stuff was either roped off or plastered with "Do Not Touch" signs.

"Can we go there?"

"Oh no," said the tour guide. "That terrible old eyesore? The whole place would probably cave in if you blew on it. Now, let's move on to the butler's pantry."

August smiled at the memory. That terrible old eyesore now sounded like the greatest place in the world.

The Wish

*E**den flung open the** front door and raced for the kitchen.

"Mom! Dad!" She skidded to a stop just in time to see her mother quickly turn away from the counter to face her, the tendrils of her wavy dark brown hair escaping her ponytail. Eden could tell from the unnatural way her mother held her arms out, using the billowing sleeves of her blouse as a screen, that she was hiding a birthday cake. The fact that her mother was also holding a pastry bag full of frosting, a yellow rosette peeping out of the tip, really gave it away. But Eden had bigger things on her mind than cake.

"You'll never believe what happened at the park," she said.

"Try us," her father said, pulling a waterfall of spaghetti out of the pot. He must've started cooking the minute he'd gotten home from the hospital, because he hadn't changed into a T-shirt yet. Instead, he'd thrown his tie over his shoulder and rolled up the sleeves of his light blue button-down.

Over her birthday dinner, Eden's parents listened intently as she told them all about the party, the broken nest, and her remarkable discovery that she could talk to the wasp queen. On her way home, Eden had been worried that her story was too incredible to be believed, but the more she thought about her mom and dad, the more confident she became that they would know it was true. They were always saying that they believed in her and knew she could do anything she put her mind to. Plus, her dad was a doctor and researcher. He was one of those humans who'd dedicated his life to helping people and learning new things.

"Overall, she doesn't trust humans," Eden said, finishing her story as she slurped down the last of her spaghetti. "I mean, why would she? But now that I've learned how to talk to her, she trusts me! And we're gonna find other people who can do it, too. Or who are willing to learn, the same way I learned kuzz-buzz. I'll show you! I'll go get my kazoo."

Eden pushed her chair back so hard she nearly knocked it over. Her parents looked at each other and smiled.

"That's an amazing story," her father said.

"Really creative. So much detail. You really need to write it down," Eden's mom said.

"No!" Eden told them. "You don't get it. This isn't a story."

"Not yet," her dad said, getting up from the table and heading into the kitchen. "Writing is hard, and it takes a lot of work. But you'll get there."

"You're not getting it, Dad," Eden said as she heard a match strike. "This happened. I helped her fix her nest, and now I'm going to help her save the planet!"

Her mother came back to the table, having just turned the dining room lights off. "That's such an interesting choice," she said. "Most kids want to be the heroes of their stories. I love that your character is an ally."

"Mom! I'm not a character. This is real!"

"I know it's real to you," her mom said, caressing her face. "It's one of the things I love most about you."

Eden glared at her mother. Apparently, there was a big difference between believing *in* someone and believing them. She wished she'd known that sooner.

Eden's father entered with the cake. The light of the candles gave his dark skin an amber glow, and she could see in his eyes and her mother's smile how happy they were to be here with her, celebrating. They sang as her dad placed the cake in front of her, but Eden couldn't stand the sound. They had no idea what traitors they'd revealed themselves to be. Eden tried to be grateful for the delicious meal and the presents stacked nearby, but her face was hot, and not from the candles. She closed her eyes and blew. This time she didn't wish that she could talk to animals. That wish had already come true.

"What did you wish for?" her mother asked.

I wished that you'd believe me, she thought. But instead she only said, "If I tell you, it won't come true."

The Lie

*A*ugust *didn't want to* lie to his mother. Just thinking about it gave him a stomachache, so he tried to think of it as acting. After all, acting and lying were almost the same thing. In acting, you had to convince the audience that the made-up story you were telling was real. As Papa Bear, he had to make the audience believe that he was a bear who lived in a human-style house. And as a boy who needed to get to Newport, Rhode Island, to find an old man living in an old house full of poisons, he had to make his mother believe that his class was going there on a field trip.

The main difference between being an actor and a liar, though, was that actors didn't have to worry about getting caught. Liars had to worry about it all the time. People went to movies and the theater because they wanted to hear stories that weren't true, but people in real life didn't like being told made-up stories at all. In fact, it made them very angry.

And that, August thought, was why people loved actors but hated liars.

He tried to tell himself that the lie he was about to tell his mom wasn't a bad one, like pretending to be sick so he wouldn't have to go to school, or saying he'd eaten his squash even though he'd actually wrapped it up in his napkin. After all, his lie wasn't designed to hurt her. It was actually designed to make her life better. On his way home from the hardware store, August remembered that his dad was so allergic to bees that he needed to carry an EpiPen with him wherever he went. August had added bees to the growing list of insects he needed to poison. Really, he told himself, how bad was a little acting-slash-lying if it could save his father's life? Still, he didn't know if his mom would see it that way. To be safe, he'd need to be as good a liar as he was an actor.

He picked up his empty plate. "Can I take yours, too, Mommy?"

August hadn't called his mom Mommy in a while, but he knew it would make her think of him as her sweet, innocent little boy even more than she already did.

"Thank you, baby," she said. "How thoughtful."

"Sure thing," he said, carrying them to the dishwasher. "Oh, by the way, my class is taking a field trip to Newport tomorrow."

"Another? Didn't you already go this year?"

"Nope," August said. "I think you're thinking of last year."

He bit the tip of his tongue, waiting to see if she'd buy it. Something he'd noticed about adults was that they didn't seem to have any trouble accepting that their minds were crumbling. In fact, they often seemed downright light-hearted about it.

"Ha! Probably," his mother said, knocking the side of her head as if it were a door. "This morning, I forgot it was Thursday. I would've missed yoga if Nancy hadn't called."

August pulled the phony permission slip he'd made from his pocket and placed it on the table beside her. He'd pulled the form off the Trampoline World website and had lightly photoshopped it, replacing the "Trampoline World" with the name of his school. His mother scrawled her name without so much as a glance. August couldn't believe the breeziness with which parents would sign away their children's safety, promising not to sue if their boys and girls came home with broken bones, concussions, or worse. It seemed like there was no risk they wouldn't take to get themselves a few free hours to see a movie or get a massage.

"Have fun," she said. "I wish I could go. I love those old mansions."

August took a deep breath, trying hard not to panic. His impulse was to shout, *No!* but that's not what a sweet, honest boy who loved his mommy would say.

"I wish you could, too," he said, wrapping his arms around her.

August felt only the tiniest smidgen of guilt as his mom hugged him back. Mainly, he felt elated. He'd done it! He'd made her believe the phony field trip to Newport was real *and* gotten her to sign the fake permission slip. It would've been wrong if he'd been lying, but since it was acting, it was basically okay.

The Escape

Eden was up and dressed before dawn. The earliest train to Rhode Island didn't leave until 6:40 a.m., but she had to leave before her parents woke up. If they knew where she was going, they'd definitely try to stop her. They warned her all the time about going places alone and how she had to be extra careful. A police officer seeing a white girl walking alone might say, *Can I help you?* but the same officer might see a Black girl walking alone as a troublemaker.

A while ago, Eden had noticed that her parents almost always referred to her as "mixed," except in certain contexts, like when they were talking about having pride or being in danger, and then she became "Black." At first, Eden resisted being described differently in different contexts. It seemed unnecessarily complicated, but her parents pointed out that complicated wasn't bad. It just meant that you had to spend more time thinking about it than you did with something simple. As a scientist, Eden liked thinking about complicated things, but sometimes she wished she didn't have to think so much and could just read and daydream more.

All that said, Eden knew that her parents were right about keeping an extra eye out for danger, and she took their words seriously, but it also seemed very unlikely that she, with her purple glasses, bright blue notebook, and lanyard necklace with a miniature magnifying lens hanging from it, would be mistaken for a troublemaker. Still, she paid close attention and did what they said to stay safe.

The fact that Eden respected and listened to her parents made things even more complicated. She'd never lied to them before, let alone done something as irresponsible as run away, but she had no choice. Since they refused to believe that she could communicate with the wasp queen, there was no point in telling them about finding the calling card and her phone conversation with the mysterious woman. And they'd certainly never believe that her appointment at the Institute for Lower Learning was real. But Eden had a hopeful feeling that it could be more than real: it could be world-changing.

Eden wasn't just thinking about the good of the world. This was also a dream opportunity for her personally. Sure, she loved spending her days in the park, reading and observing insects, but she was getting tired of observing life from a distance. It was lonely watching it go on around her. If she could find the Institute, and if it was truly a place where humans and insects could intersect and talk together, she'd find hundreds—no! literally *trillions*—of creatures she could understand and who could understand her. And maybe she could find the friend she'd always been hoping for: someone who would grab her hands and jump up and down and shout, *Exactly! Me too!* instead of smiling and shaking their head like she was sweet but a weirdo. She'd be immersed in the noise and bustle of life, instead of watching it from the sidelines.

She thought of these possibilities now, as she assembled a PB&J in the dark. She put her phone and notebook into her backpack, scribbled a note that said she'd left for school early to check on an experiment, hopped on her bike, and headed out. She hadn't anticipated how cold the morning air would be, and she zipped up her track jacket to protect herself from the chill. When she got to the train station, she chained her bike up and hoped it would be there when she got back. *If I get back,* she thought with a shudder, then took a deep breath, reminded herself not to be melodramatic, and headed inside.

No one looked twice when she bought a ticket to West Kingston, Rhode Island, from the machine. The train wasn't due to arrive for another half hour. She slumped low on the long, dark wooden benches that curved around at the ends, eating the cinnamon cruller she'd bought at the coffee shop. There had been a tray of muffins under a glass dome on the counter, which made Eden remember that today was Final Friday, and her parents were going to show up at school with cupcakes for the class's birthday celebration. How could she have been so sloppy? She'd gone to all the trouble of sending the school a note from her dad's email account explaining her absence. She'd triple-checked the bus schedule to make sure she'd be home by dinner. Eden had been so proud of her perfect plan. She'd arranged everything to make sure her parents wouldn't even know she'd missed school, let alone gone to Newport. Now they'd know for sure. But no matter how much she wished she'd done things differently, she couldn't change the past. All she could do was make sure she didn't make any more mistakes. She forced herself to choke down some coffee, dousing it with half-and-half until it was nearly as white as milk. She hated the burnt taste, but it was worth it. She needed to make sure she stayed extra alert.

When the train finally pulled into the station, she hopped on with relief. She usually loved heading north on an Amtrak train. Her parents would sometimes put her on a train to visit her aunt in Boston, and she always grabbed a window seat that faced the shore, so she could watch the gleaming water as the train sped by. This time, she barely glanced over, spending the journey replaying her travel plan in her head. She'd arrive in West Kingston at 8:40 a.m., then run to the bus stop, where she'd catch RIPTA bus number sixty-four at 8:52. If she managed all that, she'd be in Newport by 9:00 a.m. The April bus schedule said that the bus stopped on Ochre Point Avenue, just a block from The Breakers. Tillie Wannaberger, the woman on the phone, had said the Institute for Lower Learning was in the Windward estate, which was right next door. It would be a close call, but she'd reviewed every detail so many times, she was confident she could execute it perfectly, as long as nothing went wrong. Unfortunately, Eden had no way of knowing that something was about to go horribly, terribly wrong.

The Plan

August lay in bed awake, watching the minutes flip on his digital clock. Normally he'd be up by now, dressed and shoveling cereal into his mouth by 7:20. Then he'd gulp his juice, brush his teeth, and head outside to wait for the bus.

August hated the bus. His stop was the last one before school, so by the time he got on, nearly all the seats were taken. He could've sat with Randall Davis, who sat in the front row and always had an empty spot next to him, but Randall, like August, Vincent Vicks, and Ivan Linsky, was an outcast. Sheila made fun of him, too, and it was obvious to August that she did it because she was jealous of Randall, who won the talent show every year for his awesome piano playing. Sheila would look like a bad sport for making fun of Randall for winning, though, so she got all her friends to tease him for getting all A-pluses and being a teacher's pet.

It seemed nonsensical that August got bullied for being the

worst in the class and Randall got bullied for being the best, but August didn't make the rules. Sheila did, and there was no point in questioning her. Randall was also the only Black kid in their class and had an Afro, so Sheila called him Dandelion, and would mime blowing on his hair whenever she passed him in the hall. August knew that picking on Randall for having hair that was different from the other kids in the class was racist and that Sheila would get into even worse trouble for that than for regular bullying. He wondered when Randall would tell on her, but Randall never did. He'd just take a deep breath and keep walking. August always had a feeling that he should stick up for Randall, but he knew that would only draw more attention to himself, and he was scared of what Sheila would do if she found out that he was the one who'd ratted her out. So just like he avoided Vincent "Nurps" Vicks, and Ivan "Dracula" Linsky, August avoided Randall "Dandelion" Davis. Being seen with any of them was just too risky.

As much as August hated taking the bus, missing it was even worse. If he missed it, his mother would drive him to school, and the nine-minute drive would include a nine-minute lecture on how he needed to be more responsible and more respectful of his mother's time. August hated being scolded even more than he hated walking past Sheila and her friends on the bus, so he always made sure he got to the bus stop on time. Today, though, he was trying to be late on purpose.

"August!" his mother shouted from the kitchen. "What's going on up there? You're going to be late!"

August leapt out of bed and padded into the kitchen in his pajamas, doing his best to seem groggy.

"Did I oversleep?" he asked, scratching his head like he'd seen actors do on TV to show they were tired.

"Yes! Why are you in your pajamas? Get moving. Don't dawdle!"

August made a show of eating his breakfast quickly and racing back upstairs as though he truly didn't want to be late, but instead of coming down as soon as he was dressed, he lingered in his room, flipping through an old *Mad* magazine.

"August!" his mother shouted. "Hurry! You have to be at the bus stop in five minutes!"

He clattered down the stairs. "I'm hurrying!"

He raced into the kitchen, grabbed his lunch, and went to grab his backpack from the hook by the front door.

"My backpack!" he shouted. "It's not here!"

"I always tell you to hang it up the night before!" his mother shouted, racing around the room looking for it. "Where is it? We have to find it!"

August ran upstairs and sat on his bed for six minutes, occasionally shouting, "I can't find it!" and "I swear it was here!" before pulling it out of his closet, where he'd stashed it the night before.

"I've got it!" he shouted as he ran down the stairs.

His mother was waiting in the front hall, her hands on her hips like an angry mom in a cartoon. August looked over her shoulder at the front window. The bus was still a block away. He had to stall a little longer, or he'd get outside in time to catch it. He couldn't let that happen. For his plan to work, he had to miss the bus. He'd have to think fast.

As his mother thrust his lunch box into his arms, August turned it upside down and yanked the zipper open. His sandwich, apple, carrots, and cookie spilled onto the floor.

"Oh no!" he said, pretending to be upset.

"August!" his mother said, genuinely upset.

August scrambled to stuff it all back in while keeping an eye on the bus, which was now pulling up to the far end of his block. He kicked the apple so it rolled into the living room, just to give himself an extra few seconds. Sure enough, by the time his mother opened the door, the bus was pulling away, moving too fast for her to flag down.

"Darn it!" she said.

Mission accomplished, August thought.

"I'm sorry," he said, doing his best to seem genuinely apologetic. "I know how busy you are. I didn't mean to miss the bus."

He wiped at his cheek with his sleeve, as if he were brushing away a tear. Sure enough, she softened immediately.

"Oh, honey, it's okay. I shouldn't have yelled. It's not that big a deal. I can drive you."

"But . . . but . . . the field trip to Newport is today, and the bus leaves right from school. I'm going to miss it."

"All right, no problem," she said. "I'll just call the school and let them know I'll be taking you myself."

August hid a smile. This was going perfectly. Gloria, who sat at the front desk, was always too busy doing her Sudoku puzzle to know or care about the details of the school's daily schedule.

"Hey, Gloria, it's Cheryl Rattice, August's mom. We're running late today, so I'll be dropping August off at his field trip myself. Okay, thanks." She turned to August. "See? All better."

"Thanks, Mom," August said, looking up at her through his long lashes. It was a little trick that always worked, and today was no different.

"No problem, sweetie," she said, pulling him in for a hug.

So gullible, he thought as he hugged her back.

RIPTA Bus Number Sixty-Four

Eden was asleep when the deer leapt in front of the bus. She was woken abruptly by the sound of screeching tires and the shouts of the passengers. The bus skidded so wildly to the side, a heavy suitcase on the top rack flew off the shelf, slamming her in the head. The bus careened off the road into a shallow ditch, landing at a steep angle like a jaunty cap on a snowman.

The deer, who had narrowly escaped being hit, was already deep into the forest, its white tail flashing among the dark green pine boughs as it disappeared.

People had been flung from their seats and were pulling themselves up off the floor of the bus. A baby was wailing, and two men were helping an elderly woman to her feet. Eden was totally disoriented. Looking out the front window, all she could see was a light blue triangle. She stared at it for a few seconds, confused, before she realized it was a wedge of sky. The bus had tilted so far to the right that the road that had stretched ahead moments earlier had totally disappeared from view.

"Is everyone all right?" the driver called.

Eden groaned. Her head was throbbing. A woman across the aisle from her looked over at her, concerned.

"We need help over here! This girl is hurt," she called.

Eden, confused, touched her forehead and was shocked to see her hand was wet with blood. She felt woozy just looking at it and gripped the sides of her seat, willing herself not to pass out.

"I'm fine," she said. "I'm okay."

"She's in shock," the woman said to the other passengers. "We need to get her to the hospital."

"No," Eden insisted. "I'm all right."

But the grown-ups on the bus were already closing in on her, determined to help. Eden didn't want their help. All she could think about was her interview at the Institute for Lower Learning. A side trip to a hospital would jeopardize that. She glanced at the window to her left, then at the bus driver, who was bustling toward her with a first aid kit. Escape was her only hope of making her interview with the Director on time, but the door of the bus was pinned by the ditch. She scurried across the aisle to the side of the bus that wasn't pressed against the ground and yanked the window open, grateful to feel the fresh air on her face. She planted her feet and pushed her body up until she was level with the opening. It would be a tight fit, but she was lean enough to squeeze through. As she swung her body into a horizontal position, the driver grabbed the handle at the top of her backpack, pulling her backward.

"It's okay, I've got you," he said. Eden gritted her teeth. Adults always thought they were helping when they were doing exactly the opposite. She could hear another passenger talking to a 911 operator and the wail of police sirens. If she hesitated another minute, she'd never be able to get away.

Thinking fast, she slid her arms out of the backpack and slipped out the window of the toppled bus, leaving her backpack and all her possessions behind. She hated to lose her phone, but she was eventually going to have to abandon it anyway. Her parents used a location tracker so they'd always know where she was, and although that had never been a problem when she was only going places they approved of, it would definitely put a crimp in running away. As for her notebook, it would be excruciating to lose months' worth of notes, but notes could always be re-created. An opportunity like this might never come again.

Eden, now crouching on the outer side of the window, looked down at the side of the bus, which plunged like a sheer cliff down toward the road. She turned her body to the right, like her mother had taught her when they were hiking the craggy basalt face at Sleeping Giant Park, and scuttled down the side of the bus before jumping over the giant wheels to the ground.

"Stop!" yelled the driver. "Someone, go get her before she hurts herself."

But the adults on board were too big to make it through the tiny gap. They could only watch as Eden, like the deer, sprinted away.

The Disguise

A gaggle of schoolchildren were getting off a school bus just as August and his mother pulled up to The Breakers.

"There's my class!" August said, grabbing the door handle. He'd gotten lucky. So many schools took field trips to The Breakers, he'd guessed that another school would also have a trip that day, and his gamble had paid off. These kids, their backs to his mother's car as they jockeyed to be the first inside, were indistinguishable from his actual classmates.

"Hang on. Let me park and walk you over," his mother said, squinting into her rearview mirror to check her lipstick, then tugging at the lapels of her blazer to make sure they were even. His mom was only a lipstick-and-blazer kind of person on days she worked, and August wished it were a non-work day. Then she'd be wearing pajama bottoms and a sweatshirt and wouldn't want to get out of the car.

"It's okay," he told her, thinking quickly. "I'll tell Mr. Lewis. I've already made you late enough."

"If you're sure," she said, glancing at the dashboard clock. "I really should get to my meeting."

Luckily, August's mother could always be counted on to cut corners. With his father away on business trips so often, his mom was "essentially a single parent." August wasn't totally sure what this meant, but he heard his mom saying it to Nancy a lot. August missed his dad being around more and knew his mom did, too, but today he was grateful that his dad was out of town, because it gave his mother much less time to wonder why she'd never gotten an email about the field trip.

He hopped out of the car and headed for the main entrance of The Breakers, waving back at his mom as he went. As soon as she drove off, however, he changed course and looped around the eastern side of the mansion, scanning the grounds. Sure enough, the old shack was right where he remembered, at the very edge of the property, mostly hidden by a stand of low, bushy pine. He was out of breath by the time he got there, but he couldn't tell if it was from running across the giant lawn or from fear. What if the know-it-all tour guide had been right, and the old, rickety building collapsed and crushed him the minute he touched it?

Finding a crack in the door, August gingerly put his eye up to it. The inside of the shack was as beautiful as the outside was a disaster. It looked like the lobby of a tiny museum: stately and serene. The walls were paneled in rich mahogany that was etched with elaborate carvings of beetles. In the center of the polished marble floor, a mosaic made of thousands of tiny pieces of brightly colored tile read "The Institute for Lower Learning, Where Humans and Insects Intersect." Just beyond the mosaic was a desk with a placard in front of it that read "Information." Sitting behind it was a very tall, white-haired woman. Her eyes were downturned, focused on a small plate of blueberry pie in front of her. She was moving her fork toward the pie so slowly that it took August a moment to realize that the fork was moving at all. She had to be the elderly mother that the hardware store man said Milton had come to live with, and the mosaic on the floor literally spelled out that this was a place where humans and insects were supposed to intersect. If these things were real, it could very easily also be true that Milton had moved back here, and that he'd hidden his poisons here, too.

August's heart jumped in his chest like a frog cupped between two hands. He'd found it! The mysterious place the scratcher and the sneezer had told him about was real! He wanted to run in and start pawing through every drawer, box, and closet he could find, but he resisted. He knew he couldn't go in there wearing the shorts and bright yellow field trip T-shirt he'd put on to con his mother. He'd go back behind the building, change his clothes, and then return, prepared to carry out the plan he'd devised the night before.

August had come up with his strategy pretty quickly, after having had several key realizations:

1. IF THIS PLACE WAS ANYTHING LIKE THE BREAKERS OR ANY OTHER OF THE NEWPORT MANSIONS, KIDS WERE NOT ALLOWED IN WITHOUT AN ADULT.

2. MILTON WAS NOT GOING TO GIVE AUGUST THE POISONS. HE'D BROUGHT THEM BACK TO NEWPORT TO HIDE THEM, NOT TO GIVE THEM TO ANYONE WHO CAME BY.

3. MILTON DID NOT TRUST ANYONE WHO HATED INSECTS.

Therefore:

1. HE'D HAVE TO PRETEND TO LOVE INSECTS.

2. HE'D HAVE TO FIND AND STEAL THE POISONS.

3. TO FIND THE POISONS, HE'D NEED PERMISSION TO ROAM AROUND THE MANSION ON HIS OWN.

4. ONLY ADULTS WERE ALLOWED TO ROAM AROUND MANSIONS ALONE.

5. AUGUST HAD TO PRETEND TO BE AN ADULT.

The plan thrilled and frightened him. It seemed brilliant but risky, since he could easily imagine it going either very well or very badly. What it really came down to was whether he believed in himself as an actor. Lying on his bed, his head dangling off the edge of the mattress, August had asked himself the hard question: could he really make someone believe that he, a nine-year-old boy who hated insects, was actually a full-grown man who loved them? He rolled off the bed and stood in front of his mirror, studying himself. If only he'd gotten the chance to play Papa Bear that morning and seen the looks on the faces of the kids as they watched him. Their faces would've shown him just how good he was. If only he could somehow watch himself.

It had suddenly occurred to him that there was a way. His mom had taken tons of videos of him in his various school plays and pageants so his dad could see them when he got home. He'd tiptoed down to his father's office and plugged the hard drive that said "Augie" into his dad's laptop. He typed in his father's password, which was easy to remember because it was August's own birthday, and opened the folder labeled "August's Shows." He turned the sound off so he wouldn't wake his mom, and watched as he capered around the stage in all his various roles: a sunflower, a mountain, Santa, a bossy pirate, and the White Rabbit. He watched his performances with as clear and critical an eye as possible, but the truth was, he was good. Like, *really* good. He could do this.

August reminded himself of all this as he crouched behind the ramshackle building and pulled his blue Papa Bear suit out of his backpack. Next, he pulled out the dress shoes he'd worn to his aunt Rachel's wedding the year before and put them on. They were a size too tight and terribly uncomfortable, but he knew he had to wear them to make his "grown man" costume complete. Obviously, there was a lot more to playing a man than putting on his clothes, but August knew he was up to it. He was confident he could play a man, because he'd spent his whole life watching his dad. Most kids whose dads didn't travel for business had the luxury of taking them for granted, barely noticing them when they tucked them into bed or made them a grilled cheese. But since August didn't see his dad nearly as much as he wanted, he stayed as close to him as possible whenever he got the chance.

Because he was always standing in the front hall when his dad came in from the garage, August knew the exact way his dad would throw his keys in the air, then catch them before putting them down on the front hall table. He'd mastered raising and lowering a single eyebrow, just like his dad did when August told him something far-fetched. And he'd gotten great at winking slyly, the way his dad did to show that they were both in on a joke. He could imitate his dad's long, rolling stride, because when they'd go to amusement parks, August wanted to keep up and not have to ask him to slow down. He could imitate his dad's low voice, and used it (plus some added growling) to play Papa Bear. August knew exactly how his dad liked his tea—no milk, no sugar—because he loved making it for him in the morning.

By the time August had finished getting dressed, he felt good about his plan again. Strong. Confident. It was showtime.

Atom and Dot

On a high counter inside the kitchen of the Institute, Atom perched on the edge of a pie pan, all six of his legs gripping the rim so there was no chance he'd fall into the depths of the pie plate. The pie inside was fresh and still warm, and he gazed longingly at the spot where the sandy bank of pie crust met the deep blue, almost purple lake of smashed, sugared berries. He fought the urge to dive headfirst into the pan and immerse himself in the soft jellied surface, where floating was effortless. When he was little, he'd learned the hard way that pie diving was dangerous. He'd done a forward pike into a pecan pie, and worker ants had had to dig him out from between the grooves of a pecan in front of the entire colony. Besides, he was already buzzing from having eaten too much sugar that morning: a crumb of coffee cake, a bite of brownie, and an entire dollop of oatmeal smothered in maple syrup. But as always, the whiff of sugar in his olfactory receptors was irresistible. For someone who didn't have any teeth, he had a powerful sweet tooth. Still, he knew better.

But as Atom stepped back from the edge, his back leg caught on the rim of the pan, knocking him off balance. He teetered, windmilling his forelegs to keep from falling forward and his middle legs in the opposite direction to keep from pitching back. Either could be fatal. His mind filled with images of the thousands of brothers and sisters he'd never see again, and the terror alone made him lose his footing. He was hurtling toward the pie, his body toppling toward the soupy filling, when a delicate leg looped around his midsection, tugging him to safety. He turned, panting, to see the grinning face of his big sister Dot.

Atom had always been struck by how beautiful his sister was. While the chitin of his exoskeleton was just a boring old black, Dot was darker and glossier, a gleaming obsidian just like their mother, Queen Mote. Atom knew that his mother and sister weren't just more attractive than he was: they were smarter, stronger, and more ambitious, too. But he didn't mind. Ever since he'd been a pupa, Atom had understood that female ants held a much more important place in society than males. In that way, they were a lot like wasps. In both communities, the females did all the labor. They were queens, workers, warriors, gardeners, nurses, and teachers, and they played as hard as they worked. They had richer, more meaningful lives than the males, who were born, gorged themselves silly on sugar, then took off with no plan or purpose. Atom had once asked his mother why there were only queen ants and no kings. *Males are wonderful, but ruling a colony is complicated. It takes a female to do it right,* she'd explained.

Atom's mother was surprised when Atom told her that he wanted to live in the colony with her and Dot forever. She warned him that life would be hard for him there, since so few males stuck around. But Atom was determined to stay. The Institute for Lower Learning was his home. His grandma, Queen Minnie, had been the founding mother along with her human partner, Milton, and Atom knew in his dorsal aorta that he belonged there, enjoying the exceptional company of exuberant, powerful females, and doing everything he could to avoid falling into a pie.

"Come on!" Dot said cheerfully, as if he'd never been in any danger at all. "Something strange is going on around here. Let's go see what's up!"

Atom shook his head and smiled. Dot's energy was infinite and her confidence unbounded. She was as wild as he was tame. She was the doer and he was the dreamer. She would focus in, while he would space out. Whenever they went adventuring, Dot racing ahead with Atom dawdling behind, every ant in the colony would exclaim that it was impossible to believe they were brother and sister. And yet they were inseparable. Of their 3,429 siblings, Atom and Dot were the closest. No one was more fun to be with than Dot, and no one was as fierce a protector. Once, Dot had spotted two daddy longlegs playing keep-away with the grain of rock candy Atom had gotten for his birthday. Atom had been caught between them, struggling to catch the nugget of candy as the long-limbed spiders tossed it back and forth over his head. Dot had not only gotten his candy back, but also managed to tie all sixteen of the daddy longlegs' limbs in a bow and leave the embarrassed spiders at Atom's feet, like a present.

Now he smiled, happy to see her and grateful that she'd saved him yet again. "What's going on?"

"Unclear," Dot said. "Clara said she'd been snacking on the front door when a male human came by, peeked through the crack, then left. At least, that's what I think she said."

Atom nodded. Clara, like most of the termites, tended to talk with her mouth full of wood slivers, and it was almost impossible to tell what she was saying. Still, if the human part was true, this was intriguing. They never got human visitors at the Institute. Atom hopped down off the pie plate, his curiosity overwhelming his natural urge to hang back.

Dot urged him forward with a wave of her foreleg. "If we hurry, maybe we'll find him before he gets too far away."

"So you're saying we should go to the entryway? Like, the main one? On the first floor?"

"Why not?" said Dot.

Why not? There were a million reasons why not. Although the Institute was their home and they were free to go any place they liked, Atom almost never had any reason to go any place other than outside to the garden, or to the other rooms on the third floor. The entrance to their colony led directly into the third-floor hall, which also held the kitchen, the magnificent sitting room with the morpho butterfly ceiling mural, the library, and the grand staircase whose slick banisters they would slide down, hooting and cheering the whole way. There was plenty to explore right there in their own neighborhood. Going to other floors was a bigger deal, reserved for family outings, vacations, and school field trips.

"Are you coming or not?" Dot asked. Dot, like Grandma Minnie, was always forging ahead, eager to experience every part of life, whether it was delightful or dangerous.

Atom knew she wasn't actually waiting for an answer. Of course he was coming. Although her schemes and adventures often made him nervous, he'd rather be scared and go with her than stay behind and be bored.

As they wound their way over the polished kitchen floor, which was inlaid with golden hexagons designed to look like a honeycomb, and alongside the walls, which were decorated with copper vines that had grown a patina so green that it looked like actual vines were climbing to the ceiling, Atom couldn't help but marvel at the magnificent palace in which they lived. His grandma Minnie and her partner, Milton, had built it only five years ago, but they had preserved the style of the Windward, the original mansion that had been built over a hundred years before. Atom loved thinking about his grandma, but it hurt, too. She'd died a few months ago at the very old age of six, and even though Atom knew she'd had a long, happy life, he still missed her terribly. She'd been a wonderful grandmother. Every night she'd tell Atom and Dot bedtime stories about her wild adventures, and his very favorite was the one about how she became friends with a human.

The story of Grandma Minnie and Milton's friendship was as surprising as it was unique. Nearly all insects thought that becoming friends, let alone partners, with humans, was a ridiculous and dangerous notion. Everyone knew that humans were vicious killers who hated insects. Every bug had a story of a relative who'd been burnt with a magnifying glass or squashed by a swatter wielded by one of those deranged, two-legged creatures. But Grandma Minnie was far too modest to describe herself as brave or revolutionary. She'd simply say, *I thought something needed to be done, so I did it,* as if devoting your life to helping lifelong enemies become friends were as simple as digging a hole.

Atom's aunts, Itty-Bitty and Dab, were the colony's official historians. Every Winter Solstice Eve, they'd gather everyone under the Solstice branch to nibble at the popcorn garlands twined around the pine needles and hear the tale of how the Institute came to be. Atom loved hearing the details of how his grandmother and Milton had met almost as much as he loved admiring the majestic architecture of the Institute that the partners had built together.

Grandma Minnie, like the rest of the family, was a garden ant who collected seeds for a living. When she was young, she'd become an apprentice to a carpenter ant, trading sunflower seeds for lessons in how to build an ant colony. And after a long day of carrying seeds in the ant brigade, Grandma Minnie would gather up loose twigs from the garden and stay up late at night, fortifying the sandy walls of their ant colony with the twigs. And by the time Grandma Minnie and Milton had decided to transform the Windward, Minnie knew enough about carpentry and architecture to design a building big enough for humans and insects alongside her human partner.

Atom loved exploring the enormous Institute, but he had to admit that while he knew his way around many of the ornate rooms, he had basically no understanding of the overall floor plan, or where various rooms were in relation to each other. He wasn't allowed to go anywhere without Dot, and when she was leading the way, he rarely paid attention to where they were going. Being the leader was Dot's job, so Atom was free to look around and daydream, which was exactly how he liked it, and precisely what he was doing when Dot turned back and threw him a look with every surface of her compound eye.

"Quit dawdling," she said. "We have a mystery to solve!"

Tillie

August pushed open the rotted door. The old woman was now asleep, nodding over her pie. Her glasses rested on the top of her head, perched among her white curls. Because the top of her head was facing him, the combination of white curls and glasses made it look like he was being observed by a very studious poodle. August stifled a laugh, since a grown-up would never laugh at that kind of thing. A kid would see it and crack up, but grown-ups, because they were usually in a hurry, would never even notice it, let alone have the imagination to see what was funny about it.

"Hello!" he said in a voice almost as low as his dad's. He didn't want to make it too low, since he knew he'd have to keep it up all day.

The woman startled awake with three short snorts. It sounded like a pony with the hiccups. Seeing her face, August could tell that she wasn't just old; she was very old.

It was totally possible that she was 120, just like the sneezer had said. He'd seen paintings of God in the museums his parents dragged him to, and this woman looked even older than that.

"Don't mind me, I was just napping," she said. "Is that you, Eden Evans?"

August tried to hide his irritation. When he was younger and his hair was longer, people would sometimes think he was a girl.

"No, Madame," he said, straining to make his voice even lower. "I am Mr. August Rattice, and I am quite pleased to make your acquaintance."

"Oh gracious, my apologies, Mr. Rattice. I was expecting a young girl today, and I rarely get any unexpected visitors around here. The last one was"—she lowered her glasses over her eyes and examined a tall stack of calendars on her desk—"three years ago."

August tried to hide his surprise. Three years ago? That was a long time. Really long. Like, ancient history.

"Welcome. The pleasure is mine. I'm Tillie," she said, offering her hand to him.

Curious about exactly how old she was, he moved closer, doing his best to copy his father's long-legged stride.

"Allow me to explain my confusion," she said. "My sight and hearing aren't what they used to be. I felt sprightly as a girl right up until last year, but the moment I turned a hundred and twenty, I began feeling my age a bit."

August nodded, now understanding. No wonder the old lady thought he was a girl at first. She was over a century old and could barely hear or see. He laughed to himself, delighted. It would be much easier to convince her that he was an adult than he'd thought. He hoped Milton would be easy to fool, too. He shook her hand firmly, just like his dad did when he met someone for the first time, then quickly let go when he saw her wince with pain. She was clearly very fragile.

"Tell me, Mr. Rattice, do you have an interview with the Director today?" Tillie asked, squinting at her calendars.

August perked up at the sound of this. He'd just walked in the door and had already gotten an opportunity to meet with the Director, who was obviously Milton. It had to be.

"An interview? Do you have a job opening?" he asked, trying to sound casual.

"We do, for a very important job indeed, but I don't seem to have you on my schedule. You didn't call ahead for an appointment, did you? It seems unlikely I would forget, since we only get one or two calls a year."

"I didn't," he admitted. "I hope it's all right that I stopped by. I've been hoping to visit for quite some time."

"You have?" said Tillie. "How did you find us? Did you see my flyer?"

"Yes, exactly," August said, bluffing. "I found your flyer . . . in the place where you left it."

"A library?" asked Tillie.

"Yes! A library. Exactly."

"How wonderful!"

"Would it be possible for me to meet with the Director right now?" August asked. "I'd like to apply for the position."

August peered over the desk and snuck a peek as Tillie checked her clipboard. Eden Evans's interview with the Director was scheduled for nine fifteen, and it was already nine thirty.

"The other candidate seems to be running late," Tillie said. "Let me see if I can squeeze you in right now."

"That would be splendid," August said. "I'd very much appreciate it."

August wasn't sure why he was speaking in such a fancy way. His dad didn't use words like *splendid* or *I'd very much appreciate*. He seemed to have fallen into talking like a combination of his dad and Santa.

"But first," Tillie said. "Which insect language do you speak?"

"Pardon?" August asked.

"For example, the other candidate we're meeting with today, Ms. Eden Evans, can speak Wasp."

"Can she now?" August asked, feeling like the guys at the

hardware store when Milton said he could talk to ants. Was this lady for real?

"So . . . which do you speak? Or do you speak several?"

"Oh, yeah. Several." August knew he was taking a real gamble, lying so boldly, but Ms. Batra always said that the key to acting was fully committing to the role. If he was going to pretend to be a bug expert, he may as well pretend to be the best bug expert in the world.

"Wonderful," Tillie said, clapping her gloved hands together. "Which ones?"

"Oh, most of them," he said, stalling for time. His mind had gone blank, the way it did when he was taking a test. He knew the answers, but sometimes he forgot them under pressure. Finally, a few names came to him. "Flea, Bee, Ant, you name it."

"How extraordinary! Our Director will be especially excited to hear that," Tillie said. "You may find this hard to believe, but I've had a remarkably hard time finding anyone who can speak one insect language, let alone many of them. I'm a lost cause. I've tried to learn Ant for years, but I can't manage a single word. But enough about me. Let's get you upstairs right away."

August watched as Tillie pulled herself to standing. She was by far the tallest adult he'd ever seen. It was like watching a baby giraffe stand up for the first time. She wobbled unsteadily as she rose to her full height. Once on her feet, she smoothed her long ivory skirt and brushed pie crumbs from the cream-colored blouse that buttoned to her neck.

"Please, follow me," she said, leading him out of the lobby and deeper into the building. She moved so slowly that by the time they reached the elevator, August was pretty sure he needed a haircut.

The elevator was an old-timey one with an ornate, wrought-iron gate. August had only seen an elevator like that in picture books. Tillie yanked the heavy gate open with surprising ease.

"The Director's office is on the third floor," she explained, pressing the button.

The elevator shuddered as if it had sneezed, and August was surprised to feel the car moving down.

"Shouldn't we be going up?" he asked.

"Oh no," said Tillie. "That's part of the architectural design of the Institute. Since many insects' nests are built underground, or into the sides of hills, the Institute was built down into the ground, where the insects would feel most at home."

"So they're loose? There aren't any on this elevator, are there?" August asked. "I mean, I hope there are. I'm so excited to see some and, uh, talk to them."

"I can introduce you to some later," said Tillie. "As of now, we only have about two hundred varieties of insect. The Director is always inviting more to come live with us, but many insects of the far north prefer to stay where it's cold, and most of our friends below the equator prefer the heat. Although the beauty and philosophy of the Institute itself is known and admired worldwide, not every insect can be persuaded to move to Rhode Island, as you can imagine."

"Completely," August said, utterly confused.

The elevator shuddered to a stop.

"Ah, here we are," she said. "Third floor."

The Light in the Hall

It was nine forty-five when Eden arrived at Ochre Point Avenue. She had no idea how far she was from her destination when she'd jumped off the bus and run away from the wreck, but she felt pretty sure she'd run about four miles.

Eden had become a good judge of distance ever since she and her dad had gotten in the habit of running two or three miles a few times a week before school (for her) and getting to the hospital for early rounds (for him). It had started when she'd told him that she'd been sleeping badly, and he'd said that getting more exercise might help her sleep better.

"How about we get up early and run a few laps around the track at my old high school?" he'd said. At first she'd resisted. Get up earlier than she already had to? No, thanks. Eden's house was old and drafty, and the sprint from her bed to the bathroom down the hall was already enough exercise for one morning. Plus, she climbed trees.

Come on, E., her father had said. *You have the strongest fingers in the world from turning pages. Let's get those legs moving, and if you hate it, we can stop.*

Finally, she agreed. It could make for an interesting experiment. As soon as she got home from their first run, she wrote her findings in her notebook:

DATE: FEBRUARY 22ND

PURPOSE: FIND OUT IF I LIKE RUNNING

RESEARCH: TRY RUNNING

HYPOTHESIS: I WILL NOT LIKE RUNNING

EXPERIMENT: RUN

ANALYSIS: TOO COLD; LUNGS BURNED; LEGS GOT SORE; RAN TWO LAPS; ALMOST THREW UP; DAD FORCED ME TO KEEP GOING EVEN THOUGH HE PROMISED WE COULD STOP IF I HATED IT

CONCLUSION: I DO NOT LIKE RUNNING

She showed her parents her findings that night at dinner. Her father chuckled as he skimmed the paper.

"You're too much, E.," he'd said, shaking his head. Eden intensely disliked it when her parents laughed at things that didn't seem funny to her at all. They seemed irrationally amused by almost everything she did. Most infuriatingly, they often grinned at each other and called her "cute" even after she'd specifically told them she had something serious to say. Eden hated being called "cute." Did people call Marie Curie cute when she discovered radioactivity? Probably not. And Eden was pretty sure no one said, *Isn't that adorable?* when Lilia Ann Abron became the first Black woman to earn a PhD in chemical engineering. Lilia Ann Abron was one of Eden's heroes, and they had a lot more in common than the obvious things. They both were deeply inspired by nature, and they had the same middle name.

"And I believe," said her mother, pausing with her fork in the air, "that you always say a scientist has to repeat an experiment several times to test whether her theory is correct."

Eden's face burned. Her mom had her there. She recorded her next experiment as well:

> **DATE:** FEBRUARY 25TH
>
> **PURPOSE:** FIND OUT IF I LIKE RUNNING
>
> **RESEARCH:** TRY RUNNING
>
> **HYPOTHESIS:** I WILL NOT LIKE RUNNING
>
> **EXPERIMENT:** RUN
>
> **ANALYSIS:** TOO COLD; LUNGS BURNED;
> LEGS GOT SORE; RAN FOUR LAPS (!)
>
> **CONCLUSION:** 200% IMPROVEMENT!
> I ~~HATE~~ INTENSELY DISLIKE RUNNING

Eden was very excited about her improvement, but she didn't show her parents her results that night. She was concerned that if they saw her success and more positive attitude, they would pressure her to keep running, and she intensely disliked feeling pressured. Eden pressured herself enough already. She didn't need anyone else to do it.

Still, she had to admit that running was not altogether horrible, and even though it was drizzling when she woke up on the morning of February 28th, she found herself in the unlikely position of wanting to go. She liked the feeling of getting better at something so quickly. Her father seemed utterly shocked. *But it's raining,* he pointed out. *Just drizzling,* Eden said with a shrug, pulling her braids back into a ponytail and tucking them into her hoodie. That day, they ran five laps, a 25 percent improvement over their previous run, and a 250 percent improvement since their first run six days earlier.

One week ago, on April 22nd, Eden noted that she and her dad had been running together three times a week for exactly two months. She studied all the data in her notebook and, contrary to all her hypotheses, made the startling discovery that the advantages of running were statistically outnumbering the drawbacks. They hadn't increased just the distances they were running (one time they'd run three and a half miles!) but also the number of topics they talked about as they ran: pranks her dad did when he was a kid, languages Eden wanted to learn, countries they wanted to visit, nineties hip-hop, and ideas for science fair projects.

She also wrote down the new things they noticed as they drove to and from the track: noteworthy dogs, crocus shoots, a new used bookstore, the reappearance of robins, a purple Corvette, and a sidewalk chalk drawing of a rainbow. By the time the end of April had rolled around, Eden realized that she'd added too many variables to her experiment at one time. She had no way of knowing if she actually liked running or just loved running with her dad, and now here she was, using the skills he'd taught her to literally run away from him. Eden hoped he'd understand. Since they'd started running, they'd developed a whole new vibe. He didn't laugh about things she told him on their runs. He stopped calling her ideas cute; instead, he just listened.

Eden knew this was partially because he was too out of breath to laugh, but she'd also observed some other changes. He didn't always give advice or tell her what he would do in her situation. Instead, he would nod or ask a follow-up question. And over the two months, she'd learned a lot more about him, too. He told her about all the ways he thought his parents didn't understand him when he was her age, and how he worried that because he only had brothers, he wouldn't know how to be a dad to a girl, and how relieved he was to find out that he didn't have to learn to be a dad to *a girl*; he just had to figure out how to be a dad to Eden. And now she was betraying him.

When she'd first snuck out of the house that morning, she'd felt so sure that running away was her only option. But now, shivering and sweating, the caked blood on her forehead starting to itch, and the scariness of the bus accident coming into sharper focus as her shock was wearing off, she realized that maybe she should've given her parents another chance. Maybe if she'd told them less about talking to the queen and focused on the part about not knowing that the Institute existed, they would've agreed to drive her, and they could've made it a family adventure. Instead, she was alone, her hands planted on her knees and her head hanging as she panted. It wasn't until she looked up, her head still throbbing where she'd banged it, that she noticed the giant mansion looming before her: The Breakers.

It was the most beautiful building she'd ever seen. It looked like it was carved out of shortbread, its tawny walls rising three stories high. Two sets of wide stairs led to three enormous entryways with gracefully arched tops. Above that, a row of windows separated by elegant columns fronted the second floor, and above that, nine small windows dotted the third floor, which sat just under a vast, red tiled roof studded with nine chimneys.

All thoughts of her parents evaporated as Eden, entranced, ran toward the northeastern end of the property in search of the Windward. It was then that she noticed the sign that read "Children Unaccompanied by Adults Not Allowed." Just beyond it, a white security guard made the rounds in a golf cart. Eden crouched behind an elm tree until he passed, then continued her raggedy lope across the lawn, ducking behind planters and topiary as she caught sight of other guests strolling the gardens, snapping selfies on the wide patio that faced the sea.

She had made it undetected to the farthest edge of the property, where the land formed a triangular bluff that overlooked the sea, when she saw it: a tiny carriage house almost completely hidden by stubby pine trees and scrub. There was no other building in sight. This had to be it. Eden knocked on a door whose wood was so rotten her hand nearly went through it. No answer. She knocked again, then pushed the door gently. It swung open at her touch. She stepped inside, careful to leave it open a crack behind her. She didn't want to risk getting locked inside the dim chamber that, as her eyes adjusted to the dark, she could see was magnificent. A grandfather clock at the back of the room chimed ten times. It was ten? Already? Eden's heartbeat, which had finally slowed down since her escape from the bus, felt as if it had stopped entirely. She was forty-five minutes late for her meeting. The information desk, where she was supposed to meet Ms. Wannaberger, was empty. Had she missed her only chance? Maybe, but she couldn't give up without investigating further. She wrote her name in neat block letters in the guest book. Putting the pen back in its shiny silver holder, she caught a glimpse of her reflection and noticed there was still a smear of dried blood on her forehead. She licked her finger and rubbed at the splotch until it was gone. Much better. Next, she scanned the hall and noticed an elevator on the back wall of the lobby, but it was the old-fashioned kind with a metal grate. She had no idea how to use it and didn't want to risk getting stuck inside that, either. But maybe there were stairs somewhere. Seeing a light coming from a hallway that curved off the main lobby, she followed it, hoping it would lead her to the Director of the Institute for Lower Learning.

The Stowaway

The wasp queen had never been interested in humans before, but she found that she couldn't stop thinking about Eden, the one she'd met the day before. Until now, the queen had only thought of humans as confusing, violent creatures. In addition to the bee massacre, she'd heard stories about long lines of ants being crushed under giant fingers just for sampling the food on the soft buffet tables the humans loved spreading out on the ground. This made no sense to the queen. If humans didn't want ants eating their food, why did they make their tables so low and comfy?

At first, the queen had found Eden confusing in her own way. She didn't understand the strange sounds the girl was making. They'd begun to make sense when the girl had started humming into the strange contraption she'd devised, but they'd only become totally decipherable when the queen had stopped trying to focus on the sounds escaping from the girl's lips and begun listening to the feelings that were emanating from her heart. Amid all the buzzing, the queen could feel the loneliness within the girl, her determination to bring more compassion to the world, and her fears of failing at it.

It was then that the queen understood not only what the girl was saying, but also why she cared so deeply about a species other than her own, and why she was so willing to undertake a potentially dangerous mission to find other benevolent humans. The queen had a sudden, frightening thought. What if, on her passionate quest to find good humans, Eden encountered bad ones instead? The queen had heard stories of humans actually hurting *each other*. It seemed as if there was no limit to the cruelty those gigantic fiends were capable of. The queen wished she hadn't let Eden go off on her own. She needed to find her.

She summoned a worker wasp to babysit and buzzed over to the tree where she'd first met Eden, desperately hoping she'd return. The queen had been waiting for an hour and was beginning to lose hope when suddenly two much larger humans, one pink and one brown, appeared from over a small hill, running straight toward the tree. Based on her months of observing humans, the queen thought it was safe to assume that the pink one was a female and the brown one was a male. Most of their bodies were covered in fabric, like all the humans she'd seen, but the queen could see that the female had long, curling straw-colored strands dangling from her head and the male had much shorter, tighter black curls protruding from his. Although males sometimes had long strands and females had short, the queen felt fairly certain that she was correct. It was interesting to her that while most wasps were black and yellow, humans came in a variety of colors. Eden, for example, was an entirely different shade than either of these humans. She was the honeyed brown of a paperbark maple, and her fur hung in long, silky ropes that twirled around themselves like morning glory vines.

These larger humans, unlike the sweet-smelling girl, were both panting and sweating, giving off a foul odor. The queen was about to fly away, disgusted, when the female ran past her toward a nearby jogger, waving a piece of paper. The female held the paper out to the jogger, and as the wasp queen hovered closer, she could see Eden's picture on the paper. For some reason, these humans were looking for her, too!

The male and female showed the paper to every other human they passed, and the wasp queen buzzed along nearby, always making sure to keep a safe distance between them. But the other humans simply shook their heads back and forth, lifting their shoulders toward their ears. The wasp queen didn't know what this gesture meant, but she guessed it was something bad, because every time it happened, the two humans would look at each other sadly. The queen tried to feel the humans' thoughts and understand them, but their frenzy and panic made it impossible for her to decipher them.

After a long search, the humans walked toward the flat lands at the far end of the park. The queen rarely went to this frightening place. Instead of being covered in sweet-smelling grass, the ground there was covered in a flat, dark gray substance streaked with thick white lines. In between the lines were rows of metal boxes so big that they could hold up to five humans, and the humans would get into these boxes at the end of the day and leave the park at a speed faster than any insect could possibly fly.

The queen watched as the two humans climbed into their dark blue box. She knew that once it sped away, she'd never be able to catch up. She also knew that it would be irresponsible to sneak into the box and go with them. It could put her in terrible danger, which would be disastrous not only for her but for all her subjects. She was, after all, their leader. Still, following the humans was the only way she could possibly find Eden. She had no choice but to follow.

The queen waited until the humans had settled into their box, then quickly snuck in behind the female. But just as she thought she'd made it past it undetected, the female turned unexpectedly and spotted her. *Ah!* the female shouted, swatting at the queen with its giant, pink . . . what was that word again? Oh, yes, *hand*. Luckily, the queen was able to dodge the massive thing, but the force of the swat created a gust of wind so strong that it blew the queen backward, deeper into the box. The female shouted something at the male, and suddenly the wasp queen heard curious noises on either side of her. Looking left and right, she saw two transparent panels sliding downward, disappearing into the sides of the box. What strange magic was this? The queen had barely had time to take it all in when the giant pink hand swatted at her again, trying to push her out of the box.

The queen, terrified, buzzed with alarm, but the sound only made the female slap at her even more urgently. Realizing that her buzzing was only making things worse, the queen held her body completely still, doing her best to remain totally silent. Luckily, it seemed to work, because after a moment the queen felt the box begin to move: slowly at first, and then faster than she'd ever moved before.

The journey, however, was short. The nest of the humans was close by, and they arrived there only moments later. The queen was astonished at how big it was. She followed the humans out of the box and toward the nest, but they were moving so quickly that she arrived at the entrance a few seconds too late. The humans had already run inside, slamming a giant wooden rectangle behind them. The queen flew all around the square nest, searching for a place to enter, but only found more transparent panels like the ones she'd seen in the box. She hovered around their edges, looking for a button she could press to lower them, but didn't find any. Next, she banged against the panels, hoping to shatter them, but they were so thick, she couldn't even crack them, let alone break through.

The transparent panels did, however, give the queen an opportunity to watch what the humans were doing inside. The female sat down, pulled out a small, silver rectangle, and pushed three buttons on it as the male ran up a tall, zigzagging ramp until he disappeared from view. The queen watched as the female tapped on the silver thing several times, then spoke into it briefly before pushing another button and throwing it down. The queen watched as the female slumped over and lowered her head, her straw-colored curls skimming the tabletop like weeping willow branches over a lake. After a moment, the human's shoulders began to quiver and water dripped from her eyes like rain off a leaf. Then she sat back up, grabbed a flimsy piece of paper, and pressed it to her eyes. Next, she ran up the same zigzagging ramp the other had gone up before.

The queen, eager to see where the female was going, flew upward until she reached another, higher transparent panel. There, she saw the male sitting in front of a strange contraption.

It was flat and silver, with a picture of an apple with a bite taken out of it. The male pried open the contraption, which had a hinge like an oyster. Inside, the bottom half was covered with black squares that had letters on them. *At last,* the queen thought, *something I recognize!* But unlike the letters in books, which were strung together to make words, these letters appeared to be in random order. But they must have meant something to the male because he pressed the buttons eagerly.

As the female entered, the male pointed at the contraption, excited. Then he leapt up and both humans ran out of the room. Although Eden's safety was the queen's main concern, she was also fascinated by the male human's behavior. Male wasps never returned to a nest they'd left, but it was clear from this male's behavior that he still lived there and went in and out regularly. She'd also never seen a male wasp do anything useful other than breed, but this human male seemed to have many talents. He could search, pass out papers, and make a box go forward. Strangest of all, the female seemed glad to have him around.

The queen darted back to the front of the nest just in time to see the humans run out and back into the dark blue box. This time, however, the queen was prepared. She soared in without being detected, hovering near the floor so she wouldn't be seen or heard. Seconds later, the box jolted backward and then forward, and even though they were suddenly hurtling along even faster than before, the queen was more excited than afraid. Plus, she had to admit that she loved the sensation of moving so quickly. Riding in a box was even better than flying.

The Ladder

Atom and Dot zipped along the marble floors of the Institute as quickly as they could. Usually when they were playing, Atom loved the feel of his feet sliding effortlessly across the smooth marble, as opposed to the uneven, sandy paths they normally trod. He and Dot would gather up as much speed as possible, then hurl themselves across the floor, their antennae blowing behind them. Sometimes they would slide so fast they couldn't stop, wiping out and crashing into a corner or sofa leg, but the occasional dents to his exoskeleton were worth it. Now, however, they were on a mission, and their inability to get any traction on the slick floor was frustrating.

"Hurry! The human's going to get away before we can get a good look at him!" Dot said.

"It's too hard," Atom complained, struggling to catch up.

"Too hard? We just started," Dot said, and Atom could

hear the usual exasperation in her voice: fond but frustrated.

It bothered Atom that his big sister, his idol, thought he was lazy. He wasn't. He was simply better suited to day-dreaming on one of the Institute's many sofas, stroking the velvety fabric with his foreleg, than going out and working in the garden. Huh. Maybe he *was* lazy. Plus, it didn't help that Dot, like all the other females, was nearly double his size and twice as strong. How could he be expected to keep up?

Still, the journey ahead seemed impossibly far, even for someone as determined as Dot. They'd set off from the third-floor kitchen, and in the past ten minutes they'd only made it about two feet. The elevator, which was "right nearby" by human standards, was still several feet away. But he resolved that he would be as strong and brave as he needed to be. He could do this! He took a deep breath and a giant step forward.

"I can't make it. My legs are falling off. Carry me!"

"You're so melodramatic!" Dot said, but she turned and scooped him up in her forelegs like she used to when he was little and they'd sneak into the flea circus together. Atom's favorite act was the Heavenly House Flies, who would dive into giant bowls of chilled soup to do their synchronized swimming routines, and Dot would lift him up so he could see over the rim of the bowl.

"Oof," she said, staggering under his weight and putting him back down. "You're getting so heavy!"

"I'm not heavy," he protested. "I just have a big exo-skeleton."

The sound of the ancient elevator door sliding open put an end to their bickering. Dot put her foreleg over Atom's thorax and protectively slid him half a millimeter behind her, in case whoever was coming turned out to be dangerous. They watched silently as a short man and The Ladder got off the elevator.

Atom and Dot knew that they weren't supposed to refer to Tillie as The Ladder. Their mother reminded them all the time that it was disrespectful, and that Tillie deserved to be treated with more appreciation, but almost all the insects called her that, and the nickname stuck, because from their point of view, being tall was the only thing about Tillie that was useful.

Atom knew that wasn't true. They'd learned in their Ancient History class that Tillie was Milton's mother, and when it came to the Institute, she wasn't just useful. She was essential. Turning the Windward into the Institute for Lower Learning had been Tillie's idea. She'd been born in the Windward over a hundred years ago, back when it wasn't a research lab but a big, fancy house where people had elegant parties that lasted all summer long. And when, many years later, Grandma Minnie and Milton had become partners and needed a place to turn their dream into a reality, it was

Tillie who insisted that they transform her childhood home from what she called "a beautiful but impractical place" into a working laboratory.

But the reason Tillie had gotten the not-very-nice nickname of The Ladder was that, as essential as she was to the creation of the Institute for Lower Learning, she was completely, hopelessly, no good at understanding or learning Ant. Atom and Dot would beg Aunt Dab and Itty-Bitty to tell them Tillie stories, and they would regale them with tales of how Tillie, between her age and her height, would take a full fifteen minutes to lower herself to the space between the bottom of the refrigerator and the floor and then squint at them as she sat cross-legged, attempting to re-create the rhythms on the washboard that Milton had taught her.

"She was awful at it," Aunt Dab chortled, her obsidian thorax gleaming as she laughed. "Her playing was literally painful to listen to and impossible to understand. Your mother and I threw a party the day she stopped trying."

"I refused to go to that party," Aunt Itty-Bitty said, shaking her onyx head. "Tillie was remarkably untalented, but I always felt for her, poor thing. I always sensed that she was trying so hard to communicate that she made it impossible for herself to relax and actually listen."

"You did? Why?" Dot asked. She always loved a story about how useless humans were.

"She was always trying to help," Itty-Bitty insisted. "Once when we were kids, Dab and I saw a dollop of dried honey, way high up on a shelf where none of us could get to it, and Tillie noticed us staring. She scraped it off the shelf and put it on the ground for us, but we didn't dare touch it because . . . why?"

"Because we never take food from humans," Atom and Dot groaned in unison. They'd heard this rule hundreds of times and knew to never break it. They wished their aunts would finally stop saying it, but also knew that would probably never happen.

"Then she put out her finger for us to climb onto, but we didn't because . . . why?"

"Because we never accept help from humans," they groaned again.

"But then we found a little shortcut," Aunt Dab said, throwing Dot a devilish grin. "She would stand very still and let us climb her! Mama Minnie had never said, 'Don't climb a human,' so it wasn't technically against the rules."

"Is that why they call her The Ladder?" Atom had asked, and Dot had rolled her eyes at him: *Obviously.*

"Did you ever try it, Aunt Itty-Bitty?" Atom asked.

"Oh no," she said. "Dab would tell me how fun it was, but climbing that high just for a dollop of honey seemed risky. I was more the type to dawdle on a window seat and hope she'd drop a crumb of shortbread while she was reading."

Atom nodded, realizing for the first time that he and Aunt Dab had that in common. It was rare to find a female ant who liked to relax now and then, and it made him feel closer to her.

"That's right," Aunt Dab said. "Follow Bitty's example, not mine. It was very dangerous, even back then, and now it's even more so. Tillie's a sweet old lady and she means well, but you stay away. She can barely hear or see anymore, so the odds that she'd accidentally step on you or fall while you were climbing her— Oh, I can't even think about it."

Atom and Dot had promised to stay away from The Ladder, but now that she was standing right in front of them, they couldn't resist a peek. She was much taller than they'd imagined, towering over the small man by her side. At first Atom thought she was so tall that her head was actually touching the clouds, but then he realized that it was just her white curls swishing over her forehead as she moved.

"Come on!" Dot said. "Let's get closer. If we can jump onto The Ladder, we can hitch a ride and find out where they're going."

"But Aunt Dab said—"

"How could she say anything? She's not even here. Ready?" She clutched his foreleg in hers. "We're gonna do it together. Bend your knees as deep as you can. One . . . two . . . three . . . Go!"

"Wait. What? Are we jumping on 'three' or 'go'—"

By the time Atom realized he'd missed the jump, Dot was already soaring toward The Ladder. She'd calculated the trajectory of her leap with the assumption that Atom would be jumping with her, but when he stayed anchored to the ground instead, she was thrown wildly off course. Instead of landing on The Ladder, she landed on the cuff of the small man's pant leg and disappeared into the black speckles of the dark gray wool.

"Dot!" Atom screamed, scanning the bottom of the trousers for any trace of her.

Suddenly her head, as glossy as a grackle, appeared just over the top of the cuff. She clung to the fabric, waving to Atom as though she were leaving for a cruise on an origami boat.

"Wait! Come back!" Atom cried.

"I can't! He's moving too fast!" Dot shouted back. "Whooo! This is amazing! Stay right there! Once I figure out what's going on, I'll come back and pick you up!"

"But I—" Atom called out, but it was too late. Dot and the humans had already turned the corner. For the first time in his life, he was alone.

The Flick

"*Wood borers,*" *Tillie said* as they turned a corner onto yet another hallway. The house, August thought, had as many unexpected paths as a maze. He wasn't particularly good at mazes or puzzles and was suddenly worried that if he were left alone he might never find his way out. Tillie stopped for a moment to show August the walls of this new hallway. They were decorated with what first appeared to be polka-dotted wallpaper, but upon closer inspection were hundreds of intricate pearl carvings of tiny, cream-colored larvae. "Hand-carved by the wood borers themselves. It took ten thousand wood borers ten hours to carve each one. As you'll soon discover, most of the Institute for Lower Learning was built and decorated by the insects in order to assure accuracy and richness of detail."

"How very interesting," August said, continuing to follow her down the hall even though what he really wanted to do was run to the elevator, get back to the main floor, race out the main entrance (if he could even find it), go home, and never come back to this horrible place again. Tillie was wrong. Bugs were nuisances at best and murderers at worst. He refused to believe that insects were helpful, creative, or artistic.

But he *did* believe that hundreds of bugs were roaming freely inside the house, and he couldn't stop imagining that they were roaming all over him, too: inside his clothes, along his scalp, down his back. He stifled the urge to twitch and slap and scratch, telling himself that the tiny rustlings he felt against his skin were as imaginary as the inescapable itch that would arise as soon as he heard someone in his class had pink eye. Still, the tickle on his ankle felt too real to ignore, which was why he pushed up his pant leg and came face-to-face with a huge, shiny black ant.

"Ah! Ah! Ahhhh!" August shouted as he sent the ant flying off his leg with the flick of a finger.

Tillie turned toward him, confused. "Did you say something?"

August quickly tried to recover. "I said, 'Ahhhh, remarkable place you've got here.'"

As Tillie turned back to lead him farther down the dim hallway, August triumphantly looked down at the limp black speck that lay at his feet. One insect down, ten quintillion left to go.

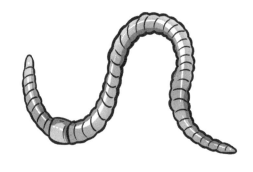

The Face in the Mirror

The narrow hallway widened as Eden moved along it, until she found herself at the top of a sweeping staircase. A gentle cascade of steps led to a grand sitting room with massive chandeliers festooned with opalescent globes. The chandeliers hung from a ceiling painted with the most exquisite mural Eden had ever seen of a blue morpho butterfly emerging from a chrysalis, against a vibrant green background painted to look exactly like the underside of a leaf. Eden knew exactly what the underside of a leaf looked like because she'd been studying leaves, flowers, and seedpods extensively since she was five and her parents had given her a kids' microscope set on the last night of Hanukkah.

Eden's family celebrated Hanukkah *and* Christmas. Eden felt bad for humble little Hanukkah, since it always got overshadowed by big, showy Christmas. Stores put up Christmas decorations and started selling Christmas ornaments and foods the minute Halloween was over, but if you weren't Jewish, you might never even know Hanukkah existed. If stores put up Hanukkah decorations at all, it was always a tiny menorah stuck in a corner of the store window, barely visible under a giant Christmas display.

It was like Christmas was the mighty oak tree and Hanukkah was the tiny acorn that got half buried in the dirt. It made sense. Christmas had Santa, stockings, a huge tree, its own Peanuts special, and a giant dinner with sweet potato pie *and* mac and cheese that Grandma Betty insisted on making all by herself. Grandma Betty preferred to spend five days doing all the work alone, just so she could get all the glory when everyone sat down at her beautiful table to enjoy her scrumptious meal.

Compared with Christmas, Hanukkah was a letdown. At Hanukkah Eden's family played dreidel, which even Eden's mom had to admit was a pretty boring game, and ate latkes, which were delicious, but Eden, who always got dragged into helping Grandma Roz make them, always wound up with scraped and bloody knuckles from grating the potatoes. *If it doesn't have a little knuckle in it, it's not a latke,* Grandma Roz loved to say. One year, after they read about the Donner party in history class, Eden asked her grandma, *If latkes have our skin in them, does eating them make us cannibals?* which was another question the entire family thought was hilarious but was so disturbing to Eden that she hadn't eaten a latke since.

But the one thing Hanukkah had going for it that made it better than Christmas was that it lasted eight days. In that way, Hanukkah was like nature; it didn't just happen all in one day. Hanukkah, like the caterpillar that becomes a butterfly, took time to reveal its true glory, and it got better as the nights progressed. First there was the menorah, a candlestick with eight branches (nine if you counted the *shamash* candle that was used to light all the others). Eden's parents let her strike the match *and* light the candles, and Eden loved watching the small pool of light thrown by the single candle grow as she lit two candles the second night and three on the third, until all nine candles crackled and gleamed on the final night, setting the whole room aglow in golden light.

And then there were the presents. On Christmas morning, she woke up to a pile of presents under the tree, which was awesome, but even Eden had to admit that by the time she'd opened them all, she could barely remember what the first one had been. Hanukkah was the opposite. Her family's tradition was to give one present each night, and they started small: a pair of socks the first night, a tea steeper shaped like a manatee the second, a box of Band-Aids printed with pictures of sushi on the third. Eden knew that a big present awaited her on the eighth night of Hanukkah, and the entire week of anticipation made that final night really exciting.

Eden literally shrieked with glee when she tore the wrapping off the microscope. It had six magnifications that went all the way up to 1200X, a built-in light, sample slides, cover slips, plastic tweezers, a plastic scalpel, specimen vials, and adjustable lenses: the whole shebang.

Eden loved using the microscope to study the intricate network of tiny veins that crisscrossed the leaves like train tracks and to learn how the veins, like the trains that carried food to faraway towns, were a perfect transport system to bring water and nutrients to the outermost edges. Having examined leaves so closely, Eden could appreciate the accuracy with which the artist had captured the complexity of the plant. Looking up at the ceiling of the sitting room, Eden guessed that the painter had not only studied leaves with a microscope but learned how to paint with a brush as slim as a needle. Maybe they worked at the Institute. Maybe they were there today, and maybe they'd be willing to tell Eden about how they blended science and fine art so seamlessly. Eden wished she'd used her birthday wish to wish that she could meet the artist, but of course she hadn't known about them at the time.

The room itself was furnished with ivory sofas and lounges, their backs and cushions tilted to offer the best views of the ceiling mural. Eden felt drawn to the room, unable to resist its opulence. The staircase's bronze handrail felt cool to the touch, its rounded edges fitting her palm perfectly, as though she'd run her hands along it a thousand times before, and she felt like a princess as she moved effortlessly down the yellow and gold striated marble. Somehow, this place she'd never glimpsed before felt as familiar to her as her own home. It was as though the entire place had been designed precisely with her in mind.

As she stepped onto the silken carpet, which was patterned with swallowtail butterflies swooping among greenbrier vines, Eden noticed that the upholstery of the ivory chairs was rich damask, patterned with intricately woven cream-colored cabbage butterflies that were so dainty they looked as though they'd been woven by the butterflies themselves. Eden knew that was impossible, but it took her a moment to shrug off the fantastical notion. In this dazzling room it seemed that anything was possible.

As she moved deeper into the room, she was caught off guard by the sight of a figure standing against one of the walls, watching her. Eden froze, startled, until she realized that the face she was seeing was her own, reflected at her from a mirror that hung between two gilt-bronze lanterns. She stared at herself, transfixed. Ever since Eden had been old enough to understand a three-word sentence, every single relative and female family friend had told her multiple times that she was beautiful. None of them ever said it casually, either. Instead, they would stop and make significant eye contact, which was usually incredibly awkward, and say in what Eden thought of as The Serious Voice, *You are Beautiful,* or *You are Beautiful, and don't let anybody tell you different,* and Eden knew that they weren't talking about how she personally looked in that moment but the bigger idea that she, as a young Black girl, was beautiful, even though most of the commercials on TV, ads in magazines, and leading parts in movies always showcased white girls with blond hair.

Eden understood why it was important to be told she was beautiful with a capital *B* and she liked hearing it, even though her mom and dad sometimes went a little overboard with The Serious Voice, but it could also be annoying when she just wanted a regular old compliment. She wished that Grandma Betty could just say, *You look great!* when Eden asked what she thought of an outfit, instead of making a grand hand gesture and theatrically announcing, *Of course you're magnificent. We are the descendants of kings and queens!*

Eden didn't feel like the descendant of a queen. She felt more like she came from a long line of court jesters. She had too many freckles, her forehead was too high, and she hated the gap between her front teeth. No one in her family would admit it, but Eden felt sure that she was not technically beautiful. At best, she was okay. But that changed the moment she glimpsed herself in the burnished mirror. The light cast by the lanterns brought out the luminescence of her skin, suffusing it with a lustrous glow. The dozens of braids her grandma would meticulously fashion for her every other month (a ritual she loved, even though Grandma Betty could sometimes tug a little too hard) that she'd always thought of as simply pretty and practical suddenly appeared regal, solid as a statue and fluid as a river. For the first time she could see that she was radiant, magnificent, and quite possibly of a royal lineage.

Eden could've stood there admiring herself forever, until she was jolted by the sight of what looked like a gigantic, eight-foot-tall emerald swallowtail butterfly. Looking closer, Eden realized it wasn't actually a real butterfly, but two enormous, stained glass double doors. They were a deep, oceanic green, splashed with the wide turquoise *V* that was the hallmark of the swallowtail, and the lines of black lead that separated the glass panes were so delicate that they perfectly replicated the butterfly's fine veining. Eden was agog at the splendor. She couldn't wait to see the beauty that lay beyond.

The Office of the Director

"**H**ow rude of me," Tillie said as she came to a stop before a door festooned with tiny enamel ladybugs. "May I bring you a cup of tea while you wait for the Director?"

August paused before he answered. He liked his tea with lots of cream, sugar, and an ice cube, but he knew that to keep his performance realistic, he should drink tea the same way his dad did. "Yes, please. No cream, no sugar, and very hot—as hot as you can make it. Because I have no worries about burning my tongue whatsoever."

"Coming right up," Tillie said, ushering August into the most impressive room he'd ever seen. He hesitated in the doorway, waiting for Tillie to warn him not to touch anything, or remind him that chewing gum wasn't allowed, like the tour guides in the other mansions always did. But the warning never came.

"Please make yourself comfortable," she said, indicating

an armchair embroidered with golden bees that faced a large desk covered with open notebooks and several magnifying glasses. "I'll be right back."

Left alone, August took a look around. The floor was made of the same elegant marble as the entryway, only here it was covered by intricate rugs that depicted scenes from the insect world: a lace bug, dainty as a doily, tending to her eggs; grasshoppers leaping in a meadow; and chartreuse aphids nestling in purple plumes of wisteria. Every wall featured jam-packed, floor-to-ceiling bookcases. But even the beauty of the room couldn't distract August from his nervousness. He was about to meet Milton, the Director of the entire Institute. And even though Milton was definitely a strange man, he was probably also a very smart one. Tillie was probably telling Milton right now that August could speak and understand lots of bug languages, when he couldn't even name ten kinds of bugs, let alone make conversation with them. August was furious with himself for making a claim he had no way of backing up, but now it was too late.

Tillie entered and placed a cup of dark, steaming tea in front of him.

"The Director will see you now," she said, sliding into the chair behind the giant desk.

"But where is he?" August asked.

"She!" Tillie said with a grin. "It's me! I hope you're not upset by my brief deception, but I find that the best test of a person's true nature is how they treat assistants and receptionists. Everyone is polite when they meet someone they think is 'important,' but you'd be surprised how many people are rude when they meet someone they think is insignificant."

"How wise of you," August said, trying to hide his alarm. Apparently, he wasn't the only one capable of pulling off a trick or two. This old lady was clearly much cleverer than she seemed.

"Please, tell me more about what you do here," he said, leaning forward in his chair. Leaning forward was a very deliberate choice on his part, and it had two purposes. One was to make it appear that he was very interested in what she had to say, which might cause her to reveal more details than she normally would, and the other was so he could plant his feet on the floor. When he'd first sat back in the chair, he'd realized that his feet didn't quite reach the ground, which he feared could blow his whole scheme.

"Well," she said. "To start at the beginning, this house was originally built by my father, Cecil, way back in 1898. It was called the Windward then, and it didn't go down into the ground. It went up into the air, like most houses do, until my son, Milton, his partner, Minnie, and I inverted it to create the Institute. The only thing I miss about the original is the way the light used to stream in. In fact, this window here used to face the ocean."

Tillie turned in her chair and clutched the edge of a dark green silk curtain behind her. "Spiders wove this with their own silk, by the way."

Before August could respond, Tillie pulled the curtain back to reveal that behind it was a window that looked onto a wall of tightly packed earth.

"But don't get me wrong," she said. "The view now that we're underground is also fascinating, possibly even more so."

Behind the glass, earthworms wriggled back and forth as they maneuvered in and out of freshly dug tunnels. Their wriggling bodies were a dark pinkish purple, like a bruise, and August was close enough to the glass that he could see they had no eyes or ears. It was a revolting sight, and it took all of August's strength to keep from turning away in disgust.

"I know what you're thinking," Tillie said. "Technically, spiders and worms are not insects, but they became so interested in the work of the Institute that we expanded our mission to include them."

"Yes, that's exactly what I was thinking," August said. "I hate when worms and spiders get left out."

"Worms are remarkable, aren't they?" Tillie said, watching them work. "They have five hearts. Five! And they're so hardworking. They dug nearly the entire foundation. Milton, Minnie, and I could barely keep up, no matter how fast we shoveled."

"This whole place was built by worms?" August asked. Her story was outlandish, but just as strange as the notion that worms dug the foundation was the image of this delicate old woman standing at the bottom of a giant hole, tossing dirt out of it with a heavy shovel. "And you helped them?"

"I know it's hard to imagine," she said with a laugh, seeming pleased to have surprised him. "When I was a girl, back in 1910, wealthy young ladies weren't supposed to do manual labor. We were supposed to be pampered little creatures, who danced and played cards while servants prepared our food and kept the house running. Now, I love cards and I adore dancing, but I didn't enjoy being useless. When my parents weren't looking, I'd slip downstairs and beg the chefs to teach me to cook, and the boiler men to show me how to load and stoke the furnace, which I still do to this day. I daresay it takes me quite a bit longer than it used to, but I manage."

"That sounds amazing," August said, and he meant it. He had no idea what a boiler man was, or what *stoking* meant, but both sounded dangerous and fun.

"And it's lucky I learned," said Tillie, "since I live here alone now."

"What do you mean, 'alone'?"

Tillie smiled. "Well, I shouldn't say 'alone.' I have the insects for company and they're lovely, but it's not the same as having another person around."

"But where's Milton?" August asked.

August regretted the question as soon as he'd asked it. Tillie's mouth twisted into a crooked line as her eyes filled with tears.

"My beloved Milton passed away last year," she said. Tears dotted her cheeks, the fat droplets magnifying her wrinkles.

"Oh, boy. Oh no," he muttered to himself, looking around nervously. Death was serious stuff. Real grown-ups didn't know what to say when they heard someone had died. How was he supposed to figure it out?

"Um, I'm sorry. That sounds really hard," he said.

"It was," she said, sniffling. "He was so young when he passed. Only ninety-nine."

August looked around for a tissue but didn't see any. He reached around in his suit pocket, found an old but basically clean paper napkin, and handed it to her. He worried she'd see the name of their local ice cream parlor printed on it in red script, but if she did, she didn't mention it.

"How very kind of you, Mr. Rattice," Tillie said, blowing her nose vigorously. It sounded like a flock of seagulls had happened upon a hot dog.

"But you got ninety-nine years with him. That's good, right?" he said, desperate to cheer her up.

"Not exactly," Tillie sighed. "My Milty grew up, as children do, and moved away. He went to college, got a job, and in the early days he wrote to me all the time, telling me exciting stories about his work as a young chemical engineer. He did good work, too. Important work. He helped develop pesticides that could wipe out millions of mosquitoes and stop them from spreading malaria."

"That *is* important. Malaria is the worst," August agreed. He didn't know what malaria was, but he could guess from her tone that it was something bad.

"Exactly," Tillie agreed. "But after having so much success devising ways to kill mosquitoes, Milton became fixated on killing *all* insects. He dreamed of a world in which unpleasant things like mite bites, lice infestations, and bee stings would be nonexistent."

August nodded solemnly, but inside he was elated. That's exactly what he wanted!

"And that's when Milton's letters changed," Tillie continued. "He started boasting about how he could paralyze thousands of bees with a single spritz of deltamethrin. As you can imagine, I was horrified by these stories, and so sad to realize that the sweet little boy I'd raised was gone."

Tillie had a row of framed photos on her desk, and she

turned one around to face August. August jumped, startled. It was a picture of him! Or at least, it could've been him. The old-fashioned clothes were the only giveaway that it wasn't. Even though the photo was in black and white, August could tell that the boy in the picture, who he now realized was a young Milton, had bright blue eyes and blond hair that swirled around his eyes, just like August's did. Maybe that was why Tillie had been so friendly to him right away. He reminded her of her son. Tillie turned the photo back to face her and continued her story. "When he was a boy, we'd spend hours in the garden watching bees pollinate the flowers and then harvesting the honey he liked to drizzle in his tea. I just couldn't understand how he'd gone so terribly wrong in his thinking."

Sounds to me like he went perfectly right, August thought, but he kept it to himself and instead nodded and said reassuring, adult-like things like "How dreadful," to make sure Tillie would think that he was on her side and never suspect that he, too, was dying to get his hands on some deltamethrin and paralyze the heck out of some bees.

"I wrote him again and again, begging him to understand the error of his ways and go back to being the kind and loving boy he once had been, but I don't suppose he liked that. After a while, he stopped writing or calling me at all," she said, clutching at the napkin. "I couldn't stand not knowing where he was. I went to psychics and palm readers and begged them: *Where is my boy? Is he alone? Is he cold? Will he ever come back?* They traced my palm until the lines wore out, but no one ever had an answer."

August thought of his mother, and how scared she'd be if he didn't come home from school that day. He felt a twinge of guilt and decided that, although Tillie's story was more interesting than he'd imagined (usually old people's stories were beyond boring), he needed to move things along so he could figure out where Milton's poisons were, steal them, and get home.

"And then what happened?" he asked, tipping so far forward in his chair that he almost lost his balance and had to grip the edge of the desk to keep from toppling right onto the floor.

"Well, I assumed I'd never see him again, but five years ago on a spring afternoon, I opened the front door and there he was, holding an enormous lollipop."

"Which is your favorite candy," August said, finishing her sentence in the hopes of hurrying her along.

"Oh no," Tillie said with a smile. "I like taffy. Lollipops are an ant's favorite candy, and sure enough, there was a large, shiny black ant riding atop the lolly, as if it were a horse."

August flinched. He knew he was supposed to be delighted

by this detail, but it sounded so gross he couldn't help but grimace. He'd never eat a lollipop again.

"He'd come home to me! And he'd fallen in love with insects again!"

"But how? Why?"

"Well, that's a story for another day," Tillie said. "The important thing is that I had my precious Milton back, and he'd brought Minnie with him."

"Wait. Who's Minnie again?" August asked.

"Why, his partner! The ant on the lollipop!" Tillie said. "We tore down the Windward, which was about to collapse anyway, and created the Institute for Lower Learning. Milton became our Human Director; Minnie became our Insect Director, and together they pursued their dream of teaching humans and insects to collaborate, for the good of each other and the world around them."

"But what happened to all the poisons?" August asked, trying to hide his impatience.

"My hope was to destroy them all," Tillie said. "But some were so powerful we couldn't take the risk of letting even one drop leak into the earth or water. We had to settle for locking them away where no one could ever find them."

"So they're here, in the Institute?" August asked.

"That's enough troubling talk," Tillie said. "Let's move on to happier matters."

The way Tillie had changed the subject so quickly made August feel certain the poisons were hidden somewhere in the building.

"Let's talk about you, August," she said. "I'm so glad you found us. You seem like a perfect candidate to be the new Human Director of the Institute for Lower Learning."

"Me?" August asked. "You just said *you* were the Director."

"I am, for now. I temporarily took over the role when Milton passed, and I do the best I can, but I can't speak to insects," Tillie said. "I certainly tried. Milton spent months trying to teach me Ant, but I was dreadful at it. Then I gave up and started to spend time by the lake, hoping to pick up Dragonfly. When I couldn't do that, I tried Earwig and Stink Bug, Lacewing and Nymph, Maggot and Mayfly, Weevil and Thrips, but it was all for nothing. Since then, I've been searching for a person who has Milton's gift to replace him. I was about to give up, but then you arrived. You have an elaborate interview process ahead of you, of course, but I have a feeling you'll do magnificently. I daresay you may be even more gifted than my Milton was."

Tillie reached out and clutched his hands in her long, bony fingers. Her skin was as delicate as tissue paper, but her grip was firm. Her intensity frightened him. But if he wanted to get his hands on those poisons, he'd need to play along.

"Yes, that's me. Very gifted," he agreed.

"I can't wait to give you a tour of the Institute and introduce you to all the insects. Especially Queen Mote, our current Insect Director. Mote is Minnie's oldest daughter, and Minnie chose her to be the new Insect Director just before she passed. She and Milton wrote in the bylaws that the departing Insect Director would choose their insect successor, and that the departing Human Director, otherwise known as me, would choose the human one. Queen Mote was the best and only choice to be Insect Director, really. She's a queen, after all, and literally a born leader. I'm very eager to find her a partner."

"Well, it'll be easy once you find the right person," August said, leaning in close. "Or perhaps you've already found him."

"Perhaps I have." Tillie smiled at him, then stifled a yawn. "My apologies, Mr. Rattice, but our tour of the Institute will have to wait until after my nap." She draped her shawl around her shoulders and headed for the door, moving so slowly that by the time she reached the threshold, August was pretty sure the tea in his cup had cooled.

"Take your time. I'm happy to wait," August lied. He didn't want to wait. The sooner he learned his way around the place, the sooner he could find the poisons.

"Meanwhile, please treat my office as if it were your own. I imagine you're eager to peruse the bookshelves," Tillie said.

"I can think of nothing more fascinating."

"Very good. I'll leave you to it. Toodles," she said, finally leaving.

"Toodles," August called after, assuming it was some strange, old-lady way of saying goodbye.

As the door was about to close behind her, August quickly wedged a book between the door and door frame, ensuring that he could make his way in and out of the office silently. He watched as Tillie headed farther down the hall to yet another mysterious room and slipped inside. He smiled to himself. He'd infiltrated the Institute and gained Tillie's trust quicker than he'd dared to dream. He was well on his way.

First Contact

*A*tom *struggled to calm* himself, taking in long, slow streams of oxygen through his spiracles. He'd panicked so badly when Dot leapt onto the small man that he'd forgotten to breathe, and his mind had gone blank. Instead of doing something—anything—he'd watched, powerless, as Dot grew smaller and smaller the farther she was carried away from him. Atom felt paralyzed. He didn't know what to do without Dot there to tell him.

He'd just steadied his breathing when he suddenly found himself cast in shadow. He looked up to see a towering figure standing above him. The figure was much shorter than The Ladder but was still tall enough that he couldn't make out the details of the face. He could, however, see the long ropes of hair that spiraled in on each other like licorice twists, and he concluded that the figure was a human girl. He knew that Dot would see the girl's long hair as an adventure and an opportunity. When Dot saw anything that rose up high or dangled down low, her first thought was *How do I climb it?* She had the spirit of a billy goat in the body of an ant, and she could somehow shinny up any obstacle and wave at him from the top before Atom had time to realize she was gone.

Once Dot had mastered the peak of, say, a kitchen chair, she would climb back down for Atom and brace herself against the tilted leg so he could climb over her body and make it to the first rung. Next, she'd nudge his butt with her head, giving him a boost. When they reached the broad plain of the wooden seat, they'd stop to rest, swinging their back legs and gazing out at the wide expanse of kitchen floor beneath them. *Look,* Dot would say. *From up here the floor looks like a checkerboard.* And then, only after she'd pointed it out, would Atom notice the pattern. It was as if nothing in the world existed until Dot taught him how to see it. Atom loved these moments with Dot, sitting side by side, surveying the world below them and feeling big.

But now, looking up at the girl, he felt small—very small. He couldn't tell if the girl was friendly or hostile, and without Dot to assess the situation for him, he didn't want to take any chances. He'd heard horrible stories of humans pinching ants to death for an offense as minor as climbing on a doughnut, so when she crouched down before him, he thought fleetingly of all the ants in the colony he'd never see again: his thousands of sisters, cousins, friends, and most of all, Dot, his best friend and fiercest guardian. She'd be furious if he died after being on his own for barely two minutes.

Atom shifted back onto his hind legs so he could look up into the girl's eyes as she looked into his. He studied her features and was surprised to see that she was looking at him with kind eyes that were as brown as wild cherry bark. But why was she studying him so intently? Was she planning to eat him? He'd heard nightmarish tales of humans dunking ants in chocolate and gobbling them like candy.

He shrank back in terror as she opened her mouth. The edges curled up, revealing white teeth, but she made no move to devour him. Who was she? What was she doing here? Her gaze was so intense that he got the distinct sensation that she was trying to read his mind. He wished he could ask her what she was thinking, but he remembered what his aunts had told him about Tillie. She'd practiced playing the washboard for months and had made zero progress. This human girl didn't even have a washboard. It seemed impossible they'd ever find a way to communicate.

But the girl surprised him once again. Instead of giving up, she put her hands on either side of her head and raised her two pointer fingers as though they were feelers, then

waggled them in his direction. Atom was stunned. He and Dot sometimes played Follow the Leader on long marches, where they'd try to copy each other's exact movements. Did this human know the same game? Atom raised his feelers and copied her gesture. Next, the girl crossed and uncrossed her fingers. Atom did the same. Next, he curled his feelers down, as if they were fiddlehead ferns, and then uncurled them. This time, it was the girl who copied him.

They stared, frozen, at each other, equally surprised by the other's actions. The girl broke the stalemate first, bending even lower and extending her finger toward him. The deep grooves of her fingerprints looked like swirling waves during a storm. Atom backed away, uncertain, considering his options. Dot, the small man, and The Ladder must be very far away by now. If Atom were to have any hope of finding them, a ride on the finger of a human would be incredibly helpful, if not necessary. And from such a towering vantage point, he might even have a chance of spotting Dot.

The girl must have sensed his uncertainty. She waited patiently, holding her steady finger millimeters from his body. The choice, she seemed to be saying, was his. He could ignore one of his aunts' top two rules and accept a human's help—literally put himself in her hands—or make a go of it on his own. He'd never had to make a decision this big on his own before, so he asked himself what Dot would do. The answer came immediately: *Take the risk!* With that, Atom took a deep breath and climbed onto the outstretched finger, clinging to it as the girl lifted him high into the air.

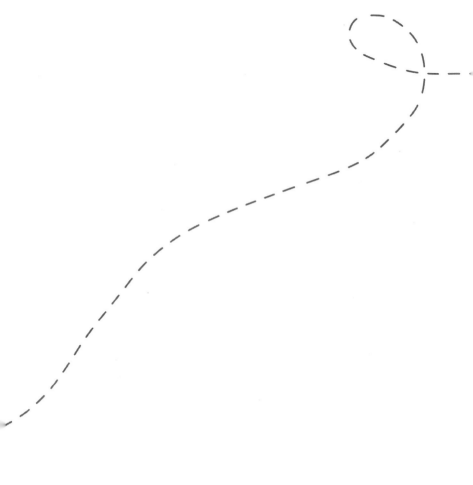

Baby Face

*E**den was amazed. She'd* almost given up on communicating with the little ant when she realized that no matter how hard she tried, she couldn't empathize with him the way she could with the queen. Maybe it was because she knew nothing about the little ant, so she didn't have enough context to understand his emotions or guess at his feelings. Or maybe it was because the ant didn't make sounds, or at least any sounds she could hear.

Eden had felt incredibly silly trying to get the ant to play Follow the Leader with her, but now she was glad she'd stuck with it. If they hadn't played together, he never would've trusted her enough to climb onto her finger. Eden realized that she'd automatically started thinking of the ant as a "he," even though she had no way of knowing its sex. Still, it felt weird to call this little creature she felt so protective of an "it," and she wondered if she'd decided the ant was a boy because she'd always wanted a little brother.

By the time she'd thought all this through, the ant had gotten himself safely onto the tip of her finger and was standing up on his back legs, which Eden took as a sign that she should also stand. As soon as she did, he gave her another direction, going back into his usual standing position, but lifting one of his forelegs until it was pointing straight out in front of him.

Go that way, he seemed to be saying, so Eden did, even though she had no idea where they were going or what they were looking for. Not having a plan made her incredibly anxious, but the little ant was communicating with such urgency that she had no choice but to follow. She prepared herself for a long and fruitless search through the seemingly endless house, so she was surprised when, after they'd only rounded one corner, he started jumping up and down then turned to face her, lifting both his forelegs up into the air. This message was totally clear: *Stop!* Next, the little ant pointed down, and when Eden looked, she could see a roundish speck with six thin spokes pointing out in every direction. It looked like someone had spilled a drop of fresh black ink, but when Eden looked closer, she could see that it was another ant: a large, wounded, trembling one. Eden realized that the little ant on her finger was trembling, too.

The injured ant was clearly important to him. Eden knelt down to examine the situation, and sure enough, the little one scurried off Eden's fingertip and rushed to its side.

Eden watched, astonished, as the little ant raced around the bigger one, examining its legs one by one, as if trying to figure out exactly where and how badly it had been hurt. Eden realized she'd started thinking of the wounded ant as a "she," since she was as glossy as the patent leather Mary Janes that Eden used to wear when she was little. She could see that the larger ant's body and legs were intact, but all six of her feet were crushed. She wished she knew how to help her but worried that if she made one wrong move, she'd damage the wounded ant even more.

Eden felt sorry for the poor little creature, but that didn't stop her from watching, intrigued, as the little ant sat up on his hind legs and rubbed his back leg against a tiny, ridged spike on his belly. The motion made a series of noises, some long and some short, that sounded like a cross between a rumble and a swoosh. It reminded Eden of the washboard that Grandpa Solomon played in his zydeco band. Suddenly, she understood. The rumble-swooshes were how the big and little ant communicated!

Eden looked around, fascinated. How could she make a sound like that? The answer was literally right under her nose. The zipper on her track jacket! She grabbed the slider and pulled it up and down. It didn't sound as close to the ant's rumble-swooshes as she'd hoped, but the little ant immediately turned his head and rumble-swooshed back at her with surprise. Eden gasped, astonished, even though she had no idea what he was saying, which confused her. Why wasn't her empathy working? She wondered if it was because the little ant was having so many thoughts at once that it was impossible for her to separate and understand them. Still, she was thrilled by the magnitude of the discovery. If humans could imitate insect noises with all kinds of everyday items like kazoos and zippers, and if insects and humans had games and gifts like Follow the Leader and empathy in common, there was no limit to how many of each other's languages they could learn and the kinds of conversations they could have. But there wasn't time for any of that now. All that really mattered was helping the injured ant.

The little ant must've felt the same way, because he turned away from Eden and started calling out to the big ant again, desperate to get her attention. Eden joined in, copying the sounds he was making as best she could, until they were rumble-swooshing to the big ant in unison. But no matter how loud they called, the big ant didn't respond. Eden wondered why she was ignoring them, especially since she was in desperate need of help. Then she remembered a fact she'd learned in a picture book called *Antcyclopedia: All the Facts from Ant to Z.* In the book, *E* was for Ear, and it explained that ants didn't have ears. And on the "V Is for Vibration" page, Eden learned that ants used their feet to hear vibrations in the ground. The big ant couldn't hear what they were saying because her feet were broken!

They needed to get the big ant some medical help and fast. But how? Eden scanned the empty hall. Where was Tillie? Was anyone in charge? Were there ant doctors? And if there were, were they ants or people? Eden's stomach lurched like a yo-yo. She felt her face get hot and her breath tighten. She could tell she was about to start hyperventilating, when she saw the little ant hop onto the toe of her sneaker. He waved his antennae at her, trying to get her attention. Eden squinted down at him. Was he trying to tell her something? Sure enough, the little ant extended both antennae toward her, then lowered them gently.

Even in her panic, Eden recognized the gesture immediately. It meant *slow down.* Slow down? Why should she slow down? Didn't he know they were in a hurry? Didn't he understand this was an emergency? Still, she followed his advice and took a deep breath. The ant made a rolling motion with his antenna: *again.* Eden took another breath, deeper this time. By the time she'd taken a third, she felt calmer. The little ant nodded at her, satisfied, then pointed at her with his foreleg.

"Me?" Eden murmured.

Next, he pointed down.

". . . Floor?"

He pointed at himself.

"You," she guessed.

Finally, the little ant pointed across the room.

". . . Wall?" Eden tried putting it all together. "Me floor you wall?"

Eden looked at the little ant, confused. What was he trying to tell her? What did he want her to do? It was like playing Charades, only there was no little piece of paper to peek at to find out what the actual answer was. Doing her best to puzzle it out, Eden started doing the motions back at him, trying different words as she pointed at her chest, the floor, the ant, and the spot across the room.

"Me down you across?"

No, that didn't make any sense, unless they were trying to solve a crossword puzzle.

"Me here you there?"

Nope, that was just stating a fact.

Suddenly, she got it. "I stay! You go! You go for help and I'll stay behind!"

To show that she understood, Eden stepped toward the wounded ant and mimed putting her arm around her. At the same time, she used her other hand to wave goodbye to the little ant, as if she were sending him off on a journey. She must've been right, because the little ant jumped up and down excitedly and hurried off, disappearing into a crack in the floor exactly where he'd been pointing.

Eden, now alone with the large ant, looked over and saw that she kept glancing at her with a mixture of suspicion and fear. She could tell the ant didn't want her coming anywhere near her, let alone touching her, but Eden knew that if she left the ant on the ground, she would almost certainly get smushed. She pulled the pale yellow calling card out of her back pocket and knelt down, sliding the card under the ant's back as gently as possible. She tried to wriggle away, but Eden continued her delicate task until the ant was off the ground and safely on the card. Eden did her best to give the ant a reassuring smile, but the ant refused to make eye contact. Eden was standing there, trying to figure out what to do next, when a boy in a blue suit ducked out of one of the many doors that lined the hall. She tucked the yellow card with the ant on it behind her back, just in case.

"Hello," she said. "Can you help me? It's an emergency."

"Who are you?" he asked. "Are you a friend of Ms. Wannaberger's? Does she know you're here?"

"I don't know her," Eden said. "But I spoke to her on the phone yesterday. I'm Eden Evans."

"Eden Evans?" he said, looking surprised. "The girl who can speak Wasp?"

"I am," she said. "Who are you? What grade are you in?"

The boy's nostrils flared with anger. "What grade am I in? I'm not in a grade. I'm Mr. August Rattice. Do I look like a child to you?"

Eden didn't know how to answer this. He *did* look like a child to her. In fact, it was completely obvious that he *was* a child, but the notion seemed to make him very irritated. Eden certainly didn't want to make a bad first impression on the very first person she'd met at the Institute, no matter how old they were.

"Oh!" she said, searching for a way to smooth things over. "Please accept my apologies. You looked so young. It must've been the light. I didn't mean any offense."

"No offense taken. Happens all the time. I'm forty years old, and I still can't seem to outgrow this darn 'baby face.'" He chuckled. "Besides, how could I expect you to tell the difference? You're just a child yourself. You can't be any more than, what? Nine?"

"Ten. It was actually my birthday yesterday."

"How wonderful. Ten is a fun age," he said, winking at her.

"Um, yes, it is," Eden said, now even more confused. Why was he winking? Was he trying to say that ten *wasn't* a fun age? How would he know? He couldn't have been more than nine.

Still, none of that seemed to matter as much as the health of the wounded ant. She pulled the yellow card out from behind her back and showed him the tiny creature. Whoever he was, maybe he could help her find Tillie. "Anyway, I'm hoping you can help me. This ant needs medical attention."

"How fortunate. I happen to be a doctor," he said.

Eden noticed that the boy's eyes widened as he said it, as if he couldn't believe the words had popped out of his mouth.

"Then why did you introduce yourself as Mr. August Rattice?"

"I, uh, I didn't want to brag."

"Are you *sure* you're a doctor?" Eden asked. She knew how hard it was to untangle herself from a fib and wanted to give him a chance to tell the truth.

"What an absurd question. Of course I am. I'm a bug doctor."

"Oh! So you're an entomologist."

"An ento what?" he asked.

"An entomologist. Someone who studies insects," Eden explained.

"Ha! Silly child. I know what an entomologist is," he said quickly. "Obviously, since I am one. The only reason I didn't understand what you said was that you were mumbling quite a bit. It's your fault. You need to speak more clearly."

"I'll try," said Eden, even though she was pretty sure she hadn't mumbled.

"So, uh, what seems to be the trouble?" he asked.

Eden held the card out closer to show him. "Her feet are broken, but she won't let me help her."

"How do you know?" he asked. "Can you speak Ant too?"

"Unfortunately not," Eden said. "I mean, I did play Follow the Leader and Charades with her friend pretty successfully, but now he's gone off to get help, and I can't tell if she isn't answering me because she's giving me the silent treatment or because she can't hear."

"Why can't she hear? Are her ears broken, too?"

Eden narrowed her eyes at him, suspicious. Any entomologist would know that ants don't have ears. Still, he seemed to be waiting for an answer.

"She can't hear *because* her feet are broken," she explained. "Ants don't have ears. They hear through their feet."

"That's right!" he said. "Obviously. Well done. Very good. That's how they hear: through their feet. I was testing you, child, and you passed! Congratulations!"

By now, Eden knew that everything the boy was saying was nonsense, and she was about to say so when they were interrupted by the sound of footsteps coming from around the corner. The steps were so slow, Eden could count to three between each footfall.

"That must be Tillie," she said. "She'll know what to do."

"No," the boy said. "I'm the expert. Not her!"

He grabbed the yellow card from Eden, snatching it so quickly that the card tilted all the way down until it was totally perpendicular. The big ant slid all the way down to the very bottom corner, which was miraculously bent just enough to keep her from sliding right off. Eden flinched. The tumble had to have hurt the creature. There was no way it hadn't. Eden grabbed for the card, but the boy spun away too quickly for her to get it.

"Stop playing around! This ant is very injured. We need an actual grown-up!" Eden insisted.

The boy's face got very red.

"I *am* a grown-up," he snarled, baring his teeth. That's when she spotted it.

"Baby tooth!" Eden said triumphantly. "I knew it! You're not a doctor or a grown-up. You're a liar who shouldn't even be here. I'm telling Tillie!"

"Don't you dare!"

"Too late! Try and stop me!"

"Oh, I will! Your wasps and ants can't help you now," he gloated. He yanked open a nearby door and shoved Eden toward it.

Eden was strong and tall for her age, but the boy had caught her off guard. She tripped on the threshold and fell into the night-dark room, landing on her hands and knees.

"Stay out of my way. I'm going to poison all those awful, disgusting bugs, and no one can stop me. Not you, not Tillie, not anyone in the world!"

And with that, he slammed the door on Eden, plunging her into darkness.

The Expert

Tillie rounded the corner only seconds after August had managed to lock the door behind Eden. He didn't have time to slide Dot and the card into his pocket, so he cupped one hand over the other, hiding them both from view.

"Ho, ho, hello!" he said with a hearty laugh. For some reason, his Santa voice kept creeping in, no matter how hard he tried to stop it.

"Ho, ho, hello to you, too, Mr. Rattice! I'm so relieved to see you're real!" Tillie said with delight. "When I woke up from my nap, I was worried I'd dreamed you. But here you are! Shall I take you on the tour?"

August sighed with relief. He'd gotten rid of Eden just in time. It was important that she and Tillie never meet. Tillie may be a hundred and twenty and barely able to hear or see, but she was definitely smart, and if she met Eden,

Tillie would know right away that Eden knew more about this bug stuff than he did. Also, Tillie and Eden would probably like each other. They were both do-gooder types who wanted to protect those icky creepy-crawlies, a job they would probably succeed at if they ever met, which was why he had to do everything in his power to keep them apart.

"Why yes, that would be delightful," he said, before suddenly being interrupted by loud, insistent pounding. It was that pesky girl, trying to get out of the dark room. August stifled a groan. He thought he'd gotten rid of her. Didn't she know she was supposed to be quiet once he'd locked her in?

"What on earth is that sound?" Tillie asked.

"What sound?" he asked, as innocently as possible.

"That knocking sound. You don't hear it?"

August grimaced. Tillie had said she was hard of hearing. Why was she suddenly so good at it now?

"Help! Help!" Eden cried. Her voice was muffled by the heavy door, but it was impossible not to hear her knocking.

"So, let's take that tour now, shall we?" August said to Tillie, offering her his arm. He needed to maneuver her farther down the hall where she wouldn't be able to hear Eden's insistent knocks. But Tillie wouldn't budge.

"Wait. Didn't you hear that?" Tillie asked. "Someone is shouting."

"I don't think so," August said through gritted teeth. "Come on, let's go."

"Help! Help!" Eden cried again.

"We're the only people here," Tillie said. "Where's that voice coming from?"

"Um, me!" August said, pounding on the outside of the door just as loudly as Eden was pounding on the inside. "Help! Help! Help me understand how these doors are so beautifully crafted!"

"Ah, yes. Remarkable, aren't they? I was hoping you'd ask," Tillie said, allowing him to steer her down the hall and away from Eden.

"Please do tell me all about it," August said, feeling grateful that he was as good at improvising as Ms. Batra said he was.

"Well," said Tillie. "During construction, Minnie persuaded the powderpost beetles and wood borers to help construct the house instead of eat it. She made every effort to get the termites on board, too, but they simply refused. For a while, it was simply ridiculous. The powderposts would build a door and then the termites would devour it. Absolutely nothing got done. All progress stopped. Finally, the termites agreed to only eat tree stumps until construction was completed. Luckily for us, most of the termites found they liked eating alfresco so much that they stopped snacking on the building. Some still insist on nibbling the furniture, but the issue is far more under control."

"That makes perfect sense," August said, using all of his acting skills to sound sincere, even though he couldn't imagine anything more preposterous.

They'd only taken a few steps when Tillie abruptly stopped and turned to him. She pushed her glasses down her nose and peered at him. "Now, just wait a moment. There's something you aren't telling me."

August gulped. Had she realized he was a boy? But how? What had given him away? He touched the buttons of his shirt. Had he misbuttoned them? That was a mistake that kids made a lot and adults never did. He cursed himself for making such an obvious error, but then realized that Tillie wasn't looking at his shirt. She was looking at the yellow calling card in his hand. He'd forgotten about keeping it hidden.

"You've already met Dot! She's a very special insect around here. She's Queen Mote's daughter and Minnie's granddaughter. You didn't tell me you'd already been introducing yourself around."

"Uh, yeah. I mean, yes. I mean, indeed," August said. It was hard to remember to use grown-up words when he was nervous. Acting was much easier when there were lines to memorize. August was good at improvising one or two funny lines now and then, but it was much harder to come up with every line on his own. He wiped his free hand on his suit pants. His hands were already sweaty from the whole door knocking thing. Now they felt drenched. "Dot and I just met. We've been getting on famously."

August didn't know what in the world *we've been getting on famously* meant, but his parents had once forced him to watch a boring old black-and-white movie with them, and a man in a tuxedo had said it like it was a good thing, and all the other characters had nodded and smiled. Sure enough, Tillie reacted the exact same way.

"Splendid," she said. "I'm sure the whole family will adore you."

"Funny, that's just what Dot was saying. Isn't that right, Dot?" August held the calling card closer to his face to make it seem like he was talking to Dot, then tilted it toward himself to make it seem like Dot was answering. August felt pretty sure that Tillie wouldn't be able to tell that he was bluffing, since she'd already admitted that she couldn't understand Ant. But Tillie didn't look pleased. Instead, she was squinting at Dot with concern.

"Oh dear," Tillie said. "I'm no expert, but she looks injured. Is something wrong with her feet?"

"Yes, they're broken," August said. At first, he was pleased with himself for remembering an ant fact, but then he regretted sharing it. If Tillie knew that ants heard through their feet, she'd know that August and Dot hadn't really been talking. "But if you think her feet have anything to do with her hearing, you're wrong. It's a myth, and anyone who tells you different is a liar."

"That's very good to know," Tillie said. "But what's important now is getting Dot into surgery immediately. Can you operate on insects like my Milton could, by any chance?"

"Unfortunately, I can't. Although I am very knowledgeable about most things, I never went to medical school." August wanted Tillie to think he could do everything Milton could, but telling Eden that he was a doctor had been a total disaster. The thought of piling more lies on top of the ones he'd already told made him anxious. He feared that, like a stack of blocks, the taller the tower, the more likely it was to all tumble down around him.

"Well, of course you didn't. Human medical schools don't offer classes in insect surgery. Milton learned by years of practicing on raspberry drupelets. Eventually, he could remove the minuscule seed from the center of each tiny nub without leaving any mark," Tillie said. "I was hoping any future Human Director would be able to do the same."

"Oh, sure. I can do that," August said. Saying he could perform surgery was as dangerous a lie as saying he was a doctor, but he knew he'd need to be at least as good as Milton to have a chance of getting the job.

"What a relief! We happen to have a fully equipped operating room right here in the Institute." Tillie pulled a huge ring of keys from her pocket.

August grinned at the sight of them. When he did find the poisons, they'd definitely be locked up somewhere. He'd need a key to get them out.

"Follow me," Tillie said. "And please tell Dot that I'll have a lump of her favorite sugar ready for her as soon as she wakes up from surgery."

"With pleasure," August said. As he looked into the ant's eyes and pretended to talk to it, he had a funny feeling that the ant was looking at him the same way he looked at Sheila. He quickly lowered the card ashamed. Even though he knew that ants didn't have feelings like people did, he still couldn't shake the feeling that Dot's fury was real.

The Breakthrough

The humans, now convinced they were alone, had finally stopped looking into the back seat. This time they rode in tense silence, barely moving at all. The male held on to the big circle in front of him with both hands the entire time, only moving them occasionally to turn the circle slightly left or right, and the female tapped her fingers on a wooden panel for the whole ride. The sound was nearly deafening, but the queen was eventually able to tune it out as she stared out the transparent panels on either side of the box. She took in her surroundings, transfixed. There was so much to look at!

First, the scenery kept changing at a dizzying pace. The queen had lived in the same tree her whole life and had assumed that the world ended at the borders of the park. Her cousin, who was a bald-faced hornet queen, had told her that there were lands beyond the park, but bald-faced hornets were known for being bald-faced liars, and the queen had never taken her cousin's declarations seriously.

But now, thanks to the box, the wasp queen had not only gone out of the park but into a city full of bustling human colonies. The queen was able to get a good look at all different kinds of human activities, because occasionally the box would stop for a bit, then start moving again.

At first these stops and starts seemed random, but then the queen noticed that every now and then there were gray rectangles hanging up above the boxes. Each of the dangling rectangles had three lights on it. The bottom light was green, the middle was yellow, and the top one was . . . The queen couldn't tell, so she assumed it was the color called "red." The queen knew that red was a color because a hummingbird had once explained to her that even though the queen couldn't perceive it, red was every bit as real as orange or violet. At first, the realization that she couldn't see all colors made the queen feel quite sad, but then a gossipy flea told her that dogs couldn't see red, green, *or* yellow, and since then she'd comforted herself with the knowledge that at least she was luckier than a dog. Now she scanned the road for boxes being driven by dogs and was relieved to see none. Unlike humans who could see yellow, green, *and* red and understand when it was time to stop and go, a dog, who was unable to see any of those colors, would probably cause a lot of accidents.

As soon as the queen was able to understand the purpose

of the dangling lights, the dark gray path in front of them changed yet again, widening until it was as broad as a river. Now the box moved faster and faster, never stopping, until it suddenly turned off the wide path and back onto a narrow one. This path, like the first one they'd been on, also had dangling light boxes and rows of human nests on either side, only these nests were much bigger and grander than the one she'd seen earlier. Also, there were huge fields of grass in front of each nest, and each blade of grass was, bizarrely, the exact same height and color.

Finally, the female turned to the male. "Farfoogde lam rpook bleh tarn ovak fridogtal," she said. Even though the queen couldn't understand her words, she could recognize from her tone and pitch that it was a distress cry.

"Enarne kal men dar swahm kotar fen sangwoh," the male replied, and this time the queen could understand that his tone was reassuring.

This pattern continued on for a while, only now and then the male would speak in the distressed tone and the female would comfort him. The queen flew back and forth restlessly in the back seat, irritated by their gibberish. Why couldn't they empathize and play the kazoo like the girl? Wasp was one of the most widely spoken insect languages. How arrogant of people to think they could successfully go through their lives only speaking human ones. Did they really think they could play a significant role in the future of the planet without being able to speak any language but their own? It was hopeless. Now she was trapped in a box with two ignorant creatures who could potentially murder her at any moment, and for nothing. She would've been better off looking for Eden on her own. Besides, listening to the two of them drone on was boring, and even though she was determined to stay alert, she found her head nodding and her eyes closing.

She was startled awake, however, when she saw the female make a sudden move with her big pink hand. The queen recoiled, prepared to sting the female before it could attempt to crush her again, but the female didn't move to swat her. Instead, she turned a dial on the front panel of the box, and suddenly the air was full of the most exquisite sounds the queen had ever heard. It was similar to buzzing, but sweeter and more melodic. It was high and piping, and listening to it filled the queen with the lovely sensation of enjoying something that was both new and familiar. It was a remarkable feeling, and it made the queen forget that she needed to be cautious. She felt drawn to the sounds, just like moths were drawn to flames. The queen had always thought moths were unwise to rush toward the very thing that could kill them, but this sound was so irresistible she couldn't stay away.

The queen found herself drifting toward the front seat, searching for the source of the magical, piping sounds. As soon as the female human noticed the queen, she became agitated and began slapping at her once again. This time, instead of retreating, the queen darted agilely around the pink hand, desperate to get as close to the magical tones as possible.

The queen, transported by the enchanting sounds, barely noticed that the female had stopped slapping at her and both humans had gone totally silent. When she turned to see if they were still there, she was surprised to see them both staring at her. After a moment, the humans began speaking to each other again, and although the queen still couldn't understand them, she realized that the sounds they were making were now soft and low, as if they didn't want to interrupt her pleasure.

Then, to the queen's dismay, the female turned the dial on the front of the box and the beautiful noises stopped as quickly as they'd started. The queen wished she were big enough to turn it back on again, but it was obviously way too large for her to manipulate. She wished the female would turn the dial again, but instead she reached her big pink hand toward the back of the box and picked up a rectangular black item. This time, the queen made no move to sting her. The female was moving slowly and calmly, and the queen could tell she had no intention of hurting her. Instead, the female opened the rectangle to reveal three shiny silver sticks. Two were studded with silver disks, and the third had a bulge with a hole in the center. It looked like a larger, more elaborate version of the stubby cylinder that Eden had put in her mouthpart. The female put the three parts together until they made one long, slender pipe, which she lifted to her lips. Perhaps she, like Eden, was trying to make contact in her own way.

To the queen's amazement, the female was able to use the stick to re-create the splendid sound that had been coming from the box. After a few notes, the female stopped playing the silver stick and said something to the queen with her mouthpart. The queen was disappointed to realize that she couldn't understand a word of what the female was saying. She despaired that they would never be able to communicate like she and Eden had. But then the queen remembered the technique she'd used to understand Eden. Sure enough, as soon as she'd closed all five of her eyes and focused on steeping herself in the female's feelings instead of understanding her words, the queen discovered that the female's emotions were similar to the ones she'd felt when her babies had been attacked: fear, heartache, and love. It made her wonder if this female was a mother, too.

The female spoke to the queen again, only this time instead of speaking directly through her mouthpart, she piped on her silver stick. "Hello? Can you understand me?"

The queen's eyes popped open with astonishment. "I *can* understand you! Can you understand me?" she asked, working hard to make her buzzing sound as much like the ethereal piping as possible.

"I can!" the female said with surprise and delight.

The queen nodded, impressed. This female, like Eden, had somehow intuited that empathy was the key to understanding. And just as it had been between the queen and Eden, it was only moments before she and the female could speak to each other in complex sentences, understanding each other perfectly with the help of the magical pipe that the queen soon learned was called a "flute."

The male, unfortunately, couldn't understand a word they were saying, so the female would pause every now and then to explain their conversation to him. The queen watched as his expression changed from disbelief to wonder. After a bit of conversation, the queen had learned that the male was called "Jordan" and the female was called "Miranda," that they were something called "married," that Miranda was indeed a mother, and that Eden was her daughter. Strangest of all, the queen learned that instead of having hundreds of babies like she did, Jordan and Miranda only had Eden, which was why they were even more desperate to find her than the queen was.

They pooled the little information they had, quickly realizing how much overlapped. The queen explained that she'd heard rumors about a mythical place where humans and insects were learning to communicate, and the humans explained that they had learned from something called "Eden's computer" that she was probably on her way to an old, abandoned place called "the Windward." It seemed unlikely that the thriving laboratory and the deserted mansion were related in any way, but it was all they had to go on. Miranda explained that with the help of the box, which was called a "car," they could get there fairly quickly. Maybe, she said, they could find Eden if they worked together.

The queen was surprised to find herself considering this far-fetched plan. She'd been taught to think of humans as being only cruel and vicious ever since she was a larva, but now that she was learning that humans cared about their children as much as wasps did about their babies, she'd begun to rethink things. Perhaps she and humans were more alike than she'd thought. After all, they were all looking for Eden, and they all knew how unique and precious she was. The queen's thoughts were interrupted by the sound of Miranda's flute.

"Will you please come help us find Eden, Your Majesty?" Miranda piped.

"It would be my honor," piped the queen.

The Notebook

Eden spread her fingers and plunged them forward into the darkness, feeling around for a door, a doorknob, anything to get her out of this place. Her eyes hadn't gotten used to the darkness, and the air felt heavy, as though someone had draped a wet coat over her. Finally, she found the knob and turned it every way she could—jiggling, twisting, tugging—but it wouldn't budge. She was trapped!

Eden gasped, literally left breathless from the realization that she'd been tricked. She forced herself to slow down and breathe deeply, just like the little ant had reminded her. She had to stay calm if she was going to figure out what was going on. What had just happened? Who was August Rattice, really? Was that even his real name? Why was he lying? And why would anyone at the Institute for Lower Learning, no matter how old they were, want to poison bugs at all?

Eden felt like a dope for trusting a total stranger. She knew better. Her parents had told her a million times: don't talk to strangers; not everyone is honest; not everyone is who they say they are. Eden took all those warnings very seriously. Her family loved to tell the story about the time when Eden was five and waiting with her mom to meet a new pediatrician, and when the doctor entered the room with a peppy *Nice to meet you. I'm Dr. Lim,* Eden lowered her *Cricket* magazine, peered over her glasses, and said, *Really? Can I see some proof?* Her mother and the doctor both thought this was hilarious, and Eden was forced to sit there, listening to them laugh until her face got so hot she was sure she had a fever. Eden was irritated and confused: Was she supposed to trust strangers or not? On the way home, as if the three shots she'd just gotten weren't painful enough, she had to listen to a lecture from her mom about understanding context.

If I take you to a doctor's office to see a doctor and someone comes in and says he's a doctor, there's a pretty good chance he's actually a doctor.

Yes, but— Eden had protested, but then their favorite song came on the radio, and she and her mom immediately stopped arguing and sang along so hard their throats burned.

Now, in the dark closet, Eden wished she'd gotten away from the boy as soon as she'd realized he was lying. She'd known something was off from the minute she'd met him, when he'd insisted that he was a grown-up. And yes, he was dressed in a suit, but nothing else about him seemed even remotely adult. His face didn't have any wrinkles or stubble, and unlike most adults, who had strong facial features like cheekbones and jawlines, the boy had a smooth, round face with big, pudgy cheeks. He was also much more temperamental than most adults. Most of the grown-ups Eden knew were able to manage their feelings; the boy looked like he was on the verge of throwing a tantrum when she'd questioned him in the mildest way. Most adults would say, "Oh, I didn't know that" when they learned something new, like that ants hear through their feet. Instead, the boy insisted that he already knew, even though he obviously didn't. Plus, he used way too many words like *quite* and *rather*, as if he were using fancy words to prove he was smart, instead of just being smart and talking regular.

But right now, he *was* the smart one. He'd gotten Eden to hand over an innocent, injured creature. For all Eden knew, he'd already killed the wounded ant. There was so much she didn't know, but the one thing she knew for sure was that she wouldn't learn anything new by staying in a locked room.

Eden paced the small space, fretting. At this point, she didn't even know if there were any other people at the Institute at all, and no one she knew was even aware that she was there. What if she never got out? What if no one ever found her? What if she got hungry, or had to pee? Was it possible she could die in that dark little room and no one would know? Almost as bad was the thought that she was losing valuable time at the Institute when she could be finding allies.

By now, however, her eyes had adjusted to the dark, and she was able to make out a pull cord hanging from a bare bulb above her head. She took off her sweatshirt and pressed it along the narrow gap between the bottom of the door and the floor to make sure no light could shine through, just in case Mr. Rattice happened to be walking by, then pulled the cord.

As the room filled with light, Eden was surprised to see that unlike the massive, well-kept rooms she'd already passed through, this one was musty and neglected. The only furniture was a plain wooden desk scattered with pens, and a bookcase with a single book on its dusty shelves. The book was bursting with index cards and sticky notes that had been inserted between almost every page as if someone had just been studying it, but the thick layer of dust that coated its cover indicated that it had been abandoned long ago. Taking the volume from the shelf, Eden realized that it wasn't a published book but a handwritten journal. On the cover, a title was written in dark green ink: *Conversations and Observations, Volume I.* Eden knew that she should be trying to escape instead of stopping to read, but the mysterious book was irresistible.

On the first page was a dedication that read "To my mother," and at the top of the next page in big green letters was the word *Fly*. As she began to read, Eden noticed that instead of having paragraphs and descriptions like most books she'd read, this book was all dialogue, as though someone had tape-recorded a conversation and then written it all down. It looked like this:

> **M.W.:** Thank you for taking the time to talk with me.
>
> **F.:** My pleasure. It's the least I can do, after you saved me from that web.
>
> **M.W.:** It was nothing.
>
> **F.:** Not to me it wasn't. *(chuckles, vomits on chair)*
>
> **M.W.:** Before we get started, can I offer you a drink or some food? I have some cantaloupe rind that's been sitting in the sun for days.
>
> **F.:** That sounds delicious, but for now just a drink, please.
>
> **M.W.:** Of course. Tea? Coffee? Sugar water?
>
> **F.:** Sugar water, please, with two thimblefuls of tea.
>
> **M.W.:** Wonderful. I'll be right back.

Eden was astonished. It was a conversation between a human and a fly! It was obvious that *F* stood for "fly," but who was M.W.? Eden needed to know, because whoever M.W. was, it was clear that they could talk to flies the same way she could talk to the wasp queen. She skimmed the book and was excited to see that M.W. had conducted many interviews with all different kinds of insects. Some she'd never even heard of, like bombardier beetles and vampire moths. The back of her neck prickled with excitement. She was flabbergasted by how quickly she'd discovered another person who could also speak to insects. M.W. could be the partner she was looking for! Plus, she was yearning to find out how M.W. had learned to speak many different insect languages. If M.W. had learned that many, maybe she could, too.

Eden knew her first priority had to be finding a way out of that room, but she couldn't help herself. She had to read at least one more chapter. She flipped ahead, stopping at "Silkworms."

M.W.: Hello—

S.W.: Aah! A human!

M.W.: Please, don't be alarmed. I'm not here to hurt you. I'd just like to interview you.

S.W.: For what? Who sent you?

M.W.: No one. I was hoping we could talk.

S.W.: Nice try, human. You think I believe you're not one of them?

M.W.: Them? Who's—

S.W.: (*twisting around to see if anyone is listening*) Shh!

M.W.: What's going on? Are you in some kind of danger?

S.W.: (*looks around, whispers*) We all are. All the time. They could be anywhere, waiting to grab our cocoons.

M.W.: Who? Who wants your cocoons?

S.W.: The silk makers! You have any idea how they make silk?

M.W.: No. I've never thought about it.

S.W.: That's because they don't want you to know. That silk tie you're wearing right now? They raided a thousand of our cocoons to make that thing.

M.W.: What? That's awful. I had no idea.

S.W.: Barely any humans do. And the ones who know don't care.

M.W.: I care. Please, join us. Let us be your allies.

S.W.: Who's us? Who's we?

M.W.: We— Wait. It probably isn't safe to talk here.

S.W.: Nowhere's safe. They're everywhere!

M.W.: Come with me to the Institute. We're having a meeting tonight, and some ants will be there whom I think you should meet.

S.W.: What ants? What Institute?

M.W.: If I told you, you wouldn't believe me. Will you come with me? Will you trust me?

S.W.: (*hesitates, then*) . . . All right, I'm in. Can I bring nine thousand friends?

M.W.: Absolutely. As many as you can! The ants and I are planning a march against insecticides.

Ants usually go marching one by one, but this
time we're going to march by the hundreds of
thousands, so we're going to need as many insects
and humans as we can get. Join us, and we can
all help each other stop cruelty, murder, and the
destruction of our earth, sea, and sky.

S.W.: Right on! Let's do this!

Eden's heart started beating like a drum in a parade. She'd
seen that the Institute was beautiful. Now she could see that
it was also a place where radical ideas were born, that there
were people who wanted to protect insects like the silkworms from the humans who wanted to hurt them and steal
their babies. Eden wanted to join them. She came from a
family that had marched and protested against injustice for
generations. Eden, her parents, her grandparents, and their
parents before them had spoken out for human rights, civil
rights, women's rights, LGBTQ+ rights, and the rights of the
planet itself. But what had happened to the big plans of the
humans and insects of the Institute? Had their march ever
happened? Why was a book that recorded the beginning of
a revolution now covered in dust? Eden skipped to the back
and saw there were dozens of blank pages. She examined
the cover again, running her fingers over the words *Volume
I.* She wondered if there were other volumes or, if this was
the only one, why M.W. and the insects would've abandoned their mission. They probably had no idea there was

an enemy plotting against them right now. She had to find M.W. and the insects. She had to stop the wicked boy.

Her best chance of escaping, she realized, was to take the door off its hinges. Unlike throwing herself against it or trying to smash through it, taking it off its hinges was something she could accomplish quietly without calling any attention to herself. She'd helped her parents put together enough IKEA furniture to be pretty confident she could manage it. Eden wished she still had her backpack. She always kept a mini tool kit in there, just in case. But maybe there was something in the room that could double as a screwdriver. She scanned the array of pens on the table, hoping to find an old-fashioned one that had a metal nib.

Eden had put the book back on the shelf and turned to examine the pens when she heard a clicking sound behind her. She turned and was stunned to see that the book was now rotating clockwise, as if it were a key in a lock. Suddenly, the whole bookcase was turning, opening like a door. And although the room it opened onto was cavernous and dark, Eden felt a refreshing breeze sweep across her face. Worried she'd never see the precious notebook again if she didn't take it with her, she snatched it off the shelf.

Eden didn't feel great about taking it. She hated stealing and any kind of dishonesty so much that she'd get upset at her dad for sampling too many grapes at the farmers market. He'd laugh and tell her to look around, and Eden would be scandalized to see that nearly every shopper was plucking grapes and cherry tomatoes off their stems and popping them into their mouths before they paid for them. The vendors either didn't notice or didn't seem to care.

Besides, Eden was planning to return the book as soon as she was done with it. And she was taking it for a good reason, wasn't she? Getting the tools to communicate with insects was the whole purpose of the Institute. Having convinced herself that she was doing the right thing, Eden stepped into the dark room. And unlike the last time, when the darkness seemed dangerous and forbidding, this time it seemed to promise something wonderful, and she felt as light and optimistic as if she were stepping outdoors into fresh air.

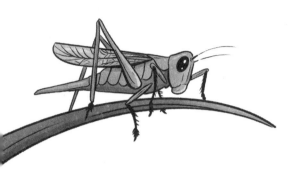

The Key

"This was Milton's operating room," Tillie explained as she led August to a wide double door. "He had a remarkable gift for healing. I once watched him perform surgery on a stick insect. Someone had mistaken him for an actual stick and jammed a marshmallow onto his head. It required nine head and neck procedures."

August had no idea bugs could be mistaken for sticks. He made a mental note never to pick up a stick again.

"No one's used this room since Milton passed away," Tillie said. "But I'd like you to have that honor."

"I am honored indeed, Tillie," he said, bowing his head in fake respect for the long-dead weirdo. "I can think of no better place to perform a lifesaving surgery on dear little Dot."

"Then let's not waste a moment," Tillie said as she unlocked and opened the door to reveal a pristine operating room. "I think you'll find everything you need."

A microscope stood atop a table at the center of the room, and alongside the table was a small stand. The stand was set like a beautiful dining room table, only it had rows of tiny surgical instruments instead of silverware. August, however, barely noticed the exquisite craftsmanship of the room. He was much more interested in the ring of keys that dangled from Tillie's fingers.

"Thank you," August said. "I'll update you on her recovery as soon as I've completed the procedure. Though obviously it's going to go perfectly, since I'm highly trained and remarkably gifted."

"May I stay? I'd love to watch you work," Tillie said, settling gingerly onto one of the low stools that ringed the operating table. She picked up a miniature magnifying glass and peered into it.

August scowled. He had to get rid of her. She couldn't know that he wasn't able to tell one tool from another, let alone perform surgery.

"I'm very sorry," he said. "But you know the old expression: a scientist never reveals his secrets."

"I thought that was about magicians," Tillie said.

"Wouldn't you call operating on insects its own kind of magic?"

"Why, yes, now that I think about it," she said.

"So scoot, my dear. And why don't you give me those keys, so I can lock up after I'm finished?" August struggled to keep his voice casual. He was certain Tillie could hear the rapid-fire pounding of his heart.

"I suppose I should," Tillie said, her smile growing as wide as the horizon. "Since they're yours now. Given all your skills, your immediate connection with Dot, and your ability to both heal and communicate with insects, I feel I can safely sidestep my usual interview process. Your final confirmation will depend, of course, on the agreement of your insect counterpart, but I would like to temporarily name you, Mr. August Rattice, the Human Director of the Institute for Lower Learning."

Tillie placed the giant ring of keys in his hand. They were surprisingly heavy and satisfying to hold. August felt a current of excitement run through him that was even more powerful than the tingle that shot through his body when he'd licked a nine-volt battery during a science experiment. He'd done it! He'd tricked her. The poisons were his to raid!

"Thank you, Tillie. I accept this profound honor, and I thank you with all my heart," August said, bowing his head in the same modest way Ms. Batra had shown him when he was playing a sunflower. "Although I would love nothing more than to celebrate this momentous event, I must ask you to leave, so I can get to work healing my lovely new friend, who

I definitely don't think is gross in any way."

"Of course," Tillie said. "And I know just what I can do while you work. I baked a nice, fresh blueberry pie this morning. Would you like me to bring you a slice?"

Blueberry pie was August's favorite. Plus, he was starving. He hadn't had any lunch or snack since he'd arrived three hours ago.

"That sounds superb," he said. "And take your time. No rush."

"I wish I *could* rush," Tillie said. "I'm afraid it's no longer an option for me these days. But I'll be back as soon as I can with a nice, hearty slice."

She moved to stand, then abruptly stopped.

"What's the matter?" August said, though what he really wanted to say was *Just get out of here already!*

"I have to stand up very carefully these days, one vertebra at a time," Tillie said, slowly straightening her spine. "Thirty-third vertebra, thirty-second vertebra, thirty-first vertebra—"

August sighed as she counted each one. He suddenly understood why his parents would get so annoyed when he sang the "Ninety-Nine Bottles of Pop on the Wall" song the whole way home from camp.

She gave August an apologetic smile. "I'm sorry to be so slow."

"Are you? I hadn't noticed," August said, digging his nails

into his palms.

"Twenty-first vertebra, twentieth vertebra, nineteenth vertebra . . ." Tillie continued.

August waited for what felt like an eternity. By the time he heard her count down the third, second, and first vertebrae and saw Tillie standing up straight again, he felt certain he was already old enough to drive.

"Oop, forgot to put down the magnifying glass," she said, gingerly curling her spine down toward the table. "First vertebra, second vertebra, third vertebra—"

"I'll get it!" August blurted, grabbing the magnifying glass and ushering her out the door.

"I'll be right back with that pie!" she called as he closed the door behind her.

As soon as she was gone, August grabbed one of the clear plastic specimen boxes, shook the ant from his hand, crammed it into the box, jammed on the lid, and thrust it onto as high a shelf as he could reach. He glanced down at the keys, eager to inspect them further. There were at least fifty, and they were arranged from biggest to smallest. The littlest one caught his eye: it was different from all the others. While the others were old, their metal teeth nearly worn smooth, the littlest key was brand-new: short and squat with a wide, round head. It gleamed as it caught the light, as though it were winking at him. It had to be the key to the room that held the poisons. August looked up at the clock on the wall. The little hand was just past the one, and the big hand was on the six. Thank goodness he'd finally learned to tell time. It was one thirty. He still had a couple of hours to search the house before his mother had any idea that there hadn't been a field trip and that he'd skipped school.

Still, he needed to hurry. August raced out of the operating room. He needed to pocket those poisons and get back to the operating room before Tillie returned with the pie. He didn't have a moment to lose.

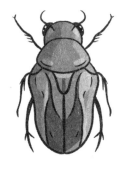

The Adventure

Digging faster than he ever had before, Atom burrowed down into the crack in the floor, searching for the rest of the colony. He had no idea where Dot and the girl had gone, and the huge distances between the rooms would make it nearly impossible for him to find her on his own. Atom had a sense of how tremendous the Institute was overall because once, on a field trip with their geography class, he and Dot had gotten to see the architectural plans that the builders had used to convert the Institute from an impractical building that rose up from the ground into a practical one that went down into it. The plans themselves were enormous, and to Atom the map of the Institute seemed as big as the actual world: each hallway as wide as a river, each staircase a mountain range, and each room a different country.

In preparation for the field trip, The Ladder had thoughtfully unrolled the plans, which had been drawn on dusky blue paper and stored on a huge spool. The plans, when spread out, stretched across the entire floor in wavy loops, and when Atom first saw it, he thought it was the ocean. Too excited to remember that oceans were outdoors and not in, he threw down his lunch crumb and ran, laughing and hollering, right into the blue waves and leaping up onto the highest one, bracing himself for a wild ride.

Everybody in the water! he'd shouted, but the paper waves barely moved, and he was left standing there, motionless, as the entire class stared.

Dude, you thought that was water? Speck had said with a nasty snort. Speck was the biggest, meanest ant in the whole class, and Atom froze, humiliated, on top of the paper wave, as he waited for the rest of the class to join in about how clueless he was. Instead, Dot stepped up to Speck, her foreleg planted firmly on her thorax.

Dude, of course he knows it's not water. Do you have, like, zero imagination? And with that, Dot threw down her lunch crumb, hollering *Cowabunga!* as she ran toward the plans, belly-flopping onto a high, paper crest.

Seconds later the entire class followed, and a chorus of voices shouting *Whoo-hoo!* and *Wait for me!* and *Is the water cold?* filled the air. Atom watched, amazed, as the entire class ran toward the paper waves, laughing and shrieking as they surfed and sunbathed, pretending the bright lamp overhead was the summer sun. In a matter of moments, Speck was the only one standing on the shore.

Come on in, Speck! Dot had shouted.

That was another thing Atom admired about Dot. She was fierce, but she never held a grudge, and soon even Speck was frolicking in the imaginary waves.

All right, all right, that's enough, Ms. Fourmi had shouted as a few ants got a little too wild, their legs kicking tiny holes in the paper. *Everyone hop off. Those are precious original documents!*

Best of all, at the end of the field trip, every ant in the class had stopped to high-two Atom and tell him how cool he was.

Thank you, he whispered to Dot as they marched home.

For what? she'd said with a wink. *You're the cool one.*

As always, she'd been his hero. And now she was missing.

"Mom?" Atom called. "Aunt Bitty?"

No answer. He called again, louder. Again, nothing. Where was everybody? He'd been counting on rounding up at least a few thousand family members to help him. Then he remembered the sunflower head they'd found lying in the grass the week before. It was as round and warm as a pizza and covered in rich golden florets. It was one of those few foods that were healthy *and* delicious. The plan had been to let it dry out for a few more days and then have the whole colony drag it inside together. Atom's hind gut churned, and he got a sour taste in his intrabuccal pocket as he realized he'd have to rescue Dot on his own.

He backtracked his way out of the crack until he found himself in the hall again. He scanned the vast chamber with dread. It was empty, and Eden was nowhere to be found. How was he supposed to find Dot and the girl? It usually took Dot and him at least an hour to get as far as the human-sized kitchen, and he was a helpless male, traveling all alone. How could he possibly search the whole house? He was standing there, pondering his next move, when the smell of pie filled his antennae. He looked toward the kitchen door just as it swung open. The Ladder stepped out, holding a piece of blueberry pie on a china plate, and began walking toward him. The Ladder! He could climb The Ladder! True, he had no idea which way she was headed, but he had no idea where he was going, either. Any direction she chose would be just as helpful as any other.

Aunt Dab's warning echoed through all two hundred and fifty thousand of his brain cells. *Stay away. She can barely hear or see . . . She could step on you . . . drop you . . . crush you . . .* Atom knew that climbing The Ladder could be deadly, but it could also save Dot's life. If their places were reversed, Atom knew that Dot wouldn't hesitate.

He waited for The Ladder to get closer, studying the movements of her flowing skirt and listening to the near-deafening clack of her heels on the marble floor. As she got close enough to step on him, he leapt as far forward as he could, landing on the hem of her skirt, and hooking his feet into one of the delicate stitches that ran along the bottom. He'd made it! Now he just needed to get to the top of her head, where he'd be able to scan the horizon. But how would he get all the way up there? In Dab and Bitty's stories about climbing The Ladder, they'd always said that Tillie, like the human girl he'd met earlier, would use her hand to help lift them up to where they needed to go. But this time, Tillie couldn't help Atom, because she didn't even know he was there. He looked upward, hoping to find some footholds in the fabric of her skirt, but all he could see was a vast, billowing cloud of cream silk.

Ants were famous for climbing vertical surfaces no matter how steep, but he knew there was no way he could chart a route through the soft fabric, which was as puffy and hard to walk in as newly fallen snow. If he wanted to get to the top of The Ladder, he'd need to find a new way up. He thought of something his mom used to tell him about digging tunnels: *Sometimes the best way to go up is by going down.* That was it! He wasn't going to climb *up* The Ladder. He was going to climb *down* her. He leaned way over, past the hem of the skirt, until he'd grabbed the very bottom with his forelegs and peered down under it. Atom had seen male and female humans' feet and shoes before, but he'd never seen a female human's foot inside a shoe quite so close up. Atom could see that the top of Tillie's foot was encased in fine white netting, over which there was a wide, cream-colored band, which was held in place by a lustrous pearl, which was then held in place by a strong fabric loop. There were so many contraptions clamped to the poor little foot, it looked like someone had strapped it down because they were worried it was going to get loose and run away.

It was hard to think while he was hanging upside down, but Atom realized that Tillie's foot was the key to getting to her hand. If he could get her to reach down and scratch her foot, he could leap onto her hand and ride it like an elevator to the upper part of her body. Gathering all his courage, he let go of the stitch with his four front legs and hung from it with his back two, as if he were on a trapeze. He pumped his legs until his entire body was swinging back and forth, and when he realized he couldn't swing any faster or higher, he let go of the stitch, hurling himself toward the pad of pink foot flesh below. He landed right in the middle of it, gasping for air. Atom was exhausted, but he still had far to go. He needed to make Tillie reach down to scratch her foot. He wriggled around on the pad, using the netting that covered it to cause as much friction as possible.

After a moment, three pale human fingers reached down to scratch the spot where Atom was wriggling, and as they did, Atom used his feelers and forelegs to drag himself onto one of the fingers. He was still wobbling on the edge of it when Tillie stopped scratching and lifted her hand back up and out from under the skirt. Atom clung to the rounded edge of her fingernail. The swirl of the fabric created hurricane-level gusts, but Atom hung on mightily. When Tillie's fingers were at the height of her waist, she gripped the edge of the china plate, and Atom was able to step off her nail and onto the plate as easily as a human would step onto a sidewalk. He relaxed, catching his breath, as The Ladder moved through the corridors of the Institute, finally stopping at a room Atom had never seen before and cautiously opening the door.

"Px, Rattice!" she called out cheerily. "G've thunquek dor blit sty!"

This time, Atom didn't bother trying to understand what Tillie was saying. Something more important had caught his attention. He was inside what appeared to be an operating room, and on a high shelf at the far end of the room was a transparent specimen box. A familiar face peered at him from inside the plastic prison. It was Dot! She was alive! Atom was astonished by the coincidence. In a building with literally hundreds of rooms, how was it possible that The Ladder had been heading to the exact same place where Dot was.

Unlike Atom, however, The Ladder didn't seem to have found what she was looking for. She wheeled around, scanning the entire room until she finally came to a stop, and Atom found himself facing the door they'd just entered. She was leaving! Atom looked down at the ground far below. He had to get off The Ladder immediately, but how?

Spying a paper napkin tucked on the underside of the plate, Atom remembered a story his Aunt Dab, who'd been an army ant, had told him about the time she'd gotten stuck on an enemy countertop and nearly smushed by a shrieking woman wielding a paper towel. Thanks to Dab's quick thinking and military training she'd managed to escape, using the very paper towel that had nearly killed her. Atom's mother used to warn him that most of Aunt Dab's war stories weren't true. He desperately hoped this one was. As Tillie turned to leave, Atom mustered his courage, then bit the edge of the napkin. He jumped off the edge of the plate, using his weight to tear off as big a paper rectangle as he could. As he plummeted down he swung his body upward, grabbing the far edge of the napkin. He was millimeters from crash-landing on the hard floor when suddenly the napkin caught the breeze, ballooning into a parachute exactly as Aunt Dab had said.

Atom whooped with excitement as the strip of napkin delivered him gently onto the ground, and he scurried out from under it as it collapsed around him. He'd done it! He'd climbed The Ladder! He'd parachuted and lived! He'd found his sister! After all the times Dot had saved him, here was his chance to save her. He wasn't just the lazy little one anymore. He'd become his hero's hero! As the operating room door closed behind him, leaving Dot and him alone in the room, he raised his forelegs up over his head in a *V* for victory. Then he heard an insistent knocking from high above. He looked up to see Dot pounding on the plastic panel of her prison.

"Hey!" she hollered. "Can you save the victory lap for later? I'm running out of air up here!"

Hidden Homes

*E*den *found herself standing* on the bank of a small pond ringed with miniature pine trees. It looked and smelled exactly like the lake behind her grandparents' summerhouse, down to the low grasses and reedy cattails that surrounded it, and the algae-covered rocks that occasionally jutted above the surface of the water. She thought for a moment that she'd somehow gotten outside, but then noticed that the blue sky above was actually a painted ceiling, and the row of larger pine trees beyond the small ones was actually painted wallpaper.

The pond's surface was dotted with lily pads as round and bright as sequins on a dress. There was no trace of any living creature, but Eden could tell from the abandoned shells of freshly shed nymph skin that draped the banks like cast-off costumes that she'd stumbled upon a dragonfly habitat. For a moment she thought she saw a glimpse of iridescent wings flitting behind a tree, but if it was in fact a dragonfly, it clearly didn't want to make its presence known.

The tiny landscape was so magical that Eden wanted to sit by it for hours, taking in all the glorious details and hoping to catch a glimpse of an actual dragonfly, but she was distracted by the sight of a narrow waterfall that spilled into the far edge of the pool. The spray of sparkling water reminded her of how thirsty she was, and she yearned for a sip. Extending a toe toward the nearest rock that poked up from under the water, she tested it to see if it would support her weight. It seemed steady enough, so she ventured forward, gingerly moving from rock to rock until she stood on the opposite bank.

Eden tucked the notebook into the waistband of her track pants, cupped her hands and held them under the cascade until they were full of water, then drank deeply. The water was so cold and delicious that she craved more and more, until she couldn't hold enough in her hands and finally just tipped her head back and opened her mouth, gulping straight from the falls. Water streamed down her chin, splashing into the pool beneath it. Eden wiped her chin, remembering all the times she had drunk straight from the hose while she helped her mom with her garden.

Eden thought about the way the midday sun would filter through the raspberry bushes, making patterns on the ground below, and she guessed it was around midday now, well past lunchtime and the Final Friday birthday celebration. Her parents must've already arrived and realized she hadn't gone to school. She imagined the box of cupcakes they'd brought sitting forgotten on the teacher's desk as they raced off to find her. She was sure they were looking for her, terrified that something awful had happened. She'd never worried them before, never even been late once. Guilt swept over her like a rolling fog.

All thoughts of her parents vanished, however, when she noticed that the wall of wet rock behind the waterfall wasn't one solid wall but two walls with a narrow gap between them. A bright light gleamed through the slender opening. Parting the rushing falls with her hands, she turned her body sideways, doing her best to slip through the gap. It was a tighter fit than she'd realized, and she sucked in her breath, making her body as slim as possible. The cold water rained down on her, soaking her clothes, and the mossy edges of the walls skimmed her sides as she pressed herself through the narrow space. Once she'd shimmied through the narrowest point, she finally had room to turn her head and saw the source of the bright light.

It was a streetlight!

Eden extricated herself from the rock and found she was standing in a room that looked exactly like a city sidewalk. The concrete was strewn with lumps of chewed gum, open candy wrappers smeared with chocolate, and a pizza box.

Every surface was dotted with what looked like tiny flecks of pepper, which Eden recognized as cockroach poop. She'd found a cockroach habitat! But it wasn't just a cockroach habitat; it was a paradise. She thought she heard a skittering sound coming from a box of jawbreakers, but by the time she got to the red and purple box, the street was silent again. She tiptoed to the pizza box, trying to keep her sopping sneakers from squelching, and lifted the lid to see if any cockroaches were lurking inside. She was disappointed that there weren't any, but she found several pieces of crust and a slice of pepperoni pizza that was deckled with tiny bite marks. The edges of the pepperoni slices curled up, making little round cups, and inside each cup was a pool of orange grease, like cups of punch set out at a party.

The entire street, like the dragonfly habitat, was empty. Eden looked at the storefronts that lined the street. They looked old-fashioned, like the ones in the black-and-white photos of downtown Chicago where Grandma Betty had grown up. There was a diner, a beauty salon, a tailor, and a bank. Each had the name of the establishment etched into its window and a sign that said "Closed." Between the tailor and the salon, however, was a door that didn't have a sign, awning, or any indication that it was a store at all. It was the kind of door you'd find inside a regular house.

Sure enough, when Eden turned the knob and stepped

inside, she found herself in a narrow closet lined with clothing rods full of hangers, and on each hanger was a beautiful wool sweater. There were hundreds, each a different color and texture, and each punctured with multiple ragged holes. Eden laughed. Her parents had lined their closets at home with cedar and sprinkled them with mothballs to keep the moths away, but now she was in the land of the moths, where sweaters had been laid out like food on a buffet, expressly to be eaten.

Eden shivered. The mysterious street didn't just look like Chicago. It was cold like Chicago, too, and since she'd arrived, a brisk wind had picked up. Strangely, it was just as chilly inside the closet as it had been out on the street, and her wet clothes only made things worse. Eden didn't feel great about borrowing one of the sweaters without permission, but there were so many and she was so cold. Plus, she was going to return it on her way back out.

She slipped a green V-neck sweater on over her track jacket. Still shivering, she also slipped a fuzzy pink cardigan off its hanger and was astonished to see that behind the row of sweaters was a staircase with checkerboard squares of green and white linoleum, just like the ones in Grandma Roz's old kitchen. Grandma Roz had moved to New Haven a few years ago to be closer to Eden and her family, but when Eden was little, Grandma Roz and Grandpa Abe used to live in an apartment in Brooklyn. Eden didn't remember much from those days, but she did remember playing a version of hopscotch on the green and white linoleum while her grandma made brisket. Even though she had no idea where this staircase led, the familiar floor made her feel as though she'd been there many times before and gave her a pleasant (though perhaps false) sense of safety and the courage to explore further, where a low hum emanated from the bottom of the stairs.

She put on the pink cardigan, then followed the sound and discovered that it was coming from a squat, avocado-green refrigerator in an old-fashioned kitchen, whose countertops were lined with bowls of brown bananas that were chockablock with tiny gouges. *Fruit flies!* Eden knew that fruit flies couldn't resist overripe fruit, and she couldn't help but wonder where they all were. She could've sworn she saw a tiny flock of them rise up from one of the bowls, but by the time she got to the counter, all she could see were motes of dust. *Maybe these places have all been abandoned,* she thought as her stomach growled. She helped herself to a freckled banana. Eden felt worse about taking the banana than the sweaters, since she obviously couldn't return the banana, but she comforted herself with the fact that the banana would've gone bad in a day or two anyway. Not seeing a trash can anywhere, she tucked the peel into the pocket of the cardigan.

Noticing that one of the kitchen cabinets was ajar, Eden

knelt down and peered into it. The cabinet had no bottom or back but instead opened onto an empty shaft that was so deep she couldn't see the bottom. A thick, gray rope attached to a pulley dangled into the shaft, like a wishing well in a storybook. Eden grasped the rope, only to discover that it was soft and made up of hundreds of thousands of delicately woven threads. *Silkworms made this rope,* she realized.

Finding it surprisingly sturdy, Eden lowered herself into the shaft. As she made her way down, she found that the dirt walls on either side were pockmarked with minuscule holes. The holes, like all the other rooms she'd passed through, appeared to be abandoned, but tiny grains of silt and sand still spilled from them, as though the ants, grubs, and mole crickets that had made them had left only a moment before. As Eden peered into the holes, a feisty brown mole cricket zoomed out of one and shot straight toward her. Eden, startled, let go of the rope. She grabbed for it as she plummeted downward, but it had already swung out of reach. Her stomach lurched as she fell, and a sour taste rose up in her throat. She tucked her head protectively, covering it with her hands, but the motion only pitched her forward, and then she was turning over and over in the dark, spinning like a planet knocked off its orbit. She fell for what felt like forever, reaching for the smooth walls in search of a handhold and feeling nothing but small, slippery lumps. She plunged deeper into the darkness, panicking at the thought of what might await her at the bottom. Freezing water? Jagged rock? But no. When she finally landed, it was on something soft and springy.

As she lay there breathless but unhurt, Eden squinted into the darkness and saw that she was in a room full of beds. Some were designed to look like race cars and others had rich silk canopies suspended from ornately carved bedposts like the ones she'd seen in museums. The bed she'd landed on had a lavender comforter with giant daisies on it that was exactly the same as the one she used to have when she was little and her parents would read her favorite books, *The Snowy Day* and *Brave Irene*, to her night after night on an endless loop. The bed was scattered with hundreds of tiny pillows, each no bigger than a paper clip. Eden shuddered. She'd landed in a bedbug refuge!

Eden knew about bedbugs from Grandma Roz. Once, when she was a girl, her bed had become so infested with them that her parents had had to throw her mattress away. *And we were so poor, we didn't have money or mattresses to throw around,* her grandma had said. *And the bites they gave me! I scratched for days. Uch, I'll never forget those nasty little vonces.* At the time, Eden had been more interested in finding out what the word *vonce* meant than hearing about all the trouble the bedbugs had caused. She'd guessed that *vonce* was a Yiddish word, since Grandma Roz would occasionally pepper her stories with Yiddish, which was such a funny-sounding language that Eden would always stop her grandma midstory and beg her to explain whatever word she'd just used. Eden was thrilled to find out that *vonce* was Yiddish for "bedbug." She had been very pleased to learn more about insects, Yiddish, and her grandma's childhood all at once.

Eden looked around, much more curious about this strange new place than worried about bedbugs. She scanned the room and saw a glowing nightlight at the foot of the bed. It was different from any night-light she'd ever seen. It had two tiny lights instead of one. And instead of bathing the room in a soft and gentle light, these two lights were piercing and focused directly on Eden. She turned her head to avoid the glare and realized there wasn't just one pair of lights trained on her but thousands. Some were high in the air, some were low to the ground, and others surrounded her on all sides. Eden gulped. They weren't lights at all. They were eyes!

Spinosad and Neem

August's lungs burned as he ran. The Institute was huge, far bigger than he'd realized, with winding hallways that twisted like tornadoes. Even worse, the underground windows that showcased the earthworms were everywhere, so no matter where he went, he could see the mushy tubes of their bodies sliding along beside him. He stopped to catch his breath. He was running out of time, and he wasn't getting any closer to finding the room that contained the poisons. He'd wasted valuable minutes trying the little key in every door he passed. It was taking too long. He needed a better strategy.

August looked down at the keys in his hand. He hadn't thought much about the fact that they were arranged from biggest to smallest when he'd first noticed it, but now he realized that their order might hold a clue. He looked down the hallway. The doors at the far end looked smaller than the ones closest to him, but August had assumed that was just an optical illusion caused by perspective. He'd paid enough attention in art class to know about that. But what if the doors didn't just look small? What if they were actually smaller? It was possible that the smaller doors took smaller keys.

August went to the door closest to him and stood as straight as he could against the wooden door frame. He reached his hand high above his head, but couldn't come close to touching the top of the frame. Then he ran past the next few doors, stopping at one near the end of the hall. He leaned flat against it and reached his hand up again. This time he could feel the very tips of his fingers grazing the top. It wasn't just an illusion. The doors were actually getting smaller.

August, revived by his discovery, took off down the hall in search of the smallest door. As he ran, the hall changed almost imperceptibly, becoming a wide, spiraling ramp. He ran down it, past the line where the fancy marble floor and elegant wallpaper ended. Here, the floor was made of rough wooden slats and the walls were painted a dingy gray. The ramp got steeper as the slats ended, finally opening onto a large room. Here, the floor was made of crumbly earth. The walls were drab concrete and lined with the many pipes that supplied the great house with water.

August felt disoriented until he remembered what Tillie had said: that the Windward had once been right-side up like a traditional house. Back then, this space must have been the attic, complete with a proper roof. But now that the house was upside-down, what was once the attic was now . . . the basement. August shuddered. This basement was even creepier than the one at home because it was several stories below the earth, and the dirt floor meant that insects could burrow in and out as they pleased. Still, he had to brave it, because built into the far wall were two wide metal doors that were just a little taller than he was. He hurried toward them, excited. This had to be it: the cabinet that held the poisons.

He pulled the key ring from his pocket and pushed the littlest key into the lock. It only went halfway in before it jammed. He tried again, but with no luck. He hated keys. He was terrible at lining up the little teeth in the narrow slot. Sometimes when he got home before his parents, and his useless babysitter, Sabrina, had her headphones on and her music turned up so high that she couldn't hear his knocking, August had to use the key his mother kept hidden in a fake rock. Most times he wouldn't be able to open the door and would wind up waiting outside in the cold until Sabrina returned to planet Earth. Once he'd jammed the key in so far it had snapped off in the lock, and his parents had made him pay for the replacement with his own money.

"For Pete's sake," his father had said. "You had the whole key in there upside down. If something isn't working, don't force it, Augie. Take a breath and try it a different way. Take it easy."

How am I supposed to take it easy when I'm freezing to death? August had thought. But while his father's words had seemed unhelpful then, they were now welcome advice.

August turned the key over so the teeth were facing up, pushed it in gently, then turned it to the left. This time, when he pressed down on the handle, the door swung open. August stepped back, amazed by what he saw. Thirteen metal tanks were lined up, side by side. The biggest one dominated the center of the cabinet. It was as tall as August and so wide that if he wrapped his arms around it, his fingers would barely touch in back. On either side of it were two tanks that were a little shorter and narrower than the biggest, and on either side of those were two more tanks that were even smaller. The tanks kept getting littler, and the smallest ones on either end were about the size of jumbo hot dogs. Etched into the front of each tank was a skull and crossbones and beneath it the name of the lethal liquid inside. There was a poison for nearly every letter of the alphabet: *acephate, borax, carbaryl, dinotefuran, fipronil, gamma-cyhalothrin, halofenozide, malathion, neem, propoxur, spinosad, thiamethoxam, zeta-cypermethrin.*

Excitement crackled through his body like Pop Rocks. He'd done it! He'd found them! But he'd miscalculated badly.

August had been imagining tiny bottles of poison that could easily fit in a pocket, not enormous tanks. He tried to lift one of the smallest ones, but he couldn't get it all the way off the ground, let alone carry it. He'd need help, but from whom? Not Tillie or Eden, obviously, and he definitely couldn't go home and ask his mom. No, he needed people who wouldn't question him and would have his back, even if things went wrong. There was a word for people like this, and the word was *friends*. The only problem was that August didn't have any. In first grade when August's mom still walked him to the bus, she'd peer inside the windows and see Randall, Ivan, and Vincent all sitting by themselves. August's mom would beg him to invite them over for playdates. He'd always said no. The thought of inviting boys he didn't really know over made him anxious: What would they talk about? What if they didn't like his toys? His mother refused to back down. She assured him that the playdates would be fun and that having kids over would be "good for him." Sometimes Ivan's, Randall's, or Vincent's parents would call his mom and invite August over to their houses. As usual, she'd plead with him to give it a try, but August never felt comfortable. He didn't like using the bathroom at someone else's house and was scared they were just inviting him over to prank him.

Please, Augie, just once, put yourself out there, she'd say, and August would refuse every time.

Now, staring at a wall of poisons too heavy to move on his own, August realized his mother's suggestions hadn't been as bad as he'd thought. If he'd made friends back then, he'd have a crew right now, when he really needed one. Going it alone all these years had been a huge mistake, and now it was too late . . . unless it wasn't. As much as he dreaded it, it was time to put himself out there.

The Bald-Faced Hornet

The queen lurched back and forth as Jordan drove even more wildly than before. And Miranda, who the queen had begun to think was at least semi-sensible, was only making things worse. Every time they approached a new, oversized human nest (which the queen had learned was called a "mansion"), Jordan would slow down just enough for Miranda to squint at the mansion and shake her head in a gesture that the queen now understood meant "That's not it," which would then cause Jordan to speed up again, until they lurched to a stop outside the next mansion and the cycle started all over again.

This behavior was confusing to the queen. Miranda and Jordan's strategy clearly wasn't working, but they continued to repeat it. This was totally unlike the practices of the wasps, who were incredibly good at problem solving. The moment a wasp realized that the colony was working inefficiently, she would alert the others, and together they would come up with a new plan and implement it immediately, unlike these humans, who kept making the same mistakes over and over. After another stop-and-start that nearly sent her crashing into the windshield, the queen couldn't take it anymore.

"This isn't working! Can we please stop at that nest—I mean, mansion—up ahead and ask for directions?" the queen piped, waving her wing at the magnificent, shortbread-colored building that loomed ahead. "Maybe someone there has heard of the Windward."

Miraculously, Miranda stopped her nonsensical behavior and nodded, which the queen now understood meant "yes."

"You're right," Miranda piped. "That's The Breakers. We'll stop there and ask."

The queen sighed, relieved, as Miranda relayed the queen's idea to Jordan, who must've thought it was a good idea, because he turned the car into The Breakers' enormous driveway. He and Miranda leapt from the car and ran for the wide rotunda of the entrance, only this time Miranda left her car door open long enough for the queen to fly out safely. The queen appreciated this gesture, although she also found it somewhat disappointing. She couldn't help but think that Miranda should've piped a humble *After you, Your Majesty,* and insisted that the queen exit the car first. But the queen also understood that these were challenging times and everyone was doing their best.

Luckily, it was lunchtime, so Jordan didn't have to wait in line to get directions. Most of the human visitors were already unfolding blankets and setting out buffets on the broad lawn that fronted The Breakers. Normally, the queen would've been tempted by the wide array of foods, but she was too distraught to eat. She couldn't think of anything but Eden: where she was, if she was safe, and how they'd ever be able to find a small girl in such a giant world.

Miranda was preoccupied, too. She'd been in such a rush to hurry out of the car that she'd forgotten her flute. By the time she and the queen had fetched it and joined Jordan, he was already deep in conversation with a giant flower.

"You didn't tell me Jordan could talk to tulips," the queen piped, impressed.

"Um, that's not a tulip. That's a person wearing green pants and a yellow shirt," Miranda explained.

"Then why is he standing in a flowerpot?" asked the queen.

"That's actually a desk," Miranda told her. "And he's not standing in it. He's standing behind it."

"Well, what's he saying?" piped the queen, frustrated that she couldn't understand what the males were saying. If only all humans could speak with flutes or kazoos, life would be so much easier. Still, she was getting better at reading human body language, and she could tell from Jordan's downturned mouthparts that the news wasn't good. Sure enough, once

Jordan had told Miranda the situation, her mouthparts were drooping, too.

"He said the Windward used to be nearby but was torn down years ago by the original owners," Miranda translated.

The queen, hearing this, was shocked.

"Present company excepted, humans are dreadful," the queen pronounced. "You not only tear down our nests, but you destroy your own as well. It's a wonder your species has managed to survive at all."

After the man behind the desk hung up one of the flyers with Eden's picture on it, Jordan rejoined them. He draped his arm around Miranda as they headed back to the dark land, which the queen now knew was called a "parking lot."

"She could be anywhere," Miranda sighed. "What do we do now?"

"We keep looking. We're going to find her," the queen replied.

"I hope you're right," Miranda said. "I'm just so scared."

The queen shook her head, mystified. *Hope? What on Earth could hope do to help this situation?* The queen understood the purpose of being scared, because being scared often led to being brave, and bravery led to taking action. The queen liked taking action because actions had a clear outcome: she would succeed or fail, and then move on. Hope, however, was confusing to her because hope didn't lead to *taking* action. It led to *thinking* about action, and a wasp's life was too short for luxuries like hoping. The queen loved every single one of the hundreds of babies she would have in her twelve-month life span, but she also understood that with so many babies, some would survive and others wouldn't. It wasn't a cruel calculation; it was just a fact.

But now, after spending time with Miranda and Jordan, the queen understood that it was different for human parents who only had one daughter and desperately wanted to believe that they would find her safe and unharmed. Miranda and Jordan needed hope. And for the first time, the queen understood that hope wasn't a luxury. It was a necessity. Having hope, she realized, might be the only way to survive a life that was too long to be measured in weeks.

Suddenly, the queen heard a kazoo in the distance. She, Jordan, and Miranda looked at each other, stunned. Eden! It had to be her! They ran toward the sound, which was coming from the picnic area where all the human visitors were eating. Dozens of families and school groups dotted the grass, and Jordan, Miranda, and the queen raced among them, searching for Eden. Jordan spotted a girl with long braids and a track jacket just like Eden's with her back to him. He clasped the girl by the shoulder and spun her around.

"Eden!" he shouted, only to see the face of a startled

stranger. Miranda, equally frantic, slipped on a patch of mud next to one of the picnic blankets and tumbled right onto a picnicking family, crushing their bag of chips.

Meanwhile, the queen flew on ahead, following the sound of the buzzing. She finally got close enough to tell that it was coming from inside an open dumpster that was parked along the back wall of The Breakers, by the old service entrance. A dumpster? Why would Eden be playing her kazoo in a dumpster? The queen soared toward the hulking bin, then peered down over the edge. There, among heaps of fat black garbage bags, was the source of the buzzing. The queen realized that it wasn't a kazoo at all, but her cousin, the bald-faced hornet queen, whose buzzing had been amplified by the walls of the dumpster. The wasp queen gazed at her messy cousin with disdain. While she had vibrant black and gold stripes, the hornet was brownish black with pale yellow patches. She looked like a mud puddle strewn with fallen ginkgo leaves. To make matters worse, she was unbearably obnoxious.

"Hello, cousin," the queen buzzed, as irritated as she was disappointed. "What are you doing here?"

"I could ask the same of you, Your Majesty, who's too scared to leave her own park," the hornet said, never able to resist the urge to tease her cousin. "What brings you by my new neighborhood?"

The queen bristled, offended. She didn't want to dignify the insult with a response.

"Glue trap got your tongue?" buzzed her cousin. "Aren't you happy to see me?"

"No," replied the queen. "I've never been before. Why would I start now?"

Before her cousin could answer, Jordan and Miranda raced up to the dumpster and peered inside. The queen watched their shoulders sag.

"I know," the queen said. "I really thought it was her, too."

Miranda looked down at the hornet in the dumpster, then lifted her flute to her lips. "Who's that?" she piped.

"This, I'm sorry to say," piped the queen, "is my cousin the bald-faced hornet. She's very . . . what's the word? Ah, yes. Annoying."

"That doesn't matter. Can she help us?"

"I doubt it. The bald-faced hornets, especially the queens, are known for their constant fabricating and fibbing. No matter what she tells you, don't believe a word of it."

"You're wrong about that, cuz," buzzed the hornet. "I've changed. Now I tell the truth fifty percent of the time."

"Congratulations. What an accomplishment," the queen buzzed sarcastically. "Now we really must be going. We're looking for a human girl who's gone missing, and we have no time to waste."

"You? Helping a human?" the hornet queen buzzed. "Now I'm the one who doesn't believe it."

"Farewell, cousin. See you at Solstice," buzzed the queen, eager to get out of there. She and her pesky cousin had never gotten along very well. She launched herself off the rim of the dumpster, but before she could fly very far, her cousin darted past her, blocking her flight path.

"Come on," she buzzed. "You've never visited me before. Give me a chance. Let me help you."

"What's she saying?" Miranda asked. "How come I can understand your buzzing but not hers?"

"What's she saying?" buzzed the hornet. "How come you can understand each other but I can't?"

"Because we have a little quality called empathy, which you sorely lack. And unfortunately for you, I have neither the time nor the desire to translate!" the queen buzzed impatiently. She was about to pipe the same to Miranda, but she softened when she saw the fear in Miranda's eyes.

"She wants us to let her help," the queen told Miranda. "But I don't recommend it. At least fifty percent of what she tells us will be a lie."

"Well, at least she'll be useful half the time."

"Very well, B.F.," buzzed the queen, giving her cousin a weary nod. "You may join us on our journey."

"Hooray!" buzzed the hornet. "It's so boring around here,

and this garbage is starting to stink. I promise you, cuz. You won't regret it."

"Is that a real promise or a lie?" the queen asked.

"I wish I knew," buzzed the hornet. "I'm such a good liar, even I can't tell the difference."

The Rope

Eden struggled to sit up, only to realize that she was tied to the bed by the thick gray rope she'd come in on. It was stretched tight across her chest and as she reached to untie herself, she discovered that her hands had been bound as well. As she looked around to see who or what was holding her prisoner, dozens of fireflies flicked their lights on all at once. Their bodies illuminated the room like hundreds of tiny torches, revealing a huge crowd of insects of all kinds staring at her.

Eden stared back in amazement, her curiosity overriding her fear. She'd never seen so many different kinds of insects at once before, and she was particularly struck by the beauty and variety of their eyes. Some had two, like humans; some only had one; and some had several bulging eyes with thousands of tiny lenses that glittered like disco balls. Some had three iridescent eyes arranged in a triangle on the top of their heads. One had six glossy eyes lined up in three rows; another had eight lusterless ones lined up in two. One had eyes perched on a platform on top of its head as if they were riding on a parade float, and some had two big eyes on the front of their face that looked forward *and* three smaller ones on either side so they could check out whatever was going on alongside them as they moved. Some of the eyes weren't even eyes, but actually just giant, eye-shaped markings designed to scare off predators.

Right now, though, these insects weren't looking out for predators. They *were* the predators, and Eden could tell from their angry looks that she was their prey. They weren't just looking at her, though. They were also looking back and forth at each other, wings, legs, and antennae flapping madly, as if trying to figure out what she was and what they should do with her. Eden strained to understand the stomp, shuffle, and flap of the insects, but she couldn't make out a word. Still, she didn't need words to see that they were angry with her. A fruit fly darted forward, pecking angrily at the banana peel she'd tucked into her pocket; a moth buzzed indignantly around the pink and green sweaters, as if it was telling her to take them off, and a team of twelve giant wetas hoisted the notebook onto their wide brown backs and trundled away with it. Even the bedbugs backed away from her, their mouths wide open, as if they'd realized only seconds before chomping down on her that she was too rotten to bite.

Eden realized with horror that these insects thought she'd stolen from them. But she hadn't been stealing. She'd just taken a couple of things that no one seemed to be using because she was cold and hungry and— She'd been stealing. Eden's face got hot. What had she been thinking? What she'd done was a million times worse than snagging a few farmers market grapes, because her crimes had a massive consequence. How was she ever going to convince the insects that the fake-doctor boy was wicked if they didn't trust her to begin with? She wished she hadn't taken, worn, or eaten anything. But it was too late for that.

Eden scanned the crowd, searching for a paper wasp who could help her communicate with her captors, but couldn't find one. Instead, she spotted a small gathering of treehoppers chatting on the headboard of the bed, their sail-shaped bodies striped with so many vibrant colors that they looked like the Maasai jewelry her grandma had brought back from her trip to Kenya. Eden thought of the notebook. She'd only skimmed the chapter about treehoppers but remembered something about how they communicated by sending vibrations to each other through plant stems. Eden, guessing that the treehoppers were using the wooden headboard to transmit their vibrations in place of a branch, pressed her ear onto the headboard to overhear their conversation. Yes! They were sending vibrations back and forth that sounded like tiny cats purring. The treehoppers were humming so quickly, Eden couldn't tell if she couldn't understand them because she didn't understand their language or they were just going too fast for her. Still, she could try to communicate with them. She rolled her tongue against the top of her mouth, doing her very best kitten imitation.

Pppptttbbbbbbbthbbbb. Pppptttbbbbbbbthbbbb.

She watched for a reaction, but the treehoppers were too busy chatting amongst themselves to hear her. Eden tried again, louder, until she could feel the purring resonate not just in her head but through her whole body, and then out into the headboard.

Pppptttbbbbbbbthbbbb. Pppptttbbbbbbbthbbbb.

After a moment, the largest of the treehoppers finally noticed her. It stopped talking with its friends, turned its great, horned crest in her direction, and stared at her with its bulbous red eyes. Maybe she was getting somewhere! Eden locked eyes with the treehopper, suddenly aware that the entire roomful of insects had gone silent, watching their interaction. Eden purred again, desperate to convey as much sincerity and passion as possible.

Pppptttbbbbbbbthbbbb, she said.

Pppptttbbbbbbbthbbb? the treehopper replied.

Pppptttbbbbbbbthbbbb! Eden repeated excitedly.

The treehopper paused for an instant, then burst out in a trill so high that all the other insects winced. Even the bedbugs covered their heads with their pillows.

Ek-ek-ek-ek-ek-ek-ek-ek-ek-ek-ek-ek-ek-ek!

Eden froze. What did that mean? What was it saying?

Ek-ek-ek-ek-ek-ek-ek-ek-ek-ek-ek-ek-ek-ek! it repeated, its sail trembling uncontrollably, and then all the treehoppers joined in.

Ek-ek-ek-ek-ek-ek-ek-ek-ek-ek-ek-ek-ek-ek!

They were laughing at her! And it wasn't just the treehoppers. It was all the insects. Bulbous crab spiders were rocking back and forth, clutching their bellies so tightly that they rolled right off the beds. Eden's face burned with humiliation. This was why she hated trying new things without enough time to perfect her technique. She never should've put herself out there. She hated being laughed at. She loathed being misunderstood. She wanted to run home and bury her face in her pillow, but she couldn't quit now. Embarrassment, unlike poison, was something she could survive.

"Stop it! This is important!" she shouted, pounding her fists against the mattress so hard that one of the stout, wooden legs at the head of the bed gave way, sending the top right corner of it thudding down to the floor. Eden, her head now considerably lower than the rest of her body, looked around, surprised. Was she really so strong that she could knock a leg off a bed? She peered over the edge of the mattress and peeked into one of the snapped-off legs. The inside of it had been totally hollowed out.

A pudgy termite sat in the very bottom of the leg, cackling at the trick it had pulled off. The cackling soon turned to coughing, however, and a cloud of sawdust flew out of its mouth as it wheezed and heaved. Finally, it recovered and crawled out of the bed leg and toward Eden. Next, it tapped the bed frame by Eden's head with its pincers six times: four quick taps, then a pause and two more. Next, it gestured to Eden, as if inviting her to attempt a reply. The termite seemed more mischievous than friendly, curious to see what the interloper would make of its offer. Still, it appeared to be willing to communicate with her, which was more than Eden could say for the treehoppers.

As Eden reached for the bed frame, the rope around her hands pulled tight. There was no way she could reach it while she was still tied up. Eden looked to the termite for help, and it must've understood her, because it gave a nod to its fellow termites, who moseyed over to the rope and plucked at it with their pincers. In moments they'd nibbled it to pieces. Her hands finally free, Eden used the tip of her fingernail to tap the bed frame four times quickly, then twice more, exactly as the termite had done. The termite nodded at her and winked. Eden shivered with excitement. They'd made a connection!

But what did it mean? The termite lifted its pincers again, but instead of tapping another pattern, it summoned the team of giant wetas, who promptly brought Milton's notebook back to Eden. Was the mischievous, wood-chomping prankster actually intending to teach her Termite?

Eden snatched up Milton's notebook, skimming the pages until the termite signaled her to stop at a page that had some sort of code on it that contained human letters as well as an array of different combinations of dots and dashes. She studied the first few:

A: . __

B: __ . . .

C: __ . __ .

D: __ . .

E: .

F: . . __ .

G: __ __ .

H: . . . .

I: . .

J: . __ __ __

K: __ . __

It continued this way for the entire alphabet and the numbers zero through nine. Eden's eyes darted back to two of the letters. The *H* had four dots, and the *I* had two. She thought about the termite's tapping: four, then two. *H*, then *I*. *H*, then *I*.

"'Hi!'" Eden shouted. "It's saying hi!"

Her shout was so loud that it startled a flock of wax moths, which were known for having the most sensitive hearing of the entire insect kingdom. She startled them so badly that they lost their grip on the ceiling and plummeted to the ground.

"Sorry," Eden whispered to the disoriented moths as they flopped around on the floor. "Sorry!"

Eden, barely able to control her excitement, gave the bed leg four quick taps, then two more. The termite fluttered its wings and tapped back the same pattern with its pincer. They'd done it! They were each saying "hi"! They were saying hi to each other!

Hoping to figure out more about the mysterious code, Eden examined the tiny page, comparing the dots and dashes at the top of the page with the key underneath until she could translate the combination of dashes at the top of the page: *M-O-R-S-E C-O-D-E*. Morse code?! Eden had learned about Morse code in history class. It was an old-fashioned way of sending messages long before texting. Eden gasped, amazed. Humans weren't just learning insect languages; insects were learning human ones, too!

Eden, having finally found a way to warn the insects, looked down at the notebook, calculating the shortest combination of dots and dashes she'd need to tell them that a fake-doctor boy had infiltrated the Institute and kidnapped an ant, and that all of them were potentially in danger. Her chest tightened as she realized that tapping out such a complicated message could take her days, if not months. She and the insects didn't have that kind of time. But as she began to brainstorm the shortest way to communicate her message, she heard a tiny buzzing nearby. Two curious bees had made their way to the front of the crowd.

Eden recalled that the queen had told her all the Buzzing languages were quite similar. Maybe Bee and Wasp were close enough that the bees could understand her, too! Eden pulled her kazoo from her pocket and lifted it to her lips, then remembered that it wasn't enough to re-create the buzzing sound. She also needed to immerse herself in the emotional life of the bees. She guessed that they might be feeling the same way she did: curious, confused, and excited by the new experience. The bees must've been imagining what Eden might've been feeling, too, because the moment she began buzzing her thoughts into the kazoo, the bees responded as if they'd understood exactly what she'd been thinking.

In moments, the air was full of all different kinds of buzzing, humming, tapping, flapping, clicking, and clapping as the bees spread Eden's message through the room. In the same way that Bee was similar to Wasp, Wasp must've been similar to Katydid, which must've been a lot like Cricket, which clearly had some similarities to Grasshopper, which must've been quite a bit like Treehopper. The news of the wicked boy who'd kidnapped Dot spread through the room like honey on toast, and within moments the entire community was streaming out of the bedbug sanctuary. As Eden watched them go, the bees explained to her that they were all heading out to find the boy and stop him before he could carry out his devious plans. The winged creatures soared up through the shaft, and the earthbound creatures made their way by crawling and slithering up its steep sides. Others disappeared into the tiny cracks and tunnels along the baseboards.

Eden, eager to join the search, tucked the notebook back into her waistband and scanned the room for an exit she could fit through, but there was no way out other than the narrow shaft. She was going to have to pull herself up by the same rope she'd come down on. But as she jumped up onto the bed to grab it, she saw that the rope was gone. Eden searched the room, confused. It had to be somewhere. A firefly had thoughtfully stayed behind to make sure she wasn't left in total darkness, and it drifted around Eden's head, also searching. Suddenly it darted to the floor, illuminating the remains of the gray rope, which lay scattered in six-inch chunks. The termites had chewed it to pieces to free her, having no idea that they'd devoured her only means of escape.

Eden looked over at the firefly, who flashed its light at her in its own version of Morse code.

__ __ __   . . . . / __ .   __ __ __, it said.

You got that right, Eden thought as she tapped the same message back.

Oh no.

The Crew

*A*ugust *pounded the buttons* in the ancient elevator. It was already two fifteen. He had to get to school before the last class ended so he could intercept Ivan, Randall, and Vincent before they went home. Like August, they left through the back doors of the school so they could be the first ones out when the bell rang. Lingering in the hallways for even a moment made it much more likely they'd be surrounded by Sheila and her crew at the most dangerous part of the day, when all the grown-ups were leaving. August rarely made his way through that awful gauntlet without suffering some injury.

The last time they'd singled him out, Paul had jammed a wet finger in August's ear, and the other outcasts hadn't gotten off any easier. August had seen Sheila and the other bullies trip Vincent, kick dirt onto Randall's sneakers, and give Ivan a bloody nose. The three of them, like August, had been bullied for so long that August wondered if they'd trust him enough to follow him back to the Institute or they'd think it was some kind of setup. Still, he had to try. But first he had to find a way to get back to school before the end of the day. Without a phone, calling an Uber was out of the question. As he pondered his options, Tillie appeared around the corner holding a piece of pie, her cap of white curls circling her head like a halo.

"There you are!" she said. "I was looking for you. Why aren't you in surgery?"

"Aaaaactualllllllyyyy," August said, drawing out the word to give himself a few more seconds to figure out a new lie. "The surgery I must perform on the dear, precious creature is far more complicated than I imagined, and I need to . . . bring in some other colleagues to assist me with the operation."

"Goodness," said Tillie. "I had no idea the situation was so severe."

"Yes," August said. "It's bad. Very bad. In fact, if I wait even a moment longer, the consequences could be downright cacophonic."

"Cacophonic?" Tillie asked. "How can consequences be noisy? Do you mean catastrophic?"

August dug his nails into his palm. Why hadn't he studied his vocabulary words more thoroughly? If he made too many more mistakes like that, Tillie might realize he was a child. He couldn't afford any close calls.

"I meant catastrophic *and* cacophonic," he said. "Because if this surgery is anything less than one hundred percent successful, I'll shout louder than anything you've ever heard."

"Well!" said Tillie. "I continue to be impressed by your passion."

"Thank you, Tillie. Your admiration means the world to me. Now, I must be off, but unfortunately my car battery seems to have died."

"That's no trouble to fix at all," Tillie said. "Years ago, my parents' mechanic taught me how to jump-start a vehicle. I'll get my jumper cables."

"You don't have to do that," August said quickly. He was stunned by how eager she was to be helpful, despite her old age. August was 111 years younger than Tillie, but he still grumbled every time he was asked to get up and find the remote. Plus, he couldn't let her see that he didn't have a car.

"Really," he said. "It would be just as quick for me to borrow a bicycle. Do you happen to have one?"

Tillie snorted with laughter. It sounded like a pig bouncing on a trampoline. "Oh dear, I haven't ridden my bicycle in a dog's age, but it's in the cloakroom, and you're welcome to use it if you like."

August didn't have any idea what a dog had to do with it, but he wasn't about to waste time arguing. He was too busy calculating how far it was from the Windward to his school. It was probably close to ten miles, but he and his mom would sometimes bike to the playground and back, and that was easily five miles each way. It would be hard, but he could do it.

"Thank you," he said. "I'll return shortly with my colleagues."

"I'm so thankful you're here, Mr. Rattice," Tillie said. "I can't imagine what would become of that poor ant if you weren't. You're a true hero."

"Uh, yeah. That's me. A hero," he said, eager to get away from her. Every time they spoke, he felt worse about taking advantage of her.

August cringed when he whipped the dustcover off the bicycle. It was worse than he could've imagined: a bright yellow beach cruiser with a cream-and-coffee-colored seat and wheels. There was a wicker basket on the front, stuffed with pink plastic tulips. It would be humiliating to show up at school on it. If Sheila saw it, she would mock him for days, but he had no other choice.

The ride was much longer and hillier than it had seemed when his class had gone to The Breakers on a school bus, but he pushed through the ache in his muscles. August couldn't stop thinking about Tillie the whole way there. Conning a trusting old woman was harder than he'd thought. Tillie was like a sweet grandma in a storybook. August had no idea grandmas like that actually existed. His weren't anything like that. One was an actress in California (she'd been in an insurance commercial where she talked to a lizard about saving money), and the other lived on a sailboat with her boyfriend. He'd never realized how lovely having a storybook grandma who made pie and had a bike with fake tulips in the basket could be.

August thought as he pedaled. Normally when he was biking, he thought about fun things, like who would win in a fight: a shark or a bear. Or what food he would pick if he only got to have one for the rest of his life (Cinnamon Toast Crunch). But today August's thoughts were more complicated, because he was thinking about heroes and villains. It was pretty clear who was who in comic books and cartoons. But in real life, it was more confusing. August was sure that his mom and Ms. Batra would think he was a hero for getting rid of insects, even though neither of them would've been thrilled by the idea that he was handling poisons. But he was equally sure that Tillie and Eden would think he was a villain for doing the exact same thing.

August thought about something Ms. Batra had said at their first play practice. She'd asked them which character they thought was the hero and which was the villain. August had thrust his hand into the air. *Papa Bear is the hero, and Sheila is the villain!* he'd shouted. The class all laughed, and even Ms. Batra had smiled as she reminded August that she'd asked him to say the name of the character, not the actor. Next, Sheila had raised her hand. *Goldilocks is the hero, and Papa Bear is the villain,* she'd said, pointing her finger right in August's face. Her silver sparkle nail polish had glinted like a knife, and even though Sheila had said the character's name instead of his, August knew Sheila was really talking about him, just like he'd been talking about her.

Let's vote! Sheila announced to the rest of the class. *If you think Papa Bear's the bad guy, raise your hand!*

August winced. Sheila was turning this into a popularity contest, which was a contest he'd never win. Kids would vote for Sheila either because they liked her or because they were afraid of her. August understood the "afraid" option. It was the "liked" option that didn't make any sense: How could anyone like Sheila? Just as he'd predicted, kids started raising their hands. Thankfully, Ms. Batra, as usual, saved the day.

Hands down, please, she'd said.

Ms. Batra went on to explain that in real life, every person believes that they are a hero and are doing the right thing. And, she told them, it was the same for characters in a play. Each character had to play what Ms. Batra called "their own truth," no matter what any other character or audience member might think of them. Goldilocks may believe that Papa Bear is a scary bully, but Papa Bear must believe he's bravely defending his family. Papa Bear may believe that Goldilocks is a nasty robber, but Goldilocks must believe she's just a lost, hungry little girl who gets attacked instead of helped.

Does that make sense? she'd asked.

August had nodded. Ms. Batra's words felt true then, and they felt even truer now. He was right to hate insects and want to save people from them. Getting the poisons *would* make him a hero. And Tillie and Eden were obviously the villains. They wanted to protect creatures who could hurt humans. Some of them even had the power to kill his own father.

Also, Eden and Tillie were obviously confused about what was real and what was made up. Even though August wished he were a strong, powerful bear, he knew he wasn't. But Eden actually thought she could talk to insects. And Tillie believed that worms had helped her build a house. Those things might have been possible in a play, but this was real life. By the time August crested the hill and looked down at the squat pile of bricks that was his school, he believed that he was, in fact, the hero, and Eden and Tillie were, if not villains, very unaware of reality.

August pulled up to the old bike rack on the far edge of the parking lot. Everyone had stopped using it ever since the school had installed new, shiny ones closer to the doors, but he and the other outcasts still used this one. Parking at the main rack basically guaranteed that his bike tires would get popped yet again by one of Sheila's minions. Sure enough, there were three bikes chained to the old rack, and Randall, Vincent, and Ivan were hanging out nearby, sitting in a circle on the grass, leaning in and laughing at something Vincent was showing them.

"Hey!" August shouted.

He was surprised to see them all together. He'd been pretty sure they all avoided each other the same way he avoided them, in the hopes of not being associated with each other. They threw a glance over their shoulders at August, offered a tossed-off *Hey*, then turned back to what they were doing.

"Guys!" August shouted as he headed toward them. Something about them seemed different. For one thing, Ivan was laughing. Hard. It was a full-on cackle that startled August, who'd never heard Ivan say anything except in class, when a teacher called on him. And even then, his voice was always only one notch above a whisper. Now he was laughing and shaking his head so hard that his bright red hair shook like a candle flame on a windy day.

Randall seemed different, too. For one thing, he'd taken off the windbreaker he always wore, even if it wasn't raining, to hide his round belly from Sheila, who'd sneak up behind him and poke it with a pencil. He was wearing a red and yellow T-shirt, which perfectly matched his red, white, and yellow kicks. It had never even occurred to August to match his T-shirt with his sneakers. He felt sure that if he dressed like that it would look too try-hard, but on Randall it looked really cool.

And Vincent, usually the least sure of himself of them all, was looking downright confident. His cape fluttered behind him in the breeze, and the guys were cracking up over whatever was written on the pad of paper he was showing them. As August approached the circle, he could see that Vincent was showing the guys some drawings he'd done of various teachers in their underpants (pretty funny) and mythological beasts (very realistic for made-up creatures).

"Cool drawings," August said.

"Thanks." Vincent nodded in a casual way that said he already knew his drawings were cool, whether August thought so or not. August realized that Vincent hadn't burped once the whole time August had been observing them. Usually, Vincent's burps were nearly constant and so strong that the smell of his sandwiches would waft through the halls. Today, however, the light breeze that drifted toward August smelled like newly cut grass, without even a hint of baloney. August was impressed. It had never occurred to him that he could just decide that what he was doing was cool without needing someone else to tell him if it was or wasn't.

"Why are you so dressed up?" Randall asked, eyeing his suit.

"Um, no reason. What're you guys doing?" he asked.

"Just hanging out," Randall said.

"Like usual," Ivan added, taking a giant cookie out of his backpack and breaking it into three equal pieces. August's mouth watered as he watched Ivan pass two of the pieces to Randall and Vincent.

"Like usual?" August asked, trying to seem casual, even though he found this news shocking. "You, uh, you hang out here? After school?"

"Yeah," Vincent said. "We have lunch out here, too."

"You have lunch together? And hang out here? Every day?" August was confused. The three of them hadn't been eating their lunches sad and separate all this time after all?

"Not every day," Randall said. "Sometimes we go to each other's houses."

"Each other's houses?" August repeated, aware that he was starting to sound like a parrot in a pet store window.

"Yeah. I invited you a bunch of times back in the day, but your mom always told my mom that you didn't want to come," Randall said.

"Plus, you never invited us to your house," Ivan added, tracing an elegant circle in the dirt with his toe.

"But that was a long time ago," August said.

"I guess," Ivan said.

August got a bad feeling in his stomach. It had never

occurred to him that they might be hanging out without him. He pushed the feeling aside, though. He had more important things to accomplish and needed to focus on the positive: convincing all three of them to go to the Institute at once would be a lot quicker than approaching them one at a time.

"Oh, that's just because I never hang out at my house," he said. "I go somewhere much cooler."

"Comic book store?" Vincent asked. "I've never seen you there."

"Oh no, cooler than that," August said. "It's a mansion. You ever been in a mansion?"

"Yeah, on field trips, like, every year," Randall said.

"This one's better," August said. "In this one, there's no rules, no tour guides, and no teachers. You can even sit on the furniture."

"Really?" Ivan asked.

"Sounds made up," said Vincent.

"Is that why you're so dressed up?" Randall asked.

"Yes! Exactly," August said. "Come check it out. We can ride our bikes there, and I promise you'll be home by dinner."

"I don't know," said Randall. "We were about to go over to my house."

"Maybe we should go with him," Ivan said, shrugging. "I mean, we've already watched basically every epic fail compilation ever created."

"That's true," Vincent said.

Randall took a deep breath. August looked at him, anxious. He could tell that whatever Randall said, the other boys would go along with.

"Why not?" Randall said, putting the last bite of cookie into his mouth.

"Sure," Ivan and Vincent said at the same time, then broke into a singsong chant. "Jinx! Double jinx! You owe me a Coke! Inky, blinky, flinky, winky. Flush it down the kitchen sinky. Alley oop! Alley oop! Duhhhh hickey! The king of France wet his pants, right in the middle of a ballroom dance. Yodel-oh lay hee hoo, yodel-oh lay hee hoo! Ner-ner-ner-ner-ner, ner-ner, ner-ner, ner-ner-ner. Huh!"

"Um . . ." said August, not sure what to say.

"It's just a thing we do," Vincent said. "My mom taught it to me. She used to do it when she was a kid."

"So you know that makes it cool," Randall said with a laugh, and Ivan and Vincent laughed, too.

August felt a prickle of jealousy. He wanted to be in on a weird, overly long in-joke. He wanted them to do the chant again, so he could learn it, too. But there wasn't time. He had bigger goals to accomplish.

"C'mon," he said, motioning for them to follow him. "Let's go!"

August threw his leg over Tillie's old bike with the tulips

in the basket. He prayed that no one would say something mean like, *Eww, that's a girl's bike,* or *I used to have a bike like that, but then my dad got a job,* or an old classic like *Nice bike,* which technically wasn't an insult but was definitely meant as one. Instead, he only heard the whooshing of the wind through their bicycle spokes as the four boys rode together toward the Windward.

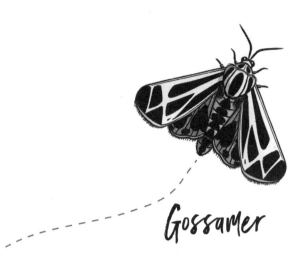

Gossamer

tom waved up at Dot, relieved to see her but also concerned about the tremendous gulf between them. He was
all the way down on the floor, and she was high on the shelf.
How could he possibly get up there? He was great at vertical
climbing, but not at doing it quickly. Then he noticed that
Dot wasn't just waving at him. She was pointing at a strand
of spiderweb that reached from the floor to the shelf. The
filament was so fine that one moment it would catch the
light and Atom could see it clearly, and the next it seemed to
disappear. As flimsy as it looked, Atom knew that the string
of webbing was his best option. Climbing it like a tightrope
would be dangerous, but it would be much quicker than
scurrying up the side of the counter, across the top, up the
wall to the shelf, along the underside of the shelf, and then
up over its edge.

He took a deep breath and made his way up the steep

strand, careful not to sever it with the spike on the underside of his belly. The strand, like the pads on the bottom of his feet, was very sticky, and the combination created a glue so strong, it was both a help and a hindrance. The glue made each uphill step a chore, but sometimes it was the only thing that kept Atom from falling off the delicate strand. Even his small breaths caused it to sway wildly.

Atom had once asked a spider who liked making her webs at the tops of doorways how she kept from getting dizzy.

Never look down, she'd said. *And stay hydrated. Always remember to drink lots of blood, even if you don't feel thirsty.*

Atom did his best to take her advice now (the "don't look down" part, not the part about drinking blood), but when he was almost at the top, he made the mistake of glancing down. The floor was so far away it looked like a checkerboard. The sight of it made the blood rush through his heart tube so fast that he lost his grip on the filament. Five of his legs slipped off of it, and as he dangled, hanging on by one foreleg, he could picture himself losing his grasp and sailing toward the ground, his legs flailing through the air as he fell. He shook off the terrible vision. He couldn't let himself die that way. He had too much life ahead of him to not fight with every bit of his strength. He reached for the filament with his other foreleg, but no matter how hard he strained, it was too far out of reach. He grabbed for it with his antennae, having no idea if they were strong enough to support his weight. He stretched them farther than he ever had before, until he finally felt one of his antenna touch the webbing. With five legs still dangling and his body feeling heavier by the second, he managed to pull himself up until he could grab it with a second leg, then the next and the next, until he was finally standing on it again.

Finally, he reached the top and scurried to the clear plastic prison. He and Dot pressed their faces against either side of the wall that parted them.

"Dot!" he cried.

"Wow, it's really nice to hear your voice again," she said with uncharacteristic sincerity.

"Wait a minute," Atom said. "You can hear me?"

"Yup," she said, shaking her forelegs at him. "Turns out these two weren't actually smushed, just crumpled, so it wasn't too long before I got some of my hearing back. But you've definitely gotta shout. Between my busted feet and this plastic thing, I can barely understand a word you're saying. Now, c'mon. Hurry up and get me out of this thing!"

Atom searched for a way to break into the box. He scaled one side, using his sticky foot pads to keep from sliding off, until he arrived at the top. Once again, Dot's climbing lessons were paying off. He was using the lifesaving skills she'd taught him to save her, and it was working!

He peered into the shallow crater on the top of the box and realized it was actually a magnifying lens designed to make the specimens inside look much bigger than they actually were. He peered through it expecting that his sister, who he'd always seen as sturdy and all-powerful, would seem even more so when viewed at five times her natural size. He was surprised to see that the magnification actually highlighted how fragile and delicate her body was. But instead of making her seem weak, Dot's obvious vulnerability only made her appear braver than ever.

"Hey!" she shouted through the plastic. "Quit the daydreaming and get me out of here!"

Atom pried at the edges of the box top, but it wouldn't budge.

"This thing is sturdy!" he shouted. "There's no way I can pry the top off. I need to find another way to get you down!"

Atom glanced back at the strand he'd just climbed. The best idea he could come up with was wildly dangerous, but it was the only one he had.

"Brace yourself!" he called to Dot, moving to the back of the box and pushing it all the way to the edge of the shelf. He placed the plastic seam that ran along the bottom of the box directly on top of the gossamer strand. "I'm gonna give you a big push!"

"Are you kidding?!" Dot said. "That sounds too risky to me,

and you know I'm a maniac!"

"I think it'll work! I've heard that spiderweb is as strong as steel!"

"Who told you that?"

"A spider," Atom said. "Though now that I think about it, she may have been exaggerating to impress me."

"All right, let's do it," said Dot. "Here's hoping we don't learn the hard way."

"Ready?" Atom shouted from the far side. "On three: one, two . . . three!"

With a mighty shove, he sent the box sailing down the filament, leaping onto the top at the last minute. It flew down the thread like a cable car gone haywire, bouncing repeatedly as it struck the tile floor.

"Aagghhh!" they shouted, until the specimen box slammed into a table leg, shuddering to a stop and knocking the top off. The force of the impact sent Dot flying through the air until she crashed onto the hard floor, landing in a heap. Atom peeled his body off the floor and dragged himself over to her motionless body. He moved to wrap his arms around her, but she'd been crushed so completely from the force of the landing that he couldn't even distinguish her abdomen from her thorax. Atom couldn't detect any life in her wrinkled torso. He cradled her body in his arms and wept.

"No, no, no," he sobbed.

"What's wrong? You hurt yourself?"

Atom, astonished to hear Dot's voice, spun around to see her army-crawling toward him with her two good legs.

"You're alive!" he shouted as he pointed, confused, at the squished brown mass beside him. "Then what's that?"

"That's a raisin," said Dot. "Now let's go. We have to find that evil little dude and bring him to justice!"

She struggled to stand, but her broken legs gave out from under her. She sat back down, wincing.

"Hop on my back," Atom said. "I'll carry you."

"It won't work," Dot said. "There's no way you can balance my weight and move fast enough for us to find him."

"Let's just get out into the hall," Atom said, wedging himself underneath her until he'd gotten her safely on his back. "We'll figure something out. I saw some stairs with long banisters. We could slide down, or—"

Atom stopped midsentence. The sight that awaited them in the hall was so fantastical he couldn't tell if it was real or a mirage. Dot's incredulous *Whoa* was the only thing that made him sure it wasn't just a dream.

Their entire colony was assembled before them like an army, each tiny ant riding a giant grasshopper. Their mother rode in front, leading the battalion. Aunt Dab and Itty-Bitty flanked her on either side.

"How did you find us?" Dot asked.

"It wasn't hard," their mother said. "You two left a trail of alarm pheromones as clear as bread crumbs in a forest."

"We knew you had to be in danger," said Aunt Dab. "So we assembled the troops."

"We *are* in danger," Dot said. "Humans have infiltrated the Institute, and they tried to kill me."

"To be fair, only one of them tried to kill you," Atom said. He still refused to believe that the girl was wicked, too.

"Are you seriously doing this to me right now?" Dot demanded.

"One is enough," said their mother. "We will find these humans and make them feel our wrath."

Atom didn't know what surprised him more: his usually gentle mother and aunts looking as regal as royalty and fierce as five-star generals, or the sight of the vast grasshopper cavalry supporting them. Ants and grasshoppers had never been actual enemies, but they hadn't ever been real friends either. Just like the old fable "The Ant and the Grasshopper" described, they were so different—the ants working hard every day to save crumbs for winter, while the grasshoppers gamboled in meadows all summer long, never worrying about the future—the two groups rarely spent any time together, which was why Atom was so surprised when two grasshoppers leapt toward him and Dot.

"Please, climb aboard," the giant creatures offered,

kneeling down until their saddle-shaped prothoraxes were low enough for them to mount. "All of our homes and lives are in danger. If we don't help each other, no one will."

Atom looked to his mother. After a giant afternoon of adventuring, he was suddenly exhausted and tired of thinking.

"Climb on," his mother said. "We're a team now."

"Plus, it looks super-fun," Dot called, dragging herself off Atom's back and onto one of the broad-backed grasshoppers. "What are you waiting for?"

Atom laughed. Even with four broken feet, Dot was still more adventurous than he was.

"Cowabunga!!!" he shouted, leaping onto the back of the other grasshopper as if he were a knight and it were a great, green horse. Atom and Dot took their places alongside their mother and together they rode, side by side, leading the battalion of ants through the halls in search of the girl and the wicked little man.

Flying

Eden had promised herself that she wouldn't cry, but she could feel the corners of her mouth beginning to point downward and her lips starting to tremble. She had to stay strong. She needed to get out of that room, find the awful boy, and stop him from carrying out his sinister plan. It seemed like a miracle that the insects had decided to trust her even though she'd given them so many reasons not to. She had to do everything in her power to help them.

Hearing a fluttering sound from above, Eden opened her eyes and looked up into the open shaft to see thousands of butterflies winging above her. They were all colors and sizes: some were tiny, mottled with gray and white, others were vibrant turquoise, and still others were the startling orange of the monarch butterfly, their wings edged with black and spotted with white.

As they swooped down on her, Eden realized that the

slippery lumps she'd passed as she tumbled down the chute were actually chrysalises. She watched in amazement as the little pods opened, revealing newly emerged butter-flies. At first their wings were slick, stuck to their bodies like freshly shampooed hair, but within moments their wings bloomed like flowers, revealing their magnificent colors. They flew down toward Eden, leaving the papery husks of their chrysalises dangling like party lanterns.

Rows of moths and butterflies landed on her arms and shoulders, curling their legs into hook shapes. They were trying to lift her! Eden admired their spirit, but she knew that she was much too heavy for them to carry. She ducked away from them, pulling off the green and pink sweaters, her track jacket, sneakers, socks, and lanyard with the mag-nifying glass. The only item that was hard to let go of was Milton's book, but she had no choice. She placed it care-fully on the bed. Ideally, she'd have a chance to come back for it.

Now wearing only track pants and a thin yellow T-shirt, Eden extended her arms for the butterflies, who were emerging from their chrysalises at an astonishing rate. Soon, thousands were clinging to the sleeves and back of her T-shirt, flapping madly. Eden suddenly felt her feet leave the ground as the butterflies soared upward, lifting her high above the room of beds, until the lavender comforter looked as small as a postage stamp. Up through the kitchen cabinet, through the closet hung with sweaters, over the city street and weedy pond they flew, until they came to the bookshelf that had launched her entire journey.

As they sailed toward the door that led to the main hall of the Institute, Eden had an alarming realization. The door had been locked when she'd first tried to open it, and now they were flying toward it at a speed so fast it would be impossible to stop in time. In a moment, she and all the butterflies would slam into the unforgiving wood. As she braced for impact, a stick insect swung out from its hiding place on the door frame and inserted itself into the lock, bending each of its legs to form a living key. The door opened a microsecond before disaster, and Eden and the butterflies flew into the hallway unharmed. They hovered in midair, Eden dangling from them, unsure which way to go.

"Look!" Eden shouted, pointing toward the glass-fronted terrariums that lined the halls. Inside them, the normally leisurely earthworms streamed downward with speed and purpose that made it almost impossible to believe that they couldn't hear or see.

"There!" Eden cried, pointing down the curving hall. "They're telling us to head down there!"

The butterflies, pulling the back of Eden's T-shirt as taut as a sail, changed course and soared down the hall. The sound of their wings as they thumped up and down in unison was as loud as Eden's heartbeat, which raced with anticipation as they sped forward, determined to find the evil boy and bring him to justice.

Boy Talk

"**W**e're looking for a place called the Windward," the queen buzzed to her cousin. "Have you ever heard of it? And please, tell me the truth."

"First you tell *me* the truth," buzzed the hornet, waggling her stinger mischievously.

The queen sighed. "Must you waggle your tail like that, cousin? Don't you think that as a queen, it might be a tad more appropriate to behave in a more dignified manner?"

"I don't think that at all," said the hornet. "What's the point of being a queen if you don't get to behave exactly how you like? Now, how'd you get mixed up with these humans? How'd you learn that Flute language? Teach it to me."

"Not now, B.F.," buzzed the queen. "We don't have time."

"Well, then," said the hornet. "If you're not going to teach me your human language, I'm not going to teach you mine."

"Oh, please," the queen muttered. "You barely speak

Hornet. There's no way you can speak a human language."

"Really?" buzzed her cousin. "Then what would you call this?"

She flew over to the lip of the dumpster and stood on her back legs, raising her wings high and wide apart, as if she were a conductor bringing an orchestra to attention.

"What's she doing?" Miranda asked.

"She claims she can speak a human language," the queen scoffed.

"Really? Which one?"

"I wouldn't get your hopes up. Do remember that bald-faced hornets are bald-faced liars," the queen said, turning back to her cousin. "Knock it off, B.F. No one's interested in your nonsense."

But that wasn't entirely true. While Miranda and the queen had been talking, Jordan had been staring, intrigued, at the shape the hornet was making with her wings. And by the time the queen had turned to look back at them, Jordan was using his arms to re-create the shape himself. The gesture, which was herky-jerky when demonstrated by a short-winged hornet, became crisp and elegant when performed by a long-limbed human. Jordan, his voice a mix of wonder and disbelief, said something aloud. And although it was only a single syllable, the queen could tell from the way his voice rose up at the end that he was asking a question.

"What's going on? What'd he say?" the queen piped to Miranda.

"He said, 'U?'" Miranda piped to the queen.

"What did she just say he said?" the hornet buzzed to the queen.

"She said he said, 'U?'" the queen buzzed back.

Hearing this, the hornet leapt up and down on the edge of the dumpster, delighted. Next, she pressed both wings down and to the left, as if she were a bullfighter waving a red flag.

Jordan repeated the gesture, then asked the hornet another question that was just a single syllable. This time, Miranda translated for the queen without her having to ask. "He said, 'G?'"

"He said 'G?'" the queen buzzed to her cousin. "Does that make sense?"

The hornet bobbed up and down even more enthusiastically. Jordan nodded back at her, equally excited.

This time, the hornet dragged her left wing low across her body on a diagonal as she waved her right wing the same way, only high above her head. The queen and Miranda watched as Jordan and B.F. matched each other, move for move. And this time when Jordan shouted out a single syllable, he wasn't asking. He was declaring.

"What was that?" the queen piped to Miranda.

"'E,'" Miranda said. "The hornet's saying 'U,' 'G,' 'E.' They're letters from the English alphabet, but I don't know what they mean all together. Uggy? Oojy? I have no idea."

"I'll find out," the queen piped. She and her cousin sailed toward each other at the same time, nearly crashing in midair.

"It's amazing, cuz! This guy knows semaphore!" the hornet buzzed.

"What's semaphore?" the queen buzzed impatiently, but her cousin had already returned to Jordan's side.

The queen, perplexed, turned to Miranda. "Do *you* know what semaphore is?"

"I do! It's a code!" Miranda piped. "Humans made it up a long time ago as a way to send messages between ships. They do it by holding flags in different positions, and each position stands for a letter of the human alphabet. No one really uses it anymore, but Jordan and his brothers learned it when they were kids so they could send each other secret messages."

The queen, thrilled, flew over to her cousin. "What's he saying?" she asked.

"You won't believe this," B.F. buzzed. "I spelled out U-G-E-T-M-E, and he spelled I-G-E-T-U right back!"

"Yugetme and Aygetu?" said the queen. "What kinds of words are those? Are they someone's names?"

"No! 'Yugetme' isn't a name. And it's not *one* word. It's three! You. Get. Me. You get me?"

"I'm afraid I don't," said the queen, her antennae spinning.

"Well, it doesn't matter," said the hornet. "Because he does. He gets me! I spelled 'You get me?' and he spelled back, clear as dew: 'I. Get. You.'"

"But how did you learn semaphore?"

"Well, after I failed Hornet, my parents sent me to the Institute for Lower Learning to make it up. They were teaching human languages, too, for extra credit."

"You went to the Institute for Lower Learning?" the queen buzzed. "It's actually real?"

"Uh, yeah. Of course it's real. Where else would I learn semaphore?"

"So you're telling me the Institute for Lower Learning is an actual place?"

"Of course it's real. Why would my parents send me somewhere imaginary?"

"And this isn't one of your lies?"

"I swear it isn't!"

"And do you swear that your swearing is real?"

"Yes! I swear that I swear!"

The queen, thrilled, shot up high into the air and twirled a figure eight before landing on Miranda's shoulder.

"I know where Eden is!" she piped. "Everyone in the car!"

"What's a car?" the hornet buzzed, chasing after Jordan,

Miranda, and the queen as they raced for the parking lot.

"It's what we call a 'box'!" the queen shouted. "You do something called 'driving' in it!"

"Why would we take a box?" buzzed the hornet. "You can't drive there."

"Why?" asked the queen, concerned. "Is it in the sky? Under the ocean?"

"No, cuz," buzzed the hornet. "It's right over there, in those woods."

She pointed a wing toward a dilapidated old shack that was tucked behind scrubby pines on the far side of the lawn. It was almost impossible to see, until one of the remaining windowpanes caught the afternoon light and glinted, like a winking eye.

The Party

"**M**r. Rattice! Esteemed guests! Welcome!" Tillie waved cheerily from behind the information desk, where she was icing a plate of sugar cookies. August clenched his teeth. How could a woman who moved as slowly as a clock hand on the last day of school somehow manage to be every single place he didn't want her to be?

August glanced over at the boys to make sure none of them were giggling or elbowing each other. He was pleased to see that they were all behaving exactly as he'd told them. *Maybe,* he thought. *Maybe we can actually pull this off.*

On the ride over, August had told Randall and the other boys that they might be meeting a woman named Tillie who was very old. August described how, when he'd first met Tillie, she'd mistaken him for a grown-up, and he planned to tell her that Randall, Ivan, and Vincent were grown-ups, too. Trying to explain that they were actually children, he said, would just confuse her. Instead, the best thing they could do was play along. Vincent and Ivan said that sounded pretty strange to them, but Randall got it right away.

"He's right," Randall agreed, puffing as he pumped his way up a hill. "My great-grandma Pearl has dementia. Sometimes when we visit her at the old folks' home, she doesn't even recognize us. One time she thought I was her little brother Elvin, which was super-weird, but my dad said I should just go with it. That felt pretty weird, too, but hey, if it makes her feel better, I'm down."

"But we're not dressed like grown-ups like you are, Augie. We're dressed like kids," Vincent said.

August paused. Vincent was right. This could be a problem.

"Actually, most grown-ups I know only wear suits when they're at work," Ivan said helpfully. "We can tell Tillie we're grown-ups who have a day off."

"Perfect," August said. "And Vincent, make sure you remember to take your cape off when we get there."

"You betcha," Vincent said. "Nix the cape."

It was already becoming clear to him that having a crew really *was* helpful. It was like they were all in a play together, with everyone doing their part to make the audience believe the story was real. Performing the part of "Mr. Rattice" by himself all day had been exhausting. Doing the fake voice was hurting his throat; his wool suit was making him itchy, and he was getting a blister from his dress shoes. But coming back with Ivan, Randall, and Vincent had been energizing and exciting. August was confident that with their help, he'd get the poisons and put an end to insects, and the entire world would be grateful. Everyone would applaud him, like the biggest audience on earth.

But now that it was time to introduce the boys to Tillie, August began losing faith in his plan. Still, there was no way to go but forward.

"Tillie, allow me to introduce you to my dear friends and colleagues: Mr. Randall Davis, Mr. Ivan Linsky, and Mr. Vincent Vicks." He glanced over at the boys and was horrified to see that Vincent had forgotten to take his cape off.

"Welcome, gentlemen. It's a pleasure to meet you," Tillie said.

"The pleasure is ours," Vincent replied, bowing so low that his cape fell forward, covering his head. He stood abruptly, pushing it back. But Tillie smiled just at him, as if everything were totally normal.

"What a dashing cape that is," Tillie said.

"Why, thank you. It's nylon," Vincent said.

"Can I interest anyone in some sugar cookies? I'm almost done decorating them," Tillie said, holding up a knife coated in pale yellow icing.

"Sugar cookies?! Yes, please!" Vincent shouted. August grimaced. Clearly, Vincent didn't know the first thing about acting like an adult. Adults didn't get that excited about cookies. They got excited about weird things, like finding parking spaces and telling each other about their doctor appointments. And they definitely knew how to control their burping.

"That's very kind of you, Tillie," August said. "But we'll have cookies *after* we perform the surgery."

"But—" Vincent said. August silenced him with a glare.

"Of course. That makes much more sense," Tillie said. "I'd ask to come observe, but I know the old expression: 'Scientists never reveal their secrets.'"

Ivan turned to Randall. "Isn't it 'magicians never reveal their secrets'?"

"Yeah," said Randall. "Scientists revealing their secrets is, like, the whole point of science."

"Anyway, now is no time to quibble," said August, jumping between Tillie and the boys and ushering them down the hall.

"Why did she call us scientists? And what did you mean, 'perform the surgery'?" Ivan asked as soon as Tillie was out of earshot. "Because I don't think I should do anything science-y. I failed our last science test. Like, really failed. Like, I got a thirty-six."

"No!" August said, frustrated. "We're not really here to do surgery. We're just here to pick something up and go."

"What are we getting?" Randall asked.

"Um, just a tank. It's in a cabinet," August said, leading the boys farther along the hall to the place where the floor began to slope downward.

"What's in it?" Randall asked.

"Um, helium," August said. He couldn't risk telling the boys the truth. What if they were like Eden and Tillie and thought killing insects was wrong?

"Helium?" Ivan asked. "Are we blowing up balloons?"

"Are we throwing a party?" said Vincent. "Is it Tillie's birthday?"

"Will there be dancing?" Ivan asked.

"I could play a song for her," Randall said. "I saw a piano in one of the rooms we passed. I'm pretty sure it was a Bösendorfer, which is super-rare. I've only seen one in a museum before."

"It's really nice of you to throw her a birthday party," Vincent said.

August clutched his belly. Hearing Vincent say how nice he was, especially after he'd lied and said Tillie had dementia when she was actually sharp and capable, made his stomach hurt. He wondered if he should tell them the truth.

"Um, guys—" he said, but Ivan, Randall, and Vincent

had already taken off running, chatting excitedly about the upcoming party.

"Whoa! Careful! This ramp is steep!" Vincent warned as he ran the last few yards and tugged on the cabinet door, which swung open. He staggered back, emitting a series of belches that filled the hall with the smell of Rice Krispies. August realized he must've forgotten to lock the cabinet door before he left. The boys stepped back, surprised by the size and number of the tanks.

"That's a lot of helium," Vincent said.

"We probably just need one tank," Ivan said.

"Let's grab the big one first so we don't run out," August said in his best casual voice. He hoped the boys wouldn't notice that he was sweating under the heavy woolen suit.

"Cool," Randall said, getting up on his tiptoes and grabbing the top of it. He tilted it back toward the other boys.

"Hang on a minute," August said. He suddenly felt tired and not sure what to do. Keeping track of all these lies was making him more exhausted by the minute. That was another way lying was different from acting. Acting was fun; lying was stressful.

"Don't worry. We've got it," Vincent said as he lifted the bottom of the tank onto one of his narrow shoulders. Ivan grabbed the middle. "The three of us can carry it ourselves."

August watched as the three boys he'd so deviously

recruited innocently hoisted the tank onto their shoulders. He didn't understand why they were being so generous and helpful, even though he'd never shown any interest in being their friend before today. Were they up to something? Were they setting him up for an embarrassing prank? It didn't seem like it. After years of being bullied by Sheila, August had a pretty good sense of when people were planning to do something mean. He didn't get that feeling at all from Ivan, Randall, and Vincent. Was it possible they were just nice guys who liked to do fun things? As the boys lugged the tank up the steep hall and disappeared around the corner, August could hear them guessing what games they would play at the party, and what kind of cake there would be.

"Cake *and* sugar cookies?" Vincent said dreamily. "This is the best day off ever."

As Ivan announced all the dances he knew and Randall listed all the songs he could play, August's stomach hurt even worse than before. Their excitement made him wish that the tank really was full of helium, and there actually was going to be a party for Tillie. He rarely got invited to actual parties, so this all sounded kind of great.

"Hey, Augie, aren't you coming?" Randall called.

". . . Yeah, I'll be right there," August said, plunking down crisscross applesauce in front of the cabinet. He couldn't stop thinking about the way the boys had gotten so excited about the idea of doing something nice for Tillie. He wondered if there was any chance they'd still like him if they found out the real reason he'd lured them here, or if Tillie could ever forgive him if she found out that he'd come to the Institute planning to kill the creatures she'd devoted her life to protecting. Probably not. Definitely not. He thought about confessing but didn't know what to say or how to say it. August had spent so much time practicing how to be a great liar. Now he wished he'd spent a little time figuring out how to tell the truth.

The Monster

*E*den *gazed up at* the undersides of the butterflies' wings as they carried her through the house. Each wing, painted with its unique array of stripes and spots of all colors, rippled and waved as the butterflies soared. It looked as if the flags of every country in the world were being flown all at once.

Eden looked down to see three boys carrying what appeared to be a silver torpedo. One was Black and had the cleanest kicks she'd ever seen. Eden spent so much time climbing trees that she'd stopped trying to keep her sneakers fresh long ago, but this boy clearly meant business. The other two boys were white. One of them was extraordinarily white. He was the palest person Eden had ever seen, and his bright, carrot-colored hair made him look like one of the orange-tip butterflies that was clutching the edge of her sleeve. The third boy, who was wearing a cape, had long dark hair and was chattering away excitedly.

They were so immersed in their conversation they didn't notice Eden hovering in the air several feet above them, let alone hear the ethereal hum created by the thousands of butterfly wings. Curious to know if they were somehow connected to August Rattice, she eavesdropped on their conversation.

"Whoa," said Clean Kicks, pausing to look into one of the windows that showcased the earthworm tunnels. "Check that out."

"That's awesome," said Cape Kid. "Earthworms are the coolest. Did you know that if one gets cut in two, it doesn't die? It turns into two separate worms."

"Actually, that's not true," Clean Kicks said.

"It is!" Cape Kid insisted. "I saw it happen in a movie."

"An animated movie?" Clean Kicks asked. "Where the worms could talk?"

"Oh. Um, yeah," Cape Kid said, rapidly losing faith in his argument.

"Either way," Orange-tip said. "This place is super-cool. What do you think it's for?" he asked.

"I don't know," said Clean Kicks, shifting the torpedo on his shoulder, which Eden now realized was a storage tank. "But this thing is getting heavy. Let's take it outside, then look around a little."

"And don't forget the cookies," Cape Kid said. He adjusted

his grip on the tank, revealing the word that was etched into its side. "Guys, I think we got the wrong tank. This one says 'spinosad,' whatever that is."

"Maybe spinosad is Latin for 'helium,'" said Orange-tip.

"Actually, *helium* is Latin for 'helium,'" Clean Kicks explained.

"Maybe we should go back and switch it out. I've never heard of filling party balloons with spinosad," Cape Kid said.

"We should check with August," suggested Orange-tip.

Eden was startled. They *did* know August. But these boys seemed curious and harmless. Sweet, even. It was odd that they were helping someone as devious as August. She didn't have time to observe any more. She had to get some answers.

"What's going on? Who are you?" she demanded.

All three boys looked up at her, surprised. Then they screamed as Cape Kid unleashed a series of epic graham cracker burps.

"It's a monster!" Orange-tip cried. "With a thousand wings and the body of a girl!" All traces of his gracefulness vanished as he leapt back clumsily, covering his eyes. The tank, too heavy for only two boys to carry, fell with a clatter. The clang of aluminum on marble scared the butterflies as well, and they shrank back in fear, accidentally letting Eden go as they soared toward the ceiling in a mass of trembling wings. Eden hurtled to the floor below, hollering as she fell. She landed hard on her butt, shouted in pain, and then bounded to her feet.

"And both halves are still alive!" Cape Kid shouted, his words garbled by a stream of belches. "Run!"

"It's not a monster. It's a girl!" Clean Kicks shouted, but it was too late.

Cape Kid and Orange-tip were already shoving past each other, trying to escape first. Orange-tip pushed Cape Kid so hard he fell to the ground, taking Clean Kicks with him. The polished marble was slick, sending Clean Kicks sliding across the floor and into Orange-tip. Like bowling pins, all three boys tumbled over, thumping against each other as they landed. Eden stood over them, taking in their toppled bodies and tangled limbs.

"Why are you boys here? Tell me!" she demanded.

"Uh, we're actually scientists?" Cape Kid said, though it was really more of a question.

"Dude, don't. It's not gonna work with her," Clean Kicks said. "She knows we're kids. She's a kid, too."

"I am," Eden said. "But unlike you and August Rattice, if that's even his real name, I was never pretending to be anything else."

"You know August?" Cape Kid asked as he and the other boys struggled to their feet. "Do you go to our school? What grade are you in? Do you wanna see some funny drawings of teachers I made?"

Eden took a deep breath. She thought of all the times she'd begged her parents for a baby brother. Thank goodness they hadn't listened.

"Focus!" Eden pleaded. "August has been tricking you. There isn't any helium in that tank. It's full of poison."

"Why would he bring poison to a party?" Cape Kid asked.

"There is no party!" Eden said. "He's planning on killing every insect in this place. And from the amount of poison he's convinced you to help him steal, I really doubt he's stopping there!"

"That's why he wanted to hang out with us all of a sudden," Clean Kicks said. "He didn't want to be our friend. He was just using us."

"But why?" Cape Kid said as a tiny burp escaped from the side of his mouth. "Because of one cockroach?"

"What cockroach?" Orange-tip asked. "I only saw the thing with the fly."

"I don't know," Eden said. "All I know is that we have to stop him. Do you have any idea where he is?"

"He's down there," Orange-tip said, pointing at the ramp.

"Thank you!" Eden said, charging past them.

"We'll come with you!" said Cape Kid.

He leapt forward to follow Eden, but his sneaker got

tangled in his cape. He reached for the tank to keep himself from falling a second time, but instead he accidentally pushed it over. The tank fell over with a clang and began rolling down the curving ramp. "Whoops! I'll get it," Cape Kid said, emitting a burp that smelled like old taffy.

"No!" Eden shouted, astounded by his clumsiness and the pungency of the odor.

"Don't worry. We've got it!" Orange-tip and Cape Kid said at the same time, then looked at each other, delighted. "Jinx! Double jinx! You owe me a Coke! Inky blinky, flinky, winky. Flush it down the kitchen sinky. Alley oop! Alley oop! Duhhhh hickey! The king of France—"

"I've got it!" Eden shouted over their bizarre chant, deeply distressed by their inability to pull it together in a crisis. She knew that even though the boys meant well, their "help" would only make things worse.

She looked up at the butterflies on the ceiling, then pointed at the boys and made a swirling gesture. She hoped the butterflies would know what she meant, and sure enough, they did. They descended upon the boys, building a tall tower around them with their bodies. They shifted and pivoted their wings as they worked, and the brilliant triangles of color created ever-changing designs that made it seem as though the butterflies weren't building a tower to confine the boys but a giant kaleidoscope for them to enjoy. The boys were too mesmerized by the magnificence of the growing tower to try to escape, until finally it was so tall that Eden couldn't see in and the boys couldn't see out.

"Later!" she shouted as she ran after the tank of poison, which was picking up speed as it rolled down the hall toward the cabinet.

The Pipes

When *August first heard* the distant rumble, he assumed it was thunder, so he kept his attention on trying to pull the key out of the lock. But the rumbling kept getting louder, and by the time August looked up and saw the enormous tank rolling toward him, he only had seconds to spare. He leapt away from the cabinet, flattening himself against the wall below the water pipes. The tank crashed into the cabinet, then bounced up, ricocheting off the pipes like a ball in a pinball game, until the pipes couldn't withstand the assault any longer and burst open. Freezing water rained down on August's head as the tank crashed to the ground, smacking against his feet and pinning them to the dirt floor, which was quickly turning to mud as water filled the narrow space. Within moments, it had risen to his knees. His woolen suit, now drenched, became unbearably heavy, weighing him down.

August heard a low hissing sound and realized to his dismay that the crash had knocked the iron spigot at the top of the tank loose, unleashing the poison. A narrow stream of toxin-filled bubbles streamed into the murky water. The man at the hardware store had said that even one drop could kill hundreds of thousands of insects. August wondered what one drop could do to him.

He reached down into the water and felt around for the spigot. When he closed his fingers around it, though, the spigot didn't feel hard and smooth, like metal. Instead, it was soft and smushy, and he could feel it moving under his fingers. Horrified, he pulled his hand up out of the water and saw that the plump, purple earthworms that had been tunneling alongside him as he raced through the halls were no longer confined behind glass. Now they were loose, squirming between his fingers.

August recoiled, disgusted. He could already imagine the repulsive things climbing up his arm and tunneling into his nose and mouth. To his surprise, though, as soon as the earthworms had untangled themselves from his fingers, they didn't continue upward but instead wriggled down his body, until they were below the surface of the water. When he reached down again to grab the spigot, he could feel that the worms had gotten there first. They were weaving between its spokes, curling and tightening their bodies around it. August wasn't the only one trying to stop the spread of the poison. These tiny creatures were, too.

August was astounded by their bravery. The bubbles of gas that had already been released into the water weren't potent enough to hurt someone his size, but August was pretty sure they were strong enough to poison the little earthworms. And yet the worms, who couldn't see or hear, persisted in their selfless quest to save the insects and humans of the Institute.

How do they do it? he wondered. *How can they be so tiny and so brave?*

August remembered what Tillie had said about earthworms having five hearts. Maybe having eyes and ears didn't matter as much as having five hearts' worth of love inside you. And in that moment, August felt his one heart expand. For the first time in his life, he realized that as small and helpless as he felt in the world, he was a giant compared to these little creatures whose limp bodies were now bobbing to the surface around him. They were still alive but too woozy from the poisons to clench their bodies around the spigot any longer. He was the only one who could save them.

August reached into the water, scooping up every earthworm he saw. Realizing he'd need his hands free to close the spigot, he draped the drowsy worms around his neck and over his shoulders, until it looked like he was wearing a thickly knitted shawl. He didn't think about the feel of their slimy bodies on his skin, only that he had to do whatever he could to do to save them. Once the worms were all safe, August reached down into the murky water and took hold of the spigot. He hesitated, unsure which direction to turn it. One way would stop the poison; the other would unleash even more. He couldn't afford to make a mistake.

Righty-tighty, lefty-loosey. The jingle his mother had taught him long ago to remember how to get the lid off a peanut butter jar popped into his mind. Now confident, he twisted the spigot firmly to the right until it was sealed tight and the poisonous bubbles had stopped flowing. He had done it! He'd saved them! But in the meantime the water had risen to his chest and was still rising. He was in trouble.

Snippets of his life flashed before his eyes like a full-color flip book. First came his earliest memories: climbing into his parents' bed on a sunny morning, the warmth of his mother's arm around him as he snuggled into the seashell curve of her body, and the first time he realized he was actually reading *Yertle the Turtle*, instead of just reciting it from memory. Then came the more recent ones: trick-or-treating, flashlight tag, getting an actual letter in the mail from his pen pal Mathilda. And then came all the terrible things he'd done that he would never be able to apologize or make up for: the five dollars he'd taken from his father's pocket; the times he said he'd walked Orso when he really hadn't; the fart he'd blamed on Angelo Gonzago during the very first nap time of preschool.

"Mommy!" he cried. He wished he'd never come to the Institute. He wished he'd never pretended to be an adult or hatched his scheme in the first place. But it was too late for wishing.

The Cookie

The smell of vanilla and confectioners' sugar flooded the queen's senses. She'd assumed the Institute for Lower Learning would be a broken-down, deserted place, and she was surprised to see a huge, beautiful room and an elderly human spreading frosting onto a cookie.

As Jordan and Miranda raced to talk with the white-haired woman, who was dressed in so many layers of white and cream that she looked like a sugar cookie herself, B.F. buzzed so excitedly that her wings looked more like a hummingbird's than a hornet's. "It's The Ladder! She's still here!" she cried, swooping around the lobby. "Everything's exactly how it used to be. There's the photo of my graduating class!"

She flew over to a collection of framed photos that lined the wall by the door. The queen joined her, and they peered at a photo of a swarm of hornets lined up in rows.

"That's our teacher, Milton, and there I am," the hornet

said, tapping the glass. The queen squinted at the picture. Her cousin's antennae were twisted together and sticking out at odd angles.

"I know," she said. "It's not a great look, but I forgot it was Picture Day and showed up with really bad nest head."

"Well, I think you look great," said the queen, telling a bit of a lie herself. "And I owe you an apology for underestimating you, B.F. We never would've found this place if you hadn't worked so hard to learn semaphore."

"Aw, it was easy," she said.

"Really? It doesn't look easy," said the queen.

"I'm lying. It was really hard."

"You're impossible," the queen said, rolling four of her eyes. But she winked at her cousin with her fifth eye to let her know how proud she really was of her.

"Go talk to The Ladder," the queen said, nudging her cousin closer. "Maybe she can help."

"Nope. We've gotta leave that to the humans," the hornet said. "The Ladder is very kind and she makes great cookies, but she can't understand a word of Hornet. Or any other insect language, for that matter."

The queen was surprised to hear this. She'd felt an immediate connection to the old woman, whose pale pink face had so many lines and creases that it reminded her of a peony. Peonies were the queen's favorite flower, and they were royal, too. They were so extravagantly beautiful that they were known as the queen of the garden, and their countless layers of petals suggested limitless depths. The queen sensed that perhaps this human woman, despite her inability to speak their languages, had levels of perception that were deeper than the eye could see.

"Still," she said to her cousin. "Let's fly over. Miranda and Jordan can translate for us."

The queen wanted to get closer to the information desk for many reasons. Of course, the first was to find any clues that could lead them to Eden, but she was equally drawn to the platter of cookies that sat alongside an open book filled with neat rows of human handwriting. Normally, the queen would be curious to see what the humans had written, but iced sugar cookies were her weakness. As ruler of her colony, it was her job to discourage her subjects from coming too close to human buffets, an activity that could be as deadly as it was tempting, and she tried to set a good example. But the call of the sugar cookies was impossible to resist. As the queen approached the desk, she didn't hover above it cautiously as she normally would have. Instead, she landed in the center of a freshly iced cookie, hoping no one would notice as she took little sips of the gleaming icing. It was delicious, and so freshly made that the icing was still warm and soft.

"What's she saying?" the queen piped to Miranda.

Miranda raised her flute to her lips, and the music she piped in response was agitated and abrupt. She explained that The Ladder, whose name was Tillie, hadn't seen Eden. Tillie had been expecting her that morning, but Eden had never arrived.

"Gronk!" Jordan said, pointing at the guest book. The queen peeked over to see Eden's name written in neat block letters.

"She *is* here!" the queen piped to Miranda. "We'll split up and search the house. You and I will go with Tillie, and Jordan will go with B.F."

By the time Miranda had relayed the plan to Jordan, the hornet was already hovering in the air, poised to fly. But as the queen raised her wings to join Miranda, she was shocked to realize that she couldn't. Something was preventing her.

"Aren't you coming?" Miranda piped.

"I—I can't," piped the queen. She flapped her wings again, harder this time, and was horrified to realize that her legs had sunk into the warm icing, which was becoming as hard as concrete as it cooled. "B.F., help!"

Her cousin soared to her side. "I've got you!" she shouted, wrapping her foreleg around the queen's abdomen and giving her a tug.

"Ow!" cried the queen.

"Sorry! I'm doing my best," she said, readjusting her grip. But as the hornet shifted her weight, the underside of her leg brushed the icing.

"Careful!" the queen called out, but it was too late. Her cousin's leg had already sunk into the goo.

B.F. flapped her wing, desperate to take off before the icing congealed around her, too, but as she struggled, the edge of her wing grazed a blob of icing that had become glued to the queen's thorax, and now the hornet was stuck to not only the cookie, but her cousin, too.

Because B.F.'s wing was stuck under her mandible, the queen couldn't turn her head to the left or right, but she could still look up. There she saw Miranda, Jordan, and Tillie staring down at what must've looked like a two-headed creature with each head facing a different direction, trying to claw its way out of a snowdrift. Jordan prodded at the icing, surveying the damage. The queen squirmed at his touch.

"Don't worry," Miranda piped. "He's a doctor."

"Get us loose!" the queen piped, only to see Jordan turn to Miranda, concerned.

"He says he can't risk it," Miranda told the queen. "The icing's so hard he's worried he might pull your legs off. You and B.F. go with Jordan, and I'll stick with Tillie."

"What's going on? What's happening?" B.F. called as

Jordan lifted the entire cookie off the plate, taking her and the queen with it.

The queen translated for her cousin, who shook her head with frustration.

"It won't work," she said. "I know the house, but I got around through the air shafts and insect tunnels. These giant humans can't squeeze into those."

"Yes, but they can fit into *that*," the queen said as Jordan hurried over to the elevator and put the cookie on the floor.

"Whoa! He's gotta slow down! I'm getting nauseated over here," the hornet said.

"Quiet! He's figuring out how to open it!" the queen said as she watched Jordan go from carefully examining the gate's levers to tugging at them willy-nilly.

"He'll never figure it out!" the hornet told the queen. "That thing is ancient, and the handle always sticks. Tell him to try the stairs off the hallway."

"You tell him! I don't know semaphore!" the queen said.

"I can't! My wing is stuck! Pipe at him!"

"I can't! He doesn't speak Flute!" The queen went silent, and she heard a shudder, then a slam. "What's going on? I can't see. I'm facing the wrong way!"

"He got the door to open and close, but he can't get the elevator to start," the hornet said. "He needs Tillie. She's the only one who knows how to work the darn thing. Is she coming to help? I can't tell. I'm facing the wrong way."

The queen peered at Tillie, who was rising from her chair at about the same speed as a peony blossoming. Miranda was doing her best to remain cool, but the queen could tell she was getting impatient.

"I think so. She might be getting up. I'm not sure. She's so slow, it's hard to tell."

"Oh, no. She was slow when I was here before. It's gotta be worse now," sighed the hornet.

"Where's Jordan? Why isn't he going to get her?" asked the queen, but the sound of the rattling gate told her the answer without her having to look. "He's trapped in the elevator, isn't he?"

"Yup," said the hornet gloomily. "Eden's lost, Miranda's stuck with the slowest woman on earth, Jordan can't figure out the elevator, and you and I are glued to a cookie. We're doomed."

"Oh dear," said the queen. "I never thought I'd be sad to hear you tell the truth."

Worms and Water

By the time Eden got to August, the water was up to his neck, and his hair appeared to be moving. As she got closer, she could see that his head was crowned with a hundred squirming earthworms, their bodies writhing and twisting as they, like the boy, struggled to stay above the rising water. Eden had read about the myth of Medusa, the magical woman with snakes for hair. Here it was, come to life before her. She stopped and stared.

"Save us!" August cried, flailing in the rising water. "My feet are stuck! We're drowning!"

"Stay calm!" Eden shouted as she kicked off her shoes and splashed into the rapidly deepening pool. "I'm coming to get you!"

"Be careful! There's poison!" he shouted as Eden dove into the water.

As she swam to the bottom, silt and dirt rose up, further

clouding the water. Her braids swirled around her face, making it impossible to see. She pulled them back and wiped mud from her eyes, until she could finally make out the shape of the giant tank. She pressed against it with all her weight, straining to push it off of August's feet, but it was too heavy for her to dislodge. She had to figure something out, and quick. She was running out of air, and the pool was getting deeper.

Eden groped around the bottom of the tank, trying to attack the problem from another angle. She could feel the floor give way under her scrabbling fingers and realized that it wasn't wood or tile, like most floors: it was raw earth. She thought of the industrious earthworms she'd seen burrowing along the hallways of the house and how they managed to dig such impressive tunnels without the benefit of hands or eyes. Inspired, Eden used her cupped hands to shovel the dirt out from under the tank, until she'd carved out a hollow trench. With no earth to hold it in place, the tank rolled easily off August's feet.

Eden used her last breath to wrap her arm around the boy's waist and propel them both upward, until they broke the surface of the water. She was light-headed and couldn't tell if her vision was blurred from lack of oxygen or because her eyes were full of water. She didn't have time to wipe them; the boy in her arms was still struggling. She pulled the sopping jacket off of him to make him as light as possible, revealing his boyish shape. How he could've thought anyone would believe he was an adult was beyond her. Cold water, still spraying from the pipes above, spilled onto her head and splashed into her mouth.

"Follow me!" she burbled.

"I can't!" August said. "I can't swim!"

Eden groaned with frustration at his helplessness. She'd never rescued anyone from drowning, but she'd once watched a lifeguard pull a struggling swimmer from the waves. She remembered how the lifeguard kept telling the man to be calm, and the way the lifeguard had flipped him onto his back, then slung her arm across his chest, towing him to safety.

"Stay calm!" she repeated, trying to throw her arm over August's chest, but the thrashing boy couldn't be still. His arms slapped at the water, sometimes striking her face. The worms' tails lashed at her, too. The force of their blows shocked Eden. The boy and the worms were both small, but the worms' determination seemed to give them super-human strength. They were all panicking, pulling her down with them. Eden struggled to stay afloat, but felt her own strength draining from her. She couldn't hold on to them much longer.

The Choice

*A*tom's mother, Queen Mote, tapped her feet against the grasshopper's flanks, urging him to go faster. The mighty green beast obliged, and its compatriots followed his lead. The army of insects galloped toward the splashing sounds, barely noticing the tower of butterflies as they passed.

"Whoa!" Atom called as the pool of water came into view. The grasshopper he was riding, who'd been bounding forward with the full strength of his powerful hind legs, skidded to a stop, nearly catapulting them both into the rising water, where they found two children struggling. The girl was grasping an overhead pipe with one hand, fighting to keep her head above the rising water, and she held on to the boy with the other. The boy didn't seem to be doing anything other than yelping, splashing, and making the girl's job even harder. But even in the midst of all the chaos Atom saw the girl notice him, her eyes sparkling with happy recognition. She *was* good. They *had* made a connection. He knew it!

"We have to help them," Atom said. "She's my friend."

"She is not," his mother said firmly. "He tried to kill Dot, and now she's helping him. The friend of our enemy is our enemy."

"Wait. What?" said Atom. "Does that mean—?"

"It means she's our enemy!" Dot said, exasperated.

Atom's mother pointed her antenna straight into the air. "Release the fire ants!" she commanded.

Hearing their name, the fire ants, which ranged in color from rust to russet and brick to burgundy, rose up on their back legs, ready for their next command. They were fierce creatures who could release a venom so powerful that one sting could cause humans hours, or even days, of pain.

"Yes! Finally! Go, Mom!" Dot hollered.

"Wait!" Atom cried as he realized that the girl wasn't just looking at him. She was winking. Blinking, actually. And way more than normal. At first the blinks seemed random, but then he noticed a pattern. Sometimes she'd open and close her eyes quickly. Other times she'd close them for a full second before opening them again.

Morse code! She was trying to communicate with him in Morse code! Atom had heard the stories of how Grandma Minnie and her partner, Milton, had learned and taught

Morse code, since it was the perfect bridge language for humans, ants, termites, fireflies, and many others. But by the time Atom and Dot were born, very few ants still knew it, and only a handful of very elderly teachers still taught it. Atom had only studied it for two months as an extracurricular, and Dot had never taken it at all. *It's not like we're ever gonna need Morse code,* she'd said. *No one ever uses it anymore.* Still, Atom had always hoped he'd get a chance to try it, and here it was.

"Wait, please! Just give me a chance to find out what she has to say," he begged his mother.

"Very well," his mother said, nodding. "Proceed."

Atom turned his attention back to Eden. Her hands were shaking from holding the pipe, her whole body was shivering, but her gaze was unwavering. Atom looked deeply into her eyes, just like he'd done when they'd first met. She opened and closed her eyes quickly, then did it again: two short blinks.

Atom searched his brain. He'd taken the class a while ago, and it was hard to remember the complicated code. Then he remembered a trick his teacher had taught him. It was called a mnemonic device. Instead of trying to just memorize the answer, he could make up a hint that would help him remember. It didn't matter how ridiculous it seemed or if it didn't make sense to anyone else. It just had to be a clue that meant something to him. The only problem was that he couldn't even remember the hint.

Great. I need a mnemonic device to remember my mnemonic device, he thought. He looked over at Dot, who was watching him as closely as an anteater. She couldn't wait for their mother to release the fire ants. Atom wished he hadn't looked at her. His whole life he'd always happily gone along with whatever Dot wanted, never questioning her judgment. *You cuties are like a two-pack of cupcakes,* Aunt Itty-Bitty would say, shaking her head. *Always a pair.* That was it! He and Dot always came in twos! The mnemonic device was "I'm a two-pack of cupcakes, because *I* am never alone." Two dots meant "I"!

He blinked two times then pointed to himself to show that he understood what two blinks meant. But instead of responding with her usual enthusiasm, the girl had no reaction at all. Atom realized there was too much distance between them. From so far away, there was no chance she could read his blinks. She probably couldn't even tell he was pointing at himself. Atom looked around, desperate to find another way of signaling to her in Morse code. What else could he use to make dots and dashes? Dot! Dot, standing by herself, looked like a dot! And three ants standing next to each other made a dash! Atom waved at the expanse of packed earth that fronted the pool and was literally crawling with his fellow ants. "Listen up, everyone! I need you all to clear this area, then do exactly what I tell you! I mean, um, please do what I tell you."

His thousands of brothers and sisters led the way, encouraging everyone to swarm to either edge of the dirt. Once a wide patch of dirt had been cleared, Atom pointed at twins he knew from Ms. Fourmi's class and called to them. "Teeny, you stand over there. Tiny, you stand ten steps away from her, and both of you hold still until I tell you that you can move. Got it?"

Teeny and Tiny started laughing.

"Oh my gosh, that's adorable," Teeny said.

"I know, right? That little male thinks he's going to tell us what to do," Tiny said, laughing.

"As if." Tiny scoffed at Atom. "You males never do anything around here. Why should we do something for you?"

"Because I said so," Dot said, stepping in between them.

"Oooh!" chorused a row of school ants, who were enjoying the drama. No one ever split up Teeny and Tiny.

"Seriously, Dot? Why are you making this a thing? Why's he even asking us to do it?"

"I don't know," Dot said. "But we're ants. We help each other. It's what we do. So get over yourselves and follow his instructions."

"Fine," Teeny huffed.

"Whatever," Tiny puffed, but they took their places on the dirt ramp exactly where Atom had told them.

"Great! Thank you!" Atom said. "Now, I need everyone else to count off by twos as quickly as possible."

"One!"

"Two!"

"One!"

"Two!"

"One!"

"Two!" A chorus of tiny voices shook the ground, and before long the ants had formed two perfect straight lines that stretched all the way up the ramp.

"Yes!" Atom said, once they'd finished. "Now, 'ones,' you're going to wind yourselves around Teeny, making as tight a circle as possible. 'Twos,' you're going to do the same around Tiny."

Soon, the entire colony was assembled in two circles as tight as licorice wheels. Atom looked over at the girl, whose eyes suddenly brightened with recognition. It had worked! She began another sequence of blinks. This time it was two long ones. What did two long blinks mean? Suddenly, Atom's mnemonic devices for the entire alphabet started coming back to him: *H* was for "horse," because the four dots looked like four little hooves; *T* was for "trick-or-treat," because the one long dash looked like a candy bar. Candy! Two long blinks meant "M" because the name of Atom's favorite candy had two *M*s in it, and Atom liked to nibble them all day *long*.

"I . . . M!" he said triumphantly. Now that he'd remembered his old system, he was able to read the rest of the girl's message pretty quickly. "A . . . F . . . R . . . N . . . D. Ima frond! Ima frond! She's saying Imafrond!"

"Or," offered Aunt Itty-Bitty, "she's saying, 'I'm a friend.'"

"Yes! That's it!" Atom said, turning to Dot. "We can trust her. She's a friend!"

"Of course she's saying that," Dot argued. "That's what every creep says to get you to trust them."

Atom hesitated. He didn't know who to believe. Would he really side with this human over his own family?

"But she's learning our languages," he said. "Why would she do that if she wanted to destroy us?"

At this, even Dot hesitated.

"See? She *is* our friend. And yes, that boy *is* our enemy," Atom said, raising his voice so he could address the entire army of ants. "But if the Institute of Lower Learning is truly the place where humans and insects intersect, we should save her because she's good, and save him, too, even though he isn't."

Atom looked from the humans in the water to his mother, aunts, Dot, and the army of ants that stood poised to either aid or attack. He'd never spoken up before. Would any of them listen?

The Shimmering Beads

August cursed himself for bailing on his swimming lessons. For a whole year, his mother had dropped him off at the YMCA every Tuesday and Thursday, trusting that he would join the other kids for the group swim class. Instead, terrified of putting his face in the water, he would hide in the locker room for the entire hour, roaming from locker to locker, idly spinning the faces of the combination locks. Moments before it was time to get picked up he'd soak his swimsuit in the sink, then run his wet fingers through his hair and across his towel until both were damp enough to seem like he'd been swimming. It had been easy to keep the lie going. When he and his family went to the beach, he'd run in up to his ankles, shout that it was too cold, and run back to the safety of the blanket. When they'd go to the local pool, he'd eat a snack as soon as they arrived, then pretend to be upset when his mother told him he'd have to wait an hour before getting in. Now, thanks to his lies, he would drown here, and he would drag these brave worms and bold girl down with him. If she'd just let go of him, she could easily carry the lightweight worms to safety.

"Let go of me!" he shouted. "Save the worms!"

"Don't give up!" Eden yelled.

"It's too late!" August gasped, pointing at the fire ants that were drifting toward them in seemingly endless waves. "Those guys look mean."

"They're not mean. They're protecting their colony," Eden said sadly. "From me. They don't trust me after all."

"So they *are* going to bite us?" August asked, unable to hide his fear.

"No. Fire ants don't bite."

"Phew!"

"They sting and inject us with solenopsin. It's a toxic alkaloid venom. It's not fatal, but I did read that the pain is so bad that it burns for days. *And* nights."

"You're not helping!" August groaned. Drowning and burning at the same time sounded awful, but August couldn't imagine that it would hurt any more than the angry glares of the insects that filled the chamber. August had come to the Institute because he hated all insects, and now all insects hated him. He was tired of being hated. He wanted to be loved for a change, and not just in the way his parents and

Ms. Batra loved him. He wanted to have friends he loved who'd love him back.

There were so many eyes watching them that for a moment, August felt like he and Eden were actors, and the insects were their audience. But real life wasn't a fourth-grade play, where he had Ms. Batra to tell him what to do and no matter how badly it went, it would be over in twenty minutes. In real life, August had to decide what to do all on his own, and he'd have to live with the consequences forever. He wished he and Eden really were actors, and he could stop the terrible scene and start over. He'd do everything differently this time. But he couldn't tell that to the large, gleaming black ant who sat proudly astride a grasshopper. He was the villain of her story, and it was too late to change the ending.

August prepared for the worst. He squeezed his eyes shut as the fire ants closed in on them. He felt Eden's grip on him loosen until she wasn't holding him at all, but he didn't sink. He felt the ants' bodies press against his, but he didn't feel any pain. His brain struggled to make sense of it all: How was it possible that he, who couldn't swim, was floating? He opened his eyes to see Eden floating beside him, looking around with wonder.

"What's going on?" August asked.

"I read about this!" Eden said. "This is what they do when their colony floods!"

Eden pointed at the water around them, and August saw that they were floating on a disc made of shimmering red beads.

"They're using their bodies to make a raft!" Eden said. "They're saving us!"

"Who is?" August asked.

"The ants!"

Confused, August peered over the edge of the raft.

"Ants," August repeated. "We're floating on millions and millions of ants."

It was the last thing he said before he fainted.

The Reunion

den's mother had just finished wrapping Eden in a warm blanket when her father carried August's limp body into the sitting room and set him down on the sofa. Even though Eden had been pretty sure that the ants wouldn't have let August and her drown, she'd been so relieved to hear her parents' voices calling her name that the sight of her mom running toward her, carrying a white-haired woman piggyback-style, barely struck her as odd.

Eden Evans! At last we meet! the elderly woman had called as Eden's mother placed her gently on the ground, and Eden realized this must be Tillie Wannaberger. Eden had no idea how her parents had found her, or when they'd met Tillie, but there was no time for explanations or greetings. The crowd of insects parted to make a path for her dad so he could walk without trampling them, and when he arrived at the water's edge, he scooped the unconscious boy into his arms.

Now that they were all clustered in the sitting room, the insects and humans, from the boys to the boll weevils, were edging closer to August and the worms with a mix of curiosity and concern.

"Please, everyone. I'm a doctor. I need you to step back," Eden's father announced. "Or, uh, fly or crawl back. We need to give this boy and the worms some breathing room."

"How can I help?" Tillie asked. "I have smelling salts and a fully stocked operating room. The surgical implements were designed for patients who are under four inches long, but perhaps you can improvise?"

"Thank you. I appreciate that very unusual offer, but first we try something simpler," Jordan said, taking August by the shoulders and giving him and the unconscious worms a firm shake as he called to them in a loud voice. "August! Worms! Are you okay?"

Luckily, that first step was enough to rouse them. August's eyes fluttered open. The worms, who didn't have eyes, began to wriggle.

"He's breathing!" Eden's father said, and then he looked over at the worms. "And they— Well, I don't know if they breathe, but they're definitely doing something."

"Oh, thank goodness," Tillie said, sitting down beside Eden and holding up the sugar cookie. "But what are we going to do about these two?"

Eden looked over at the cookie and gasped. "Your Majesty?" She leaned closer, realizing that the queen was not only trapped in the thick icing, but that her body was tangled around another, very similar-looking insect. "Or should I say, Your Majesties?"

Both little faces looked up at her blankly, and Eden realized that neither could understand her without her kazoo. But she didn't need words to know how to help. "Allow me," Eden said, taking the cookie from Tillie. Tillie watched as Eden breathed gently on the hard sugary crust until it softened just enough for the queen and her friend to fly free.

"So you don't just talk to insects. You help them, too," Tillie said to Eden, her voice full of wonder.

"I do my best," Eden said.

"Thank you, my dear," the queen buzzed, shaking clumps of icing from her legs. "It is such a relief to see you safe and well, though I have half a mind to sting you for giving me such a scare."

"I was thinking the same thing," Eden's mom piped to the queen.

"Wait a minute, you two can talk to each other?" Eden asked her mom.

"We can!" her mother said. "Thanks to a very strange combination of buzzing, flute playing, and empathy."

"For me it's buzzing, empathy, and kazoo!" Eden

exclaimed. She glanced over at her dad to see if he could understand the queen, too, but he was busy striking strange poses at the queen's friend, who was doing the same back at him.

"Who's that with dad?" Eden asked her mom. "And what exactly are they doing?"

"B.F., this is my daughter, Eden," her dad signaled as he and the hornet joined them. "Eden, this is my new friend, the bald-faced hornet queen. And bizarrely enough, we both know semaphore. It's unbelievable, like everything else that's happened today. But we still shouldn't have doubted you. Sorry, E."

"Thank you," Eden said, hugging him.

"What *did* happen?" Tillie asked, so Eden, Jordan, and Miranda told her the whole remarkable story, filling in each other's gaps, as Ivan, Randall, and Vincent set out sugar cookies for all the insects.

"But there's one detail I don't understand," Tillie said to August as Eden and her parents wrapped up their tale. "Did you really think you'd convinced me that you were anything other than a little boy?"

August's face turned from light to hot pink. "Wait," he said, and Eden could hear the astonishment in his voice. "You know I'm not a man?"

Heroes and Villains

"**W**hen did you realize I was a boy?" August asked Tillie.

"A moment or two after we met. And I'm sure I would've known right away if my ears and eyes were still up to snuff. Besides, it never even occurred to me that you were trying to trick me," Tillie said, looking over at Vincent. "What grown man wears a cape, for goodness' sake? I thought we were playing. Milton and I used to play all kinds of make-believe when he was a boy."

"I wasn't playing make-believe," August said indignantly. "I was acting."

"Oh, I didn't mean it as an insult," Tillie said. "I love make-believe. Acting is simply make-believe at its very best. But what you were doing wasn't either of those. You were simply lying. Did you think you could fool me just because I'm old?"

August looked away, trying to avoid Tillie's eyes. "Um, yeah. Kinda."

"You should also know that I'd *prefer* to have a child as the new Human Director," Tillie said. "Milton wasn't technically a child when he created the Institute, but he led like one because he'd finally regained the most childlike parts of himself: playfulness, curiosity, imagination. Luckily, this room is full of humans and insects who share those qualities, and their ability to collaborate is the only reason these precious creatures survived your barbaric efforts to extinguish them all."

August looked around the room. Some of the insects, like the termites and fireflies, seemed to be looking at him sympathetically. Others, like the big ant, were giving him some serious stink eye. He noticed an actual stink bug glancing his way and couldn't tell if it was giving him stink eye intentionally, or if that was just its normal face.

"How *did* they all survive?" August asked. "I thought just one drop of that poison was enough to kill every insect for miles."

"Oh, no. The poison in the large tank is fairly weak. That's why Milton made so much of it. The poison you're referring to is so strong that Milton only needed to make a very small amount. Besides, I would never keep anything that dangerous in a cabinet. I keep it somewhere much safer."

"But why would you keep any at all?" August asked.

"It's too dangerous to throw away, since it has the potential to contaminate our rivers, oceans, forests, and farmland. I have no choice but to keep it," Tillie explained. "And I also have no choice but to ask you to leave, August. I normally believe in second chances, but you have lost the trust of everyone here, from our proud queens to our humblest fleas."

August didn't want to go. He wished Tillie had offered him an opportunity to prove that this remarkable day at the Institute had changed him. He thought about the sign on Ms. Batra's wall:

ALL THE WORLD'S A STAGE,

AND ALL THE MEN AND WOMEN MERELY PLAYERS:

THEY HAVE THEIR EXITS AND THEIR ENTRANCES,

AND ONE MAN IN HIS TIME PLAYS MANY PARTS.

August knew he couldn't undo the past. But if all the world really was a stage, he still had time to play a lot of other parts. He'd been a villain, but that didn't mean he couldn't be a friend and helper next, or even a hero one day. He took the ring of keys from his pocket and handed them to Tillie. "I apologize for everything, Tillie. And you'll see. I'll teach myself at least one of their languages so I can start being helpful around here as soon as I earn the right to come back."

"Learning an insect language isn't as simple as it sounds,"

Tillie warned. "I desperately wanted to talk to bugs, but I wasn't born with the gift."

"Actually, it isn't a gift. It's a skill," Eden said. "Anyone can learn."

"But how?" August asked.

"There are so many ways. Some of the languages are like playing music. Others are like cracking codes. And many insects speak more than one," she said, gesturing at Atom. "He can blink in Morse code *and* play his belly like a washboard. You can read all about all the languages in the notebook and learn as many as you like."

"What notebook?" Tillie asked.

"It's incredible. I'll show it to you, as soon as I can get back to the bedbug habitat," Eden said. "It's filled with detailed language lessons and interviews between insects and M.W., whoever that is."

"M.W.?" Tillie said. "That must be my Milton! He never mentioned that he was writing a book, but it has to be his."

"I don't understand," August said. "If teaching humans and insects to communicate was so important to him, why didn't he share it with you?"

"I think I know," Tillie said. "My Milton was a perfectionist. Ever since he was a little boy, he'd never share any stories or drawings with me until he was sure they were perfect."

"But that's good, isn't it?" August asked.

"Oh no," Tillie said. "Nothing is ever perfect, so waiting until it is means you wind up waiting forever."

"Do you think we should share Milton's notebook now?" Eden asked.

"I don't know," said Tillie. "That's a question for our new Human Director. You'll have to ask her."

"Really?" Eden asked, scanning the room. "Can I meet her? Where is she? What's she like?"

"She's wonderful," Tillie said. "She's wise, she's kind, she's brave . . . She's you."

"Me?" Eden said.

"Provided that your parents and insect counterpart agree," Tillie said. "I hope that Queen Mote will make her choice shortly. In the meantime, you must have a lot of questions to ask before you decide—"

"Yes!" Eden blurted. "It would be my honor."

August was surprised to realize that he was smiling. When he'd first met Eden, he'd seen her only as an enemy and a threat, and he'd treated her as badly as Sheila treated him. But now everything was different. He actually felt happy for Eden, and despite all the bad things August had done, he had faith that they would become friends one day. It was a wonderful feeling.

The Successor

While the humans had been talking, a small colony of lice, who'd been living just above the ears of humans for so long that they'd become fluent in English, had decided to pitch in and were helping the girl, whose name was Eden, translate the humans' conversation for the assembled insects. When Atom heard that Eden was going to be the new Human Director, he scurried to his mother's side, excited.

"Mom! Did you hear that? The girl—I mean, Eden—is going to be the new Human Director! You're gonna pick her to be your new partner, right?"

"Well, she won't be *my* partner," his mother said as she gathered him, Dot, and their thousands of siblings into a circle. "Your grandma Minnie made it very clear that she always wanted a young ant to be her successor, so we decided that I would do the job temporarily until we discovered which one of you would be the most natural Insect

Director. And, based on the events of the day, we have come to our decision."

"That's amazing! Go, Dot!" Atom shouted, his dorsal aorta filling with pride. He was happy not just for his big sister, but for the Institute and all the creatures living in it. The quest to develop insect-human communication that had ended when Milton and Grandma Minnie had died would begin again. He began a chant that quickly spread throughout the family. "Dot! Dot! Dot!"

"Whoa, now. Slow down," his mother said, quieting them all. "Atom, my dear, as wonderful and bold as your big sister is, she will not be our new Insect Director. Your aunts and I have searched our dorsal aortas, and it's clear that you are the one who carries our mother's spirit most deeply inside you. There's no one better suited to carry out her dream and guide us forward than you. This is a great responsibility, my love, and we know that you will rise up to meet it."

"But I can't handle such an important job. I'm just a male," he said.

"Sometimes, your spirit is more important than your gender," his mother told him. "You can do this, my son. But only if you believe you can."

"I'm not sure," Atom said.

"Then I'll be sure for you, until you are," Dot said.

"But wait," Atom said. "It has to be you, Dot. You're the

leader, not me. You're the one who's strong and confident and—"

"Yeah, yeah. I know all that," Dot said. "Obviously. But the other stuff? The teamwork? The collaborating with humans? Ugh, that's not me."

"But—"

"It's you," she said. "I mean, don't get me wrong. Being the Insect Director sounds awesome. And you're gonna kill it. But you know what job sounds even better to me? Five-Star General. I want to run the army! Can I, Mom? Please?"

"One day, sweetheart," her mother said with a smile. "But first we need to get your feet fixed."

"This is gonna be great," Dot told her little brother. "With me in charge of war and you in charge of peace, we'll be unstoppable."

"Then I accept the job. That is, if Eden accepts me," Atom said, though he knew already that she would. "But if I'm any good at being a leader, it's only because I learned from the best." Atom waited for his sister, who always had an answer for everything, to respond, but she didn't say a word. "Dot? Hey, Dot. Wait. Are you crying?"

"What? No. I'm not crying. You're crying," she said, swatting him with one antenna and wiping her eye with the other. Atom swatted her back, laughing, until their mother stepped between them.

"There will be plenty of time for tears and laughter later," she said. "But now is the time to think of the future. You and Eden have a lot of work ahead of you."

"Yeah," said Dot, nodding in August's direction. "Number one is getting that rotten kid out of here."

Atom looked over at the boy and thought of all the ways he had hurt his sister, and all the harm he meant to do to Atom's home and community. Even Tillie thought he should leave. But then Atom thought about Grandma Minnie and what she would've wanted.

"Little boy, Tillie and my sister are right. You must go," Atom said. He watched the boy's head droop and shoulders slump as Eden translated his proclamation to English. "But you've said you want to change, which is most important. Go out into the world and do what you can do to make it better. And over time, if we see progress, we'll think about letting you come back. Does that sound all right to you?"

"Why do you care what he thinks?" Dot grumbled. "He should be grateful you're even thinking about giving him a chance. He's lucky we're not stinging and biting his butt six ways to Sunday."

"Don't worry. I'm not asking him," Atom said. He nodded at his new partner. "I'm asking her."

The Partners

Eden studied Atom's eyes as he sent her a series of blinks. "O-K?"

"O-K," she blinked back with a grin.

Atom extended his foreleg toward her. Eden, feeling pretty sure that he was encouraging her to speak to the group, panicked. What should she say? She'd only said yes to Tillie moments ago, but she was already doubting herself. Was she really ready for this big a job? Would the insects accept her? Respect her? Her first day there, she'd fallen down a hole, humiliated herself in front of the treehoppers, and needed to be rescued from drowning. She'd barely survived, let alone proved she could lead. There was still so much she had to learn. There had to be someone out there who was more qualified than she was. She could feel the sharp claws of anxiety scratching away at her, until she felt her mother's breath by her ear.

"Sweetheart," she whispered. "You've got this."

Eden took a deep breath. Maybe her mother was right. Eden had always spent a lot of energy worrying that anything she had to offer would never be perfect or groundbreaking enough to make a difference, but now she understood that all she needed to offer was herself. She'd been born with the giant, Christmas-morning-sized pile of gifts that were her sprawling family and beloved parents, whose love had been bridging two cultures since its very beginning. And she also had the Hanukkah-sized gifts of curiosity and empathy, which grew bigger and cast more light with every passing day. These gifts were her birthright and her superpower, and now she saw how she could use them to help people and insects look at the world as one giant nest and understand the importance of banding together to protect it. She looked down at a smiling louse who was watching her patiently, ready to translate her words to the crowd. It was time.

"My new partner is very wise," she said. "It's time to open our notebooks and our hearts to each other. Insect friends, please be patient with us. You're small and nimble, able to shift with the seasons and sensitive to the smallest changes to our planet. We humans are large and clumsy. We're slow to change and quick to assume that we run the world single-handedly. But as my friend and mentor the queen has taught me, we need you far more than you need us. Without you to pollinate the plants, everything would die. There'd be nothing to eat: no fruit, no vegetables, no wheat, no corn, no fish, no birds, no cows, no milk."

"Would there still be pizza?" Ivan asked.

"No pizza," Atom said, and the room became quiet as Eden and the louse shared this dire message with the crowd.

"But I love pizza," said Ivan.

"So do I," said a fly.

"I love Cinnamon Toast Crunch," sighed Randall.

"Me too!" said August.

"And strawberries," said Eden's mother.

"And skin cells," said a cluster of flea larvae.

And soon everyone was calling out all the things they loved to eat most. With the help of the lice, who were teaching the humans and insects helpful phrases in each other's languages, everyone began chatting with each other, eager to try out the new words they were learning. Eden could barely keep track of who was speaking for themselves or translating for someone else, but no one really seemed to care. All that really mattered was that they were sharing.

"Spaghetti!"

"Popcorn!"

"Pollen!"

"Ice cream!"

"Blood!" chorused the mosquitoes, who then glanced

around the suddenly quiet room. "Seriously? No one else is into blood?"

"We are!" a of cloud black flies hooted in agreement.

"Me is!" said a baby flea, who was so tiny he was literally microscopic.

Everyone laughed, delighted. The queen flew to Eden's side and they marveled at the happy chaos of fresh collaboration all around them. The kind of communication they'd dreamed about only one day ago was already in motion. Eden was pretty sure that most of the conversations bordered on nonsensical: a mish-mosh of mistranslations like a huge, intra-species game of Telephone. But, she realized, that's how most conversations between strangers began: they started out clunky and clumsy, then got looser and more fun as everyone got to know each other.

Eden couldn't help but notice that once again she was in her familiar role of observer instead of participant, but this time she relished the opportunity. She was standing apart by choice, watching the impromptu party as a proud host instead of a bashful stranger with no one to talk to. All she had to do was take one step forward and she'd be in the middle of this beautiful, unruly group, having finally found a place where she truly belonged. And she felt calm and happy, knowing that feeling at home in this underground world was a step toward feeling the same way in the larger one above. But for now, she was content to revel in the sight of all the faces: insect, human, old, young, vivid, plain, kind, fierce, bristled, bearded, rough, smooth, showy, and camouflaged, all eager to learn from each other.

"This is how we'll do it," Eden told the crowd. "We'll try new things, and whether we flourish or flop, we'll always be there to pick each other up. Humans, insects: each of us individually is an insignificant speck in an infinite universe, but together, we small creatures have great power."

She and Atom turned to Tillie. "It's time to open the doors of the Institute for Lower Learning again," they announced.

The insects cheered. Even the butterflies, who were so exhausted from carrying Eden that they lay draped over the backs of the sofas like doilies, managed to clap their wings. The thumping of their applause sounded like the soft and steady beat of a spring rainstorm, the kind that leaves the air fresh and clean and inspires the dogwood to bloom.

Eden breathed deep and smiled at her new partner. She could already smell the pink and white blossoms.

One Year Later

"**M**ake a wish," *Tillie* said to Eden, placing a birthday cake in front of her.

Eden looked at the cake. It was her favorite (yellow, with chocolate frosting) but instead of candles, eleven fireflies plus one to grow on hovered above it.

"I don't know what to wish for," Eden said, gazing down at their bright little lights, thinking of all she and Atom had accomplished in the past year. "I already have everything I could dream of."

Thanks to Eden and Atom's powerful partnership, the Institute for Lower Learning was thriving. Eden was studying many of the insect languages in Milton's notebook, and Atom was studying several human ones in Minnie's. The new Language Laboratories were packed to capacity every day. At first, many people had been reluctant to take an insect language class because they were worried they'd never get the hang of it, but Eden, who wasn't perfect at not needing to be perfect but was getting better at it, encouraged them to come and give it a try anyway. Pretty soon, the classrooms were abuzz with the sounds of humans and insects making mistakes and learning from each other.

August had earned the right to come back to the Institute after having spent the entire summer mounting a Free the Fireflies campaign, teaching all the neighborhood kids that catching fireflies in jars was just plain cruel. He'd managed to pick up Firefly pretty fast, once he'd learned that Morse code could also be communicated with flashing lights. Being afraid of the dark had actually come in handy, since it had made him an expert at flicking a flashlight on and off quickly. He'd taught his parents Morse code, too, and they watched proudly as August taught Human-Firefly Flashlight Tag to all the neighborhood fireflies and kids. He even let Sheila play. They hadn't become friends or anything. August didn't want to. He was busy hanging out with his new friends, Randall, Ivan, and Vincent, but Sheila had finally stopped calling him Nigh, which he did appreciate.

Ivan, Randall, and Vincent had each picked up an insect language as well. Randall was excited to learn that treehoppers communicated best through vibrations. He felt sure they'd respond to his piano playing, and he persuaded Tillie to get the Bösendorfer tuned. At first, he'd tried playing the keys like he usually did, but the treehoppers laughed at him, just like they had at Eden. Realizing that they were a bit snobbish and responded best to much more sophisticated vibrations than the keys were capable of producing, Randall propped open the massive, caramel-colored lid of the piano and played the strings directly, as if they were a harp. The treehoppers, impressed, responded immediately, and they soon became the best of friends.

Ivan was delighted to learn that bees communicated through something called a "waggle dance," which had quite a bit in common with ballet. The waggle dance involved a lot of running in giant figure eights, while ballet involved spinning in tiny, precise circles. Both made the dancers very dizzy, and after they'd practiced for hours in Ivan's mother's dance studio, they'd flop onto their backs and laugh until the room stopped spinning.

Vincent, who couldn't dance or play an instrument, was worried that he'd never learn an insect language, until he discovered that moths communicated by smelling pheromones. Realizing that his nervous burping condition could actually be useful, Vincent learned to burp on cue, and soon he and the moths were able to understand each other based on the scents they released. He'd used his set-building skills to make a fort in his backyard, and the moths would occasionally come over for sleepovers. They'd wake up early and play in the crisp dawn air, Vincent's new orange cape spreading behind him like wings as he ran.

The four boys had convinced their school to add the Institute for Lower Learning to their field trip schedule, and Tillie loved welcoming crowds of children into its halls, delighting in the sound of footsteps and laughter echoing through her home once again. Today, the halls were extra-crowded with kids who'd come to celebrate Eden's birthday.

"Let's eat!" August said, flicking a mini-flashlight on and off at the fireflies. "Scooch over, so I can cut the cake."

"But first, presents," said the wasp queen, nudging a small package toward Eden.

"Absolutely! Presents first," Tillie kuzz-buzzed. Over the past year, Eden's mother had bought Tillie a kazoo and taught her to play it. Tillie had been pleasantly surprised to learn that as soon as she relaxed and stopped straining so hard to learn insect languages, her ability to speak and understand Wasp came quickly. Between her profound empathy and her mastery of the kazoo, Tillie and the queen had become close confidants. Tillie had even taught the queen, who'd already lived a whole year longer than her normal life span, the secrets to her longevity (plain yogurt, good posture, laughing).

"This ribbon is magnificent," Eden told the queen, and the silkworms who'd made it wriggled with pleasure as the wide band of pink silk fell away. Eden tore off the wrapping paper, revealing an exquisite notebook made of paper crafted by the queen and her hive. On the front cover, a title was stamped in dark green ink: "Conversations and Observations, Volume II."

"You've learned everything you can from Milton's interviews," the queen said. "Now it's time to conduct your own."

"Thank you," Eden said with a smile. "I've already chosen my first subject."

Eden took a pen from her pocket and wrote "Paper Wasp" in neat script at the top of the first page. She turned to the queen.

"Tell me," she said. "When did you first learn you could communicate with humans?"

MORSE CODE

ALPHABET

A	B	C	D	E
·−	−···	−·−·	−··	·
F	G	H	I	J
··−·	−−·	····	··	·−−−
K	L	M	N	O
−·−	·−··	−−	−·	−−−
P	Q	R	S	T
·−−·	−−·−	·−·	···	−
U	V	W	X	Y
··−	···−	·−−	−··−	−·−−
		Z		
		−−··		

NUMBERS

1	2	3	4
·−−−−	··−−−	···−−	····−
5	6	7	8
·····	−····	−−···	−−−··
	9	0	
	−−−−·	−−−−−	

SEMAPHORE CHART

A/1 B/2 C/3 D/4 E/5 F/6 G/7

H/8 I/9 J K/0 L M N

O P Q R S T

U V W Q Y Z

Ready Cancel Error / Attention

Number

1 2 3 4 5

6 7 8 9 0

```
.__ ._ .. _ ./ ._/ _. ___ _ ./_ ___/_ .... ./
.. _. ... _ .. _ ._ _.

_ . ._.. ._./ ._ ... /___ ___ .. _./
.._ ._ ... _ ___ _. .. _ .
.__. _ _. _/ ___ .._/_ .... ./ ._. ___ ___ _._/
._ _. _..
__. . _/ ._/ ._. ___ ... _ _. _ _. _.. /
_... ._ _._ _._

__. ._ .. ._.. / ._.. . ._ ._ . _
.. _. ... _ .. _ ._ _ . ./ .._ ___ _.
._. ___ _. _ . ._./ ._. . _._ _ _. .. _ _._
._.. ___ ___ / ._.. ___ ___ _.._ /
... __ ___ _. ..... ._ ___ _ .....
._.. ___ ... / ._ _. _ . . ._. . ... / _._ ._
___ ___ _ __ _ ___ ___ ... __ ___ ___ _.
```

ACKNOWLEDGEMENTS

Special thanks to my earliest readers: Keryl Brown, Dorrie LaMarr, Nadya LaMarr, Courtney Lilly, Corey Nickerson, Nina Palmer, and Peter Saji. Your love, emotional support, creative expertise, and encouragement are unparalleled. This book is so much better because of you. Extra special thanks to the twelve-and-unders: Jackson Chavis, Benji Greenwald, Sky Morino, and Sam Peterson. Your openhearted delight and ruthless honesty is, quite simply, the best.

A whole separate category goes to Betsy Lerner, who both demands and deserves it, for being my writing role model and earliest editor, and for opening the door to the major leagues.

Special shout-out to Sarah Burnes, my wonderful agent, who saw my potential in the early days and pushed me to improve every day after. Also to Marlene Zuk, the most knowledgeable and whimsical bug expert a girl could ask for. And to Stacey Barney, my extraordinary editor, whose love for my characters and faith in me never ceases to astound. Your one-two punch of gentleness and rigor inspired me to demand more of myself than I knew I could.

My endless love and gratitude to the members of my family who are no longer on earth but are forever in my heart: my mother, Roz Lerner, who let me stay up late reading, and my father, Howard Lerner, who let me stay up late telling jokes. Most of all to my beautiful children, Ruby and Hart Campbell (the real Atom and Dot), whose young lives were stolen by a drunk driver. I miss you every moment.

Finally, to Colin Campbell, the best husband and father I can imagine. Your wise notes on story and structure are exceptional, but it's your optimism, courage, humor, and boundless love in the face of despair that really do it for me.